HOT SHOTS

To Chris: *signature*

Also by Anne Marsh

His Dark Bond
One Hot Cowboy
Burning Up
Slow Burn
Reburn
Hot Zone

Also by Lynn LaFleur

"The Right Number" in *Nightshift*
"Trouble in Boots" in *In a Cowboy's Bed*
Smokin' Hot

HOT SHOTS

ANNE MARSH

LYNN LaFLEUR

STACEY KENNEDY

APHRODISIA

KENSINGTON PUBLISHING CORP.
www.kensingtonbooks.com

APHRODISIA BOOKS are published by

Kensington Publishing Corp.
119 West 40th Street
New York, NY 10018

All Kensington titles, imprints, and distributed lines are available at special quantity discounts for bulk purchases for sales promotion, premiums, fund-raising, and educational or institutional use.

Special book excerpts or customized printings can also be created to fit specific needs. For details, write or phone the office of the Kensington Special Sales Manager: Kensington Publishing Corp., 119 West 40th Street, New York, NY 10018. Attn. Special Sales Department. Phone: 1-800-221-2647.

Aphrodisia and the A logo Reg. U.S. Pat. & TM Off.

ISBN-13: 978-0-7582-8895-0
ISBN-10: 0-7582-8895-6
First Kensington Trade Paperback Printing: March 2014

eISBN-13: 978-0-7582-8896-7
eISBN-10: 0-7582-8896-4
First Kensington Electronic Edition: March 2014

10 9 8 7 6 5 4 3 2 1

Printed in the United States of America

CONTENTS

Fired Up

ANNE MARSH

*This one's for my fellow Divas on Romance Divas.
Not only are we rowing in the same writing boat, but,
with you all, it's no dinghy. It's a big cruise ship of
fun with plenty of hot cabana boys. Thank you.*

1

―――――――

"You found our private channel." Her hotshot's rough, smoky voice flooded the airwaves and the small lookout cabin. Too big for the 14×14 space, his sinful Cajun accent had Hannah imagining long bayou nights.

"Wouldn't miss it for the world." Her fingers slipped from the dial.

"That's good." His familiar, low rumble reached her clearly despite the fifty-odd miles between them. "I'd hate to think I was the only one countin' down the hours."

Oh, she liked that. Cole Henry, waiting for nightfall and her. Some days, the days when the Big Bear Rogues got called out into the field on fire duty, ten o'clock came and went without hearing his voice. He stood her up those nights, but so far he'd always come back.

He didn't apologize, though. Her Cajun was too matter-of-fact; he'd told her the fires came first. Based on the size of the smokes she'd spotted from her watchtower earlier today, she was damned lucky he wasn't out in the field again.

"You had a busy day today." Please don't let him be too

tired. The watchtower fifty miles east had spotted an impressive smoke yesterday. After that call in, it had been all hands on deck, and she'd known the Big Bear Rogues would be headed out. Maybe the fire hadn't burned as hot or as long as expected, or maybe her Rogues had managed to hit the sweet spot.

"You spotters keep us busy." She heard the slow smile filling his voice. Her shyness amused him, but he always gave her these few minutes of conversation.

"Busy's good." The breathless catch was back in her own voice. God, why was she so aroused just chitchatting with him?

Because she knew what was coming next.

"A one-hundred-fourteen-acre burn. Eight hours digging line and we barely contained the fire." His bald words painted an all-too-clear picture of the harsh conditions he'd faced down in the field. "We had the trucks out and the tankers dropping slurry all afternoon. Summer's only going to get worse. Things are heating up in the park."

"I should let you go." She ran her fingers along the mic, rubbing the cool metal with her fingertips. She was too damned hot.

That soft male chuckle filled her tower again, followed by the unmistakable rustle of fabric. "Not a chance in hell, *sha.* Lie back."

Not a question or a suggestion.

An order.

Like always, her pulse skipped a beat. *Dangerous.* She didn't need a man to give her orders, but Cole did it so well. And there was something about him. She wanted to give him everything he asked for. He shocked her and pushed her. And some part of her enjoyed that, enjoyed the erotic nervousness that filled her up whenever she heard his voice. She'd never meet him face-to-face, which made doing this so much simpler. That, and the dark night outside. Just her and the lonely airwaves, alone in a fire watchtower fifty miles from the nearest base camp.

No one had to know.

"Hannah." The warning growl of his voice stroked over her nerve endings like he was right there touching her skin as he bared her. He always knew when she didn't obey. So she loved pushing him, knowing there was nothing he could do, but so, so many things he *would* do if he ever got his hands on her.

This was fantasy, she reminded herself. Naughty, but not explicitly forbidden, although only because the employee handbook hadn't been updated since 1960. She knew better than to take on one of the hotshots in real life, because the real-life Big Bear Rogues lived up to their name—big, rough, sensual men who would take no prisoners in bed. She didn't need or want that kind of intensity on a permanent basis.

"Give me a moment." Dragging the microphone with her, she lay down on her mattress and positioned the mic on the floor by her head. If he wasn't out in the field, he always called her right on the stroke of ten, so she should have been ready for him. She always made him wait, though, because she loved drawing out their game. The wash-worn cotton sheets were deliciously soft, and her old UC Davis T-shirt rode up over her hips and belly. That shirt and a pair of silky panties were all she had on. The cabin didn't come with curtains, but fifty miles inside Sequoia National Park in a thirty-foot-high watchtower, she wasn't worried about Peeping Toms.

"Lose the panties."

Her fingers curled obediently in the lace ribbons. Taking his orders was her decadent secret, a naughty self-indulgence she didn't have to explain away. Arousal flooded her pussy, full and warm. The sensations would only get better the longer they played. She'd take what he offered simply because she wanted it.

Wanted him.

His breathing hitched louder, grew rougher. "Is your pussy bare?"

She sighed, hearing that betraying catch. "I'm pulling my panties down my thighs now."

Let him imagine *that*. He wasn't the only one who could play this game. She pulled the scrap of fabric down slowly, spinning out the moment and the sensations. With no one to see, she gave herself over to the erotic rub of the silk and lace against her sensitive skin. Drawing her legs up, she tugged the panties free and set them beside her on the mattress.

She turned her head toward the mic. "Your turn."

Buttons popped free from a pair of worn blue jeans as booted heels hit the table fifty miles away. His cock would spring free, the heavy length probably stretching deliciously far up his flat belly. She'd never seen him, but she'd seen enough of the Big Bear Rogues to know that her hotshot would be as fine looking as he was rough around the edges.

"Talk to me," she said.

"Talkin's not what I wan' to be doin'."

Maybe not, but she wasn't ready to take on the real man. Cole Henry would be every bit as much in charge in the flesh as he was over the airwaves. This way, he was *her* fantasy and she was ultimately the one in control. One flick of her finger hitting the switch beside the mic and the connection between them vanished. Besides, even if she wanted more than a fantasy lover, the distance between her watchtower and base camp was too great. No one would make that trek for casual sex.

"Imagine this." His voice grew rougher and deeper, a needy masculine growl. "You're naked on this mighty fine desk I have here in my office and I've got you all spread out, so I can touch you."

Shifting on her sheets, she imagined the cool, slick surface. The erotic shock of being naked and exposed where she shouldn't be.

"This way, see, when I step between your pretty thighs, you

can't shut me out none. I'm right there and you're open and goin' nowhere. You know that, right?"

"Yes."

"I'm goin' to put my hands on your thighs, press you wider still. I want to look at you some, see where I'll be puttin' my fingers and my tongue. My dick. Make sure you're wet and ready to take me."

"How?"

"You got me on my knees, *sha*." There was nothing submissive about his words, however. No, his words were pure dominance. Even on his knees, he'd be the one in charge, controlling her pleasure and her body with erotic ease. "One small tug and there you are, right on the edge, and I'm feastin'."

The hard edge of the desk digging into her ass, leaving her off balance. Knowing he could see all of her and how very much she needed his touch. Yearned for him. God, she loved his imagination.

"All I got to do is lean forward to taste you. You like the thought of that? My tongue dragging up through your folds, learnin' how sweet you are? First one side, then the other. I'm takin' my time, lickin' real slow. You wan' me to suck your clit?" He paused and she knew he'd wait for the words—all night if he had to, because Cole Henry was one patient man.

"Please."

His throaty chuckle unlocked something in her. "I should make you say it, *sha*. You're awful shy, sweet thing."

Only in real life. *This* didn't count. Putting her fingers on her pussy because she was done waiting for him, she pressed hard, then bucked as a spasm of intense pleasure ripped through her. Oh, God.

"Of course, maybe we should be payin' more attention to your nipples. Just so you don' come so fast. You don' want this to be over quick, do you?"

She didn't want to. No, she wanted to stay right where she

was, swirling her fingers in her heated folds. Her small whimper gave her away.

"Uh-uh," he said. "You're almost there. That means we're goin' to slow things down."

"Cole—"

"Reach up under your shirt," he instructed. His firm voice only aroused her further. He knew what she needed and he'd give it to her. On his terms. "Touch your nipples."

She did as he commanded, sliding her hands beneath the T-shirt and rubbing her palms over the sensitive curves. Her fingers stroked up, cupping her breasts and trailing her fingers higher.

"Pinch the nipple." He wouldn't make this easy for her.

Carefully, she closed the fingertips of her left hand around her nipple and squeezed gently.

"Harder, *sha.*"

He knew her so well. He always pushed her further.

"Leave a hand there on your tits. Now you can touch your pussy with your other hand."

Christ, Hannah coming was the sexiest thing Cole had ever heard. Yeah, he'd give anything to be there in that watchtower with her, his tongue buried in her pussy, his fingers working in deep. She exhaled hard, a soft, low pant that picked up speed, her breathing coming faster and faster as her orgasm rippled through her. Then he heard that happy, sated sound she made, like every muscle in her body had just turned to water and she was ready to curl up and nap some.

He wanted to see her face as he worked her body over, as he drove her right to the edge and made her wait for it. Face-to-face with her, would he be so attuned to the small gasps, the way she sucked in a breath right before her pleasure broke and she came? If he was closer, with his dick deep inside her, riding her hard, would he notice these things?

Fuck.

He couldn't imagine not noticing. He'd notice everything

about Hannah. It was driving him pure crazy not having a face to put with the sultry voice reaching out to him over the airwaves.

She'd got hers, so now it was his turn. Ladies first, then him. That was part of their date night, too. Him rubbing one out fast and hard, his hands slapping against his cock, pulling up and tensing as the sensation in his balls tightened. No lube because he wanted the raw feeling tomorrow, to go through his day with that reminder of what they'd shared tonight. Plus, she'd hear every stroke.

She always listened.

Hannah. His balls constricted. Grabbing his T-shirt to catch the evidence, he came in long, hard jerks. She was miles away, where she couldn't possibly see him, but he'd never felt more stripped bare—or closer to a lover. Funny how touching wasn't everything, how just hearing her breathing over the airwaves did it for him.

"Cole . . ." Her sated, sleepy voice floated over the airwaves to him.

Whatever question she had, whatever words were coming on the heels of his name, didn't matter because right then thunder boomed over the line. *Too close.* Summer lightning storms were a serious threat in the national park. More than one watchtower had sustained direct hits.

He cursed, shooting to his feet. "Hannah?"

The microphone fell over, almost muffling the sound of someone dressing rapidly. A second clap of thunder was followed by what sounded like the whole damn watchtower vibrating.

"Talk to me," he bit out. "Tell me what's happening. Now. You okay?"

"Thunderstorm," she said, a low laugh escaping her. "Talk about ending on a bang. It's gorgeous." Static broke up her voice. *Hell.*

"Those strikes are damned dangerous, *sha.*" He bit back a curse. This was not your average afternoon thunderstorm. "There are better ways to live on the edge of danger." He should know. He'd tried them all and settled on fighting fire.

"I'll be fine." She dismissed his concern.

"You need to get out of the tower." Like many of the watchtowers in the park, the Widow's Peak tower was perched on top of a ridge. With its metal observation deck, it was the perfect lightning magnet. "Get out of there, lie down on the ground, and play it safe until the storm passes."

"This from you." Amusement colored her voice. "Hey, hotshot, maybe you should try taking a walk on the safe side of things. See how you enjoy that."

She had no idea.

He opened his mouth to say something, but a second loud boom rolled over their connection, followed by a burst of static. Pulling up his jeans, he ran scenarios in his head.

Her voice broke up. "Radio . . . hit . . . going . . ."

Christ.

No way he wanted her out there alone without a radio. He wanted the connection to her, but he also wanted her to have that lifeline back to base. Shit sometimes happened in the forest. There were plenty of possibilities for disaster once he let his imagination get rolling. The trails were open to anyone, so all kinds of low-life, crazy hikers could cross her path. There were bears. She could fall in a river and drown, because God knew more than a few park visitors died that way each year. There were rock falls. And, of course, the goddamn fires he fought.

He knew which watchtower was hers. He'd made a point of looking it up after the first morning he'd heard her reporting signs of smoke. That sweetly sexy voice of hers caught his imagination, had him imagining carnal acts he had no business thinking about. But he had.

Hell yeah, he had.

Hannah Green's watchtower was thirty-nine degrees north, eight-four degrees west. That put her fifty miles inland. Thirty of those he could cover on the fire roads, but the last twenty were a brutal hike in. He glanced at the clock. He'd leave as soon as he'd squared his absence with his team leader. Push hard and he'd reach Widow's Peak tomorrow at sunset.

Special delivery.

2

Cole slammed out of the radio tower at base camp. Lightning forked down from the night sky, lighting up a nearby ridge. The next bright slash temporarily blinded him, but that didn't matter. His dumb ass could stare at the fireworks display as much as it wanted, because he knew the path to Sam Clayton's RV blindfolded.

His team commander's RV was parked where it always was. The lights were off, but at least the camper wasn't rocking. Sam's fiancée wouldn't appreciate a meet and greet in the middle of banging Sam's brains out, and Cole needed Sam in a good mood.

An amenable Sam would make this easier.

He pounded on the door, jiggling the latch while he counted off the seconds. One Mississippi. Two Mississippi. And . . . fuck politeness. The handle opened easily, because no one bothered locking up in base camp. Shoving the door open, he put his head in. Sam liked to stick to a schedule, so the giant mound beneath the covers on the bed was likely him.

"Rise and shine," he said, knocking hard again on the open

door. One way or the other, Sam was going to get up. Next step? He'd go in there and wrestle the man. Christ, he really hoped this was one of those nights when Olivia was traveling for work. As an FBI agent, Sam's fiancée didn't always stay put.

"What the hell?" Sam shot up in the bed, shoving back the covers.

The sleepy protest from Sam's companion had Sam shooting daggers at him. Yeah. No luck. Olivia was having a sleepover. "Cole?"

Sure enough, Olivia sat up. She made the fire department T-shirt she was half-sporting look damned sexy. The fabric slid down her bare shoulders and he caught a glimpse of long legs as Sam stood up and headed his way.

"Stay in bed, honey." Sam definitely did not sound happy. "I'll be right back."

Cole caught the snort of feminine amusement and frustration loud and clear. He was also fairly certain she added, "You wish, Sam." But he wasn't stupid. Get in the middle of that argument and he'd still be standing here next week—and he was leaving just as soon as he'd given Sam the heads-up.

"Tell me the forest is on fire." Sam propped an arm on the door frame. Now that Sam was vertical and listening, Cole stepped back, leaning against the wall of the RV. He tipped his head back and stared up at sky. All those stars lit up the camp. Right on cue, though, there was another distant roll of thunder and bright spike of light.

"That's the problem, right there." He flipped a bird at the horizon and the summer lightning storm.

His fear for Hannah's safety didn't make any fucking sense. He'd never met the woman, no matter how many hours he'd spent talking to her on their private channel. He didn't even know anything about her—her deepest sexual fantasies aside. And yet he really, *really* needed to go out and see for himself that she was fine.

"Cole?" Sam stared like Cole was crazy, and maybe he was. He'd pulled Sam out of bed and the man was standing there in just his boxers. Cole was damned lucky Sam didn't sleep naked. The whole situation was ludicrous. There just was no good explanation and, honestly, he didn't care.

But some part of him *did* care about Hannah Green and the bad situation she could be in.

Fuck. He was burning time and somehow he needed to explain the unexplainable to Sam. He should be focusing, but instead his mind was fifty miles away in a watchtower with a woman whose face he wouldn't recognize if she walked past him.

"I need to head out." There. That was plain enough.

"Right this second?" Sam drawled the question, even though Cole's midnight presence on his doorstep had to be an answer.

"Pretty much." Ten minutes. He'd spare that much. He had a feeling he wasn't going to be able to relax until he saw Hannah for himself.

"Because we got us a new fire?" Sam eyed him, like he thought Cole had lost it. "Or you got bad family news?"

A feminine hand waved a pair of jeans over Sam's shoulders. "You boys might want to take this over to the office."

"Yeah." Taking the pants, Sam turned and pulled Olivia into his arms. Cole looked front and center because he liked Olivia and he wasn't sure how she'd feel about an audience. Still, there was no shutting out the soft sound of kissing and the low murmur as the pair exchanged intimacies.

"You can look now," she said dryly. "It's safe."

"You bet," he agreed, turning his head and smiling. Sam was a lucky man. Olivia tucked her hair behind her ear and grinned at him. His intrusion didn't matter to her. For just a minute, Cole imagined what it must be like having a woman like that waiting in his RV for him. Olivia and Sam came from two different worlds, but they'd worked something out. Sam, clearly, was happy. Good for him.

"Come on," Sam growled, stepping into his jeans and buttoning as they walked away from the RV. "We'll talk in the office."

Sam Clayton's "office" was a beat-up supply depot where he'd crammed a desk and a chair for those days when the paperwork couldn't be put off any longer. Flicking on the light, Sam dropped into his desk chair. "So hit me. What urgent piece of business has you banging on my door after midnight?"

Sam swung his feet up on the desk and papers crunched as the small mountain of paper covering the desktop dropped by a half inch or so. Cole shot a quick prayer of thanksgiving heavenward that he'd been spared the team lead. No way could he buckle down at that desk like Sam. Being shut up in here would be hell.

Instead, he laid out the bare facts. "Thunderstorm knocked the radio out at Widow's Peak."

Sam steepled his fingers, leaning forward in his desk chair. The tension in the man's body was hard to overlook, but he didn't point out that Widow's Peak was fifty hard miles away, or mention certain basics like cell phone reception and phone lines. "You sure of that?"

"Damn sure. Heard it myself. Two near strikes and possibly one dead on."

"Uh-huh. And your new secret superpower is long-distance hearing?" Sam's dark gaze watched him calmly. Yeah, this was the part Cole would have preferred not to share. He hadn't bothered dating these last few years, but he remembered enough. Kiss and tell was definitely on the no-fly list. Sam Clayton wasn't much for office hours or protocol. The man went out and he got the job done. He was a damned fine hotshot and park ranger. He also was no fool.

That was the thing. None of the Rogues was a saint, but Cole was more devil than any of them. Sam knew that, so the look on the other man's face—wavering between suspicion and resignation—was hardly unexpected.

"No." He flashed his team boss a quick grin. "You know how, Sam."

"Not sure that I do. Explain it to me."

"Sometimes I talk with the lookout at Widow's Peak. Off-hours. On the radio."

"Just to pass the time. Uh-huh." Sam tilted his chair and re-arranged his booted feet up on top of his desk. He didn't seem to mind the number his steel toes were doing on all that paper-work. Instead, he contemplated the 1960s popcorn ceiling like it was holding all the answers. "This would be our young female lookout? The only one who isn't past the age of forty and sporting a dick?"

True enough, but Cole wasn't fool enough to describe the situation quite like that. "I like talkin' to Hannah."

Sam sighed. "I'll bet that you do, although I'm also betting there's at least a half-dozen park regulations that say she's off-limits."

"None that I know of," he pointed out, because he never had been able to keep his mouth shut. He supposed he should keep his opinions to himself, but Sam's words were too close to an ultimatum. He didn't need the list of all the reasons why he couldn't have Hannah Green.

She was *his.*

She'd talked to *him.*

He'd liked the sound of her voice from that first morning, when he'd heard her answering watchtower roll. The way she said those two words, *Widow's Peak,* shot straight to his dick. He'd immediately wanted more. More of her voice, more of her. More of a chance. And, if there was one thing he'd learned in the military, it was radios. A little B and E, and he had access to the base camp radio. He'd put out a call to her tower and she'd answered. The rest was history.

"She didn't have to talk to me," he pointed out.

Sam shook his head. "Management makes sexual harassment training mandatory for a reason, Cole. You've got to lay off her. When she comes down for her days off, then you see where she wants to take this, but no more late-night calls. That's an order."

Sam's eyes bored into Cole's, clearly demanding agreement, but that was just another thing that was destined not to happen. Hannah Green was an addiction Cole had every intention of feeding. He'd spent way too many hours imagining a face and body to go with the voice. His current fantasy featured real dark hair that hit her butt and a pair of legs that went on for days. But, because this wasn't the time to fight that battle, he nodded. "I hear you."

"But you're still planning on doing this your way." Sam swore. "Hell, Cole."

His name paired with a curse word was a familiar refrain he'd heard all his life. Even the military hadn't succeeded in erasing his rebellious streak. Rule breaking was his everyday behavior. He saw something he wanted, he went for it. Run farther, dig faster, fight harder. Those were the things he did. It was just that somehow, sometime this summer he'd gotten Hannah Green in his sights instead of fire.

None of which mattered because she was out there alone with no radio.

"Lightning strike?" he prompted. His behavior wasn't the issue here. He wasn't changing, and they both knew it. The only question was when or if Sam would file disciplinary charges or boot his ass off the team. His two years with the Rogues had been damned fine ones, but he'd never expected the job to last forever. He was no team player.

"Fuck, yeah." Sam sat up, running a hand over his head. "Give me the deets."

Cole ran through the lightning strike he'd heard and Hannah's comments. "Her radio's out," he finished. "She needs a new one. I can head out now, bring her a new kit, and check up on her. You know if she's armed?"

She was a woman alone. She'd damned well better have brought protection with her, and he didn't mean the condom-variety either.

"Shotgun," Sam said absentmindedly, clearly running through Cole's 411. "In case of bear."

"Good." He hoped like hell she plugged anyone who threatened her. Lots of people carried but then couldn't pull the trigger when they needed to. Hannah was soft and she had a real feminine side. She also had plenty of backbone, though, and his instincts said she wouldn't let any attacker—four-legged or two-legged—push her into an impossible corner. "I'll grab a new radio and be on my way."

"You shouldn't go." Sam's gaze held his.

"I'm goin'." He put a whole lot of implacable in his voice. This was non-negotiable.

"Cole—"

"I'm goin'," he repeated. "I've got R and R due to me. We'll count this."

Sam spared the duty roster pinned to the wall a glance. "We're already stretched tight. I shouldn't be sparing even one man."

That sounded like agreement to him.

"I don' need company." He'd take care of Hannah. Whatever had happened out there at Widow's Peak, whatever was going down now, he'd haul ass and he'd have her back.

"Play by the rules." Sam slapped his hands on the desk. "You do the right thing, Cole. Take the new radio out there and do a quick welfare check. Then you turn right around and come on back. Four days. No more."

Cole got the other man's anger. Cole was a big, rough bastard, and no one in his right mind would want to unleash him on some unsuspecting woman. Sam didn't know what kind of conversation he'd been having with Hannah, but no matter what those midnight calls had covered, no one wanted Hannah backed into a corner. And that included Cole. Scared or *harassed* didn't cover what he wanted Hannah Green to feel when he came knocking. Yeah, he'd done the training. He knew precisely where the line was and, while his steel toes might be pressed up right against it, he wouldn't cross it until she asked him.

Sam didn't know that, however, but justifying his actions went against the grain. Snapping the other man a two-fingered salute, he spun on his booted heel and strode away. He had preparations to make. He'd hit the road now. He didn't need sunrise to cover the distance to the fire trail with his pick-up. By the time the sun was well over those mountaintops, he'd be on the trailhead.

Volunteering to be the man who hiked out to the watchtower was a no-brainer. He wanted to know his Hannah was safe. Although hell if he knew when he'd started thinking of her as *his*. Maybe, he grinned, when she'd let him make her come. He wanted more than words now. Hell, he planned to get his fingers and tongue just about everywhere a man could. His dick, too. So, yeah, hiking to the watchtower wasn't a hardship.

What happened after he reached Widow's Peak was up to Hannah.

He wouldn't do a damned thing she didn't ask for.

Yeah.

He was looking forward to all the *asking* she'd be doing.

3

The watchtower at Widow's Peak was a decades-old cabin perched on stilts thirty feet up in the air. It took ninety steps to reach the trapdoor in the catwalk floor from the ground, her calves burning all the way. If that wasn't enough, reaching the place at all took a ten-hour drive up the fire roads from Big Bear Lake, followed by a brutal hike in by pack trail. Her piece of the park for the summer came with a big dose of welcome peace and quiet, plus million-dollar views. Hannah got up each morning to a panoramic, ringside seat looking out over mountains and forests, and a hundred-plus miles of pure visibility.

Unfortunately, running water was limited.

Her bathing choices were stream, pond, or go dirty. The pond was already choking up with algae as the water levels dropped further with each passing day, so Hannah headed for the stream. After losing her radio—*and Cole,* a little voice in her head said—falling asleep had been hard. She'd have to decide if she was hiking out tomorrow to pick up new gear or if she wanted to sit tight for a couple of days and hope base camp figured out her dilemma. Maybe a little cold water would clear her head, make things clearer.

Because the images from last night's conversation were seared into her brain, she'd spent the morning alternately staring sightlessly out at the horizon and looking at the veterinary textbook she was supposed to be reviewing. She had exams this fall and being too prepared was impossible. Unfortunately, Cole made a far better bedtime story than animal anatomy. Right now, her dreams had nothing to do with the veterinary degree she was mere months from earning.

Back home, she would have been plenty concerned about running around a public stream naked. Sequoia National Park was different. *She* was different here. There simply weren't that many people, and the ones who did come out this far were visible miles away. Yesterday's thru-hikers hadn't met anyone else on the trail for days, so she could enjoy her solitude. No one would bother her today. All the same, she brought her rifle with her, just to be on the safe side.

She picked a deeper spot, where the water running off the rocks gave her some way to wash the biodegradable soap out of her hair. "One, two, three and in," she muttered to herself, like saying the words out loud would psych her up enough to make the plunge palatable.

No such luck. She went under and came up gasping. The water was still ice cold, although the day's heat had warmed it up a few degrees. A few, meaning "not enough to make a damned bit of difference." This was going to be the world's quickest wash. In. Soap and rinse. And out.

She closed her eyes and got busy with the shampoo. A cold shower was just what the doctor ordered. Since she had no radio, she wouldn't be talking to her hotshot tonight. Tomorrow, she'd think about packing down to base camp and picking up some new equipment. Tonight, however, she was good and alone.

Leaning back, she let the water rinse the peaches-and-cream suds away. The movement exposed her breasts, cold pebbling her nipples when they broke the stream's surface and met the air. The erotic burn and tingle had her wishing Cole was there.

Cole. What kind of face would go with that sinfully rich, sweet molasses voice? His sexy rasp got her wet in seconds and she wouldn't get her next fix until she acquired a new radio. So all she could do now was fantasize. He'd be a big man, she decided, given his work as a hotshot. A stubble-roughened jaw, because shaving went by the wayside out in the field, with a powerful, loose-limbed sprawl. That Cajun accent of his promised he'd be dark haired and dark eyed. All yummy things.

She slowly dragged the washcloth over her breasts.

The day's temps were headed well north of ninety.

Cole was fairly certain he'd spotted a new smoke.

And there wasn't a cloud in sight, while the humidity index kept climbing. The Big Bear Rogues would have the aftereffects of last night's lightning storm to contend with along with the summer's fires.

"Laissez les bon temps roulez," he growled.

The good news? He was outside. This part of Sequoia National Park was all wide-open space broken only by tall stands of ponderosa. The place had a rough beauty, but when Cole looked closely, plenty of fire scars, too. Still, the faster he beat feet, the faster he'd see for himself that Hannah was doing okay.

He'd been hiking for forty minutes when Cole hit pay dirt.

Oh, yeah.

Unless he was seriously lost or the park's visitors were a way better-looking crew than he'd run into before, his lookout was having herself a bath in the stream. As he came along the trail, eyes scanning left and then right, he caught the sound of a whistle. A little hum and splash, followed by an unmistakably feminine gasp. He'd bet that water was still a cold son of a bitch despite the hot summer temps.

He didn't need a porn star. That made for good times in his head, yeah, but what he really wanted—*who* he really wanted—was the woman standing watch at Widow's Peak.

Tall, short, fat, thin—he wanted a face to go with the name and the voice.

Whatever she looked like, he'd enjoy her.

Silently, he prowled to the top of the trail. The stream was down and to his right, a real pretty jumble of mountain boulders and a nice, smooth entry. Despite the waist-deep water, the current was a lazy dog, rippling gently around a pile of boulders four feet in. Those rocks made a convenient waterfall for the mermaid washing her hair.

The buck-naked mermaid.

She was definitely safe. That was his first thought, followed by an adrenaline rush of relief that fucked with his knees almost as much as it messed with his head. Whatever had knocked out her radio, she was fine.

Hell, way more than fine.

His day had definitely improved.

His first view of Hannah Green was nowhere near as close-up and personal as he'd fantasized, but his hard-on didn't seem to mind. This close to Widow's Peak, he figured his mystery bather had to be Hannah. There was no pack or gear in sight to mark a thru-hiker or even a day-tripper. She was definitely local.

With her head back, the delicate arch of her throat tempted him to run his mouth over the vulnerable curve. Water-darkened hair spilled down a sun-kissed back, the soapy rush half-masking her body with a sudsy curtain. Her hands worked the mass of hair, separating the strands and, wouldn't you know it, the water was clearly every bit as cold as he'd expected, because her breasts—Jesus, her nipples were hard, greedy nubs. He wanted to flick them with his thumbs, cup those generous mounds, and tease her good.

He shouldn't have looked.

He sucked in a harsh breath, fisting his hands on his thighs. Not looking was an impossibility. She arched her back, running her hands through all that hair again, then slicked the water off her face. Her eyes closed, blissed out, but her hands stayed busy, running over her cheeks and along her shoulders like she was enjoying the simple touch.

"Lower, *sha*," he growled to himself, because he didn't want to break this spell she didn't know she'd cast.

And it was definitely his lucky day, because, as if she'd heard him, she obediently smoothed her hands lower, trailing her fingers over the tantalizing slope of her breasts. She didn't slow, going right for the gold, her fingers finding and shaping those nipples, and he swore he heard her pant. Her pretty pink lips opened right up and a throaty moan boiled out.

He loved that sound.

Hell, he *knew* that sound. Splashing and half-humming, half-singing an off-key song, she had a voice he'd have known anywhere.

Hannah Green.

Had to be, and he had to get a closer look.

Shower time over, however, her hands fell away from her breasts and she started wading toward the bank. She was finished, even if he was barely getting started. He watched her come toward him and saw that his mermaid wasn't buck-ass naked after all. No, she was wearing a pair of miniscule panties that had his heart pounding against his rib cage and his dick lifting. Soaked through, the scrap of white nylon and lace pressed against the dark arrow of hair covering her pussy. Then, Holy Jesus, she made his day. Right there, she bent over, wriggling the wet panties down her thighs.

She was killing him.

He ran options in his head. Walking down to meet her wasn't his best plan. He'd scare the shit out of her; plus, he'd tip his hand. She'd know exactly what he'd seen. No, the safer bet was meeting her back at the tower. Decided, he hauled ass to the watchtower and was waiting for her on the bottom steps when, ten minutes later, she finally finished up and came back to the tower, trailing clothes and gear. She hadn't bothered getting dressed at all.

No, she rocked a towel and a pair of hiking boots, all long, muscled legs and bare skin.

He'd tried to be a gentleman, but some things just weren't meant to be.

"Evening, *sha*."

Maybe he should have called out earlier, given her some more advance warning, although he enjoyed the look of surprise on her face. The shotgun she leveled on him? Not so much. Knowing his luck, she'd be loaded for bear and Sam would laugh his ass off.

She cursed like a trucker, the obscenity a turn-on coming from that innocent-looking mouth. Of course, he already knew she liked to curse. And that there was nothing she wouldn't say.

Her clothes hit the ground as she racked the shotgun. The bra that bounced toward him didn't match the panties she'd shucked back there in the stream at all. Her bra was pink-and-white checks and all smooth, padded curves. He imagined it on her, wanted to run the backs of his fingers along those lines, explore the softness for himself.

She gestured with the gun, but he didn't take his eyes off her face. Up close, she was even prettier than he'd thought, although he liked her best without the towel. He still hadn't recovered from those little panties.

"Start talking," she growled.

He could explore later. If she didn't accidentally kill him first.

"You got a hell of a way of welcomin' a man."

* * *

Holy. Shit.

The man lounging on her steps was one hell of a welcoming committee. As her brain pinwheeled frantically, trying to process his presence, her libido registered his body—his large, well-muscled, *hard* body. He had to be well over six feet tall, and she drank in every inch, starting with the T-shirt pulled tight over his chest and then moving down over his Nomex-clad thighs. Given the way he was sprawled, there was no missing his package. He sure had one hell of a *welcome* for her.

Handsome, laughing eyes examined her from an even better-looking face, his skin sun-bronzed from hours outdoors. Dark hair brushed against his jaw in thick waves, but stubble roughed his jaw from at least a day on the trail. His watchful attitude screamed former soldier, but that hair was pure bad boy. No standard military issue there. He flashed her a wicked hint of a dimple as he winked, confirming her rule-breaker impression, and he'd have laugh lines before he was forty from the smile lighting up his face.

"Wow." She watched her stuff hit the ground in slo-mo and hoped like hell her jaw hadn't followed. She hadn't expected company, with the next supply drop not scheduled for another two weeks, so this man was an unexpected bonus. Hopefully, the bottle-green Nomex he was sporting meant he was Forest Service and not some random hiker who'd found his way to her watchtower. She'd relax more if she could pretend someone, somewhere, had checked into this man's background and bona fides before unleashing him on the world.

"Truer words." He grinned at her, a slow, sexy tug of his lips, and leaned forward, snagging the satin cups of her bra. She wasn't sure if it was better or worse that she'd passed on the practical white cotton or that she had the underwear taste of a high-class hooker.

He extended the bra to her, like she didn't have a shotgun trained on him. "Yours."

"Thanks." She was fairly certain her face was on fire, but not dropping the towel was paramount. Yet, the longer she looked at him, the more she wanted to peel that Nomex right off of him and kiss her way south. Three words and his Cajun accent melted her.

His Cajun accent.

Oh. My. God.

"Surprise," he said dryly, watching her carefully as she lowered the gun.

Nothing could have prepared her for meeting this man. Exchanging sexy chitchat wasn't like her. And doing it over the airwaves? God. Her face flamed. He wasn't supposed to be *here*. He was *never* supposed to be more than a voice.

And he definitely wasn't supposed to have a body that was even better than his voice. She'd mentally given him a hundred different faces, depending on her mood. Nothing could have prepared her for the reality. Tall, clocking in at well over six feet, with dark eyes and harsh cheekbones in a rough-hewn, hard face, Cole Henry was the kind of man any woman would look at. Twice.

"Cole Henry." He stuck a hand out. Since her dignified choices were few and far between at the moment, she took his hand with her free one. Calloused masculine fingers closed around hers.

"Why are you here?" Instantly, her blush got worse—God, what had she *said* to him? Surely, he knew those conversations were fantasies and not some kind of sexual rain check he could cash in?

There was no way she was going to do any of those things.

No matter how tempting he looked.

Right now, though, he was eying her incredulously. "Your radio went out during last night's thunderstorm and I couldn't raise you afterward."

He'd come all the way to check on her? Warmth flooded her.

"Damned straight I was comin' out here," he continued. "I'm your delivery boy."

"Excuse me?"

He liked the way her eyes widened. "Your radio is busted." He jerked a thumb toward his pack. "I brought you a replacement, *sha*."

Was that a flash of disappointment he saw on her face? Or was he looking for something he wouldn't find?

"Oh." She chewed on her lower lip. "Well, thank you, Cole Henry. I've always wondered . . . that's not a Cajun name." She looked him up and down like she wasn't standing there all but buck-ass naked. If the small talk made her happier, though, he was game. Usually, talking about himself was right up there with lobotomies and trips to the dentist, but he'd make an exception for her. Although he still hoped she'd hurry up and get comfortable with him, because his ass was falling asleep on her steps.

"My *maman* was the Cajun. Not my daddy. He stuck while he could, but my mother raised me."

His father had been a career soldier who'd eventually been killed in the line of duty. Before that, though, the man had always been shipping out, at least to hear his *maman* talk about it. The last time had occurred when Cole was five, leaving him only the briefest flickers of memory of a big man with gentle hands and hard eyes. That man had taken care of his family both before and after his death, but the checks that came couldn't replace the man duty had taken from them, even if the money made his mother's life easier.

Hell. He was a one-nighter and a ship-out man like his daddy. He wasn't made to stick.

He didn't think his Hannah was harboring long-term thoughts, but being clear never hurt.

"I'm stoppin' for one night. Tomorrow I'll be headin' back down the trail."

"So, how about you lettin' me up? I'll get your new radio set up."

Cole's dark voice did unspeakable *things* to her libido. Hannah was fairly certain the simple question wasn't meant to be so arousing. The plain truth, however, was that she found everything about Cole Henry sexy. Still, she considered the options in her head, not sure if he meant for her to take his words at face value or if there was subtext.

In.

Or out.

She stared at him, wishing the answers to the questions she didn't know how to ask were written on his face. Had he come here just to drop off a radio—or had he come here for *her*? And if she was the real reason for his pit stop, how did she feel about that?

"You want to check the place out, be my guest. I won't leave you down here where the bears can get you. Come on up. Do what you need to do." She gestured for him to go first, though, because damned if he needed to know what she was—or was not—wearing beneath her towel. Having his hands and his eyes all over her second-best bra was embarrassing enough.

"Sure, *sha.*" Rising gracefully to his feet, he swung himself up the ladder and started climbing hand over hand.

The man certainly had a spectacular ass. She gave him a head start, hanging back some, because taking an inadvertent boot to the eye was painful and the view from here was fantastic. The muscles in that toned ass flexed beneath the Nomex with each step he conquered.

When he reached the top, he shouldered open the trap door and reached down a hand for her gun. Giving up the weapon went against the grain, but she handed the shotgun over when he waggled his fingers. Honestly, this close, he could hurt her a half-dozen ways and they both knew it. Either she trusted him or she didn't, and so far, he'd been nothing but honest with her.

She could always shoot him later. The thought made her snort, and he shook his head. "You find somethin' funny?"

Yeah. He had her veering between homicidal and horny as hell, so he was lucky she'd opted for laughter.

Another day, with a less *male* companion, and she might have taken a moment to appreciate the panoramic view of mountains and forest unfolding around the watchtower. She had a real sweet setup. He didn't seem to care, though, because as soon as he'd gotten his boots on the platform, he shifted her stuff to his left arm, bent down, and hooked his right beneath her elbow, giving her a quick boost and pull. The towel hitched, slipping lower over her breasts.

Hope you enjoyed the show.

She headed inside, snagging her stuff as she pushed past him.

Somehow, she wasn't surprised when he deftly blocked the closing door with a booted foot. Yeah, clearly he wouldn't put it past her to slam the door in his face. He wasn't wrong either. Seeing him here in her private space evoked a visceral reaction. The small cabin seemed even smaller, pulling her toward him.

"You sleep in here?" He stepped in after her and gestured toward the mattress on the floor. The words came out as a question, although the truth was obvious. Of course, she did. Some of the other lookouts preferred to camp below their towers or had small cabins nearby, but she'd always enjoyed the sense of security and privacy she got from being so high above the forest floor. Nothing could get to her up here.

"This is my place." She thought maybe he flinched a little at her words, but she had a hard time imagining a big guy like him being put off by a cabin in the sky. He was certainly no stranger to rough-and-tumble.

"Not too much room to spare." He drawled the comment from her doorway, clearly in no hurry to come inside despite his claims earlier. So, okay. He was so far out of her league, it wasn't funny.

She crossed her arms over her chest. His eyes followed and her nipples puckered in response. He took his time looking, in no hurry to drag his gaze back to hers. She didn't know if she should be offended or turned on.

His slow smile decided her.

Turned on.

The folds of her pussy were swollen and overly sensitive, making each step she took an exquisite agony. If Cole would just make himself scarce, she had no doubt her battery-operated boyfriend would give her an orgasm in minutes.

"I've got a roof," she volunteered when the silence stretched on for too long and he showed no signs of leaving. No, the damned man just stood there, watching her. "And there's plenty of space between me and the wildlife. That works for me."

"*Oui.*" He shrugged. "Me, I'd rather be outside."

She bet he would. His feet would hang off that mattress, and they'd be banging knees and elbows. This couldn't, wouldn't work, and the sooner her libido got that message, the better.

Now that she got a good look at him, she saw the warning his face broadcast. Not only was he a big, hard brute of a man, but the scars alongside his jaw and throat said someone or something had tried to slice the skin there and almost succeeded. If his body were a map of where he'd been and what he'd done, he was clearly dangerous because of what he'd survived. He even moved with the sure, confident prowl of a wild cat. He *knew* he was in charge and that his very presence sucked the air out of the room. She should have grabbed the radio from him and sent him packing down the mountain.

She should *not* be imagining forty different ways to keep him there.

"Turn around," she demanded, because standing here in her towel was a bad idea. "Or get the hell out. Today's peep show is over."

He shrugged, like he didn't understand what the big deal

was, but he turned and she got the unmistakable feeling this was the first and last time he would take orders from her. While she studied his broad back and the way the faded cotton stretched over powerful muscles, he scanned the horizon. She did that, too, when she wasn't distracted by sexy hotshots, automatically looking for smokes. Tonight, the forest was real quiet. Close by, a hawk screamed and dove, hunting dinner, but the canopy of treetops spread away unbroken by new smokes.

The rustling sound of the towel hitting the floor seemed overly loud. She didn't know whether she wanted Cole to stay put—or to move. God, she'd bet he could move.

His next words were a surprise. He didn't comment on the view or even the potential for trouble brewing out there on the horizon. Instead, the man she would have sworn would avoid anything personal headed right there.

"I scare you." His declaration was matter-of-fact.

"Some," she admitted, because it was the truth. Having him here was like being shut in with a large tiger. She had no idea what he really wanted, or even *if* he wanted something.

"We'll work on that." A powerful shrug of his shoulders accompanied the easy declaration.

That just confused her further, because he was only here for one night. Looking at him made her think about sex—hot, nail-clawing, fierce sex—but he hadn't said that was what he wanted. Instead, she pulled on clean clothes: panties and a cotton tank top, shorts, and flip-flops. She skipped the bra because her skin was hot and the idea of anything binding her was unbearable.

"It's safe now," she said dryly.

"Tell me about last night." He didn't look away from her million-dollar view. "The lightning-hittin'-things part."

She shrugged and hung up the towel. "It's not your problem."

"Like hell it isn't." His words lacked any heat, though. "We talk every night for two weeks, *sha*, and then you go off radar? Of course I'm comin' here and checkin' you out."

The words hung there in the air between them, a potent reminder of sex. *Don't go there.* She didn't know what she wanted.

Or, if she was being honest, she knew *exactly* what she wanted—she just didn't know how far she'd let herself go.

"I don't need protecting," she said, when the silence stretched on for too long.

He turned away from the window. "You still shouldn't be out here alone." Outside, night rolled in, slowly wrapping the watchtower in shades of gray.

4

He was hot. She hadn't a date in months. And he didn't feel like a stranger.

"I'll buy you dinner," she decided.

"You're feedin' me?"

"Sure." She grinned at him. "If you eat veggie burgers."

She gave him credit. He didn't flinch. "Sounds good."

The cooking part of things went surprisingly well. She played chef while he manned the coals. They chatted while she got things going, but the conversation remained in neutral territory. He didn't mention seeing her in her skivvies or their late-night calls. Instead, he caught her up on the park news, describing a couple of recent calls. She didn't have much to contribute. She loved sitting in the watchtower, loved the peace and quiet of it all, but those calm days didn't make for exciting storytelling. What was she supposed to say? I saw a bear yesterday? Or, hey, I called in that smoke you spent ten hours busting your ass to knock down—glad I could help?

Honestly, she wasn't sure what she'd expected—maybe for him to pounce or make some kind of reference to their late-night calls—but Cole Henry was a gentleman. He didn't get in her space. Much. Sure, he brushed past her a time or two as she worked and his fingers touched hers when he handed her the frying pan or a spatula. He was all kinds of rumpled, sexy gorgeous, too. Just looking at him was the highlight of her day. She sighed. Maybe he was disappointed now that he'd got a good look at her. Or maybe he'd only been interested in phone sex. Or he had a girlfriend back at camp and she'd been a little side cheat that didn't quite count—although something told her Cole Henry would never, ever cheat. He'd been blunt, earthy, and raw on those calls. If he was done with a woman, he'd tell her. Nicely, maybe even gently. But he'd walk.

Still, working beside him was enjoyable. They fell into an easy rhythm like they'd made dinner together a thousand times before. Again, that was something unexpected. Not surprising was his expertise with the coals. He knew exactly how to coax her fire pit to life and build up a hot bank of coals for her to cook on. He hummed, too. The low, slightly off-key thread of sound was nothing identifiable, but she definitely liked the smile tugging at his lips as he worked.

He was easy on the eyes, too. She wanted to peel off the Nomex low on his hips, push up the faded cotton T-shirt, and run her hands over the washboard abs underneath. And his wide shoulders definitely begged a gal to hang on. Yeah, she couldn't even pretend she wasn't checking him out, so she looked him over and let herself imagine all the places she could be kissing him. Like the strong, tanned column of his throat and—he reached for her bowl of burger fixings—down his back until she reached his delicious ass. Part of her definitely wanted to pop all his buttons and forget about dinner. Looking at him was even better than listening to him.

She'd had supplies packed in at the beginning of the week, so she was pleasantly stocked up and had fresh food to offer him. His hands expertly wielded a knife, chopping lettuce and tomato while she flipped their burgers in the cast iron over the fire. He was confident and sure as he went all Ginsu on the produce.

"You're starin'," he said, not turning around.

Yeah, well, this wasn't the way she'd imagined her day ending. Not by a long shot. "Maybe you're imagining things," she countered.

"Don' think so." He finished on the lettuce and pulled a tomato over onto the board he'd balanced on her picnic table. One of the previous watches must have built the damned thing from scratch, because no way Park Service had packed it in. The table had definitely seen better days, but she liked the memories and love stories scratched into its weather-beaten surface.

He looked over at her and smiled. Slowly. "I always know when a pretty girl is watchin' me."

"Really?" Yeah, he was all hotshot. She was fairly certain the Forest Service passed out that brand of cocky confidence with the Nomex.

"Now you're thinkin' I'm overconfident." He looked up from his handiwork and his slow grin set something on fire in her belly. God, he really was one hundred percent bad boy. Their radio exchanges should have been her first clue.

And they still hadn't discussed where he was sleeping tonight.

"I like the way you look at me," he continued.

"Really?" she drawled. Again. Yeah, she was winning all sorts of prizes for conversational brilliance tonight.

"And you should know I'm lookin' at you." He winked and went back to chopping.

Well, then. There was that.

She finished her burger handiwork and transferred the patties to the plates. Her melamine was all pretty Target ware, blue with white swirls. The little pretend flowers were like nothing she'd ever seen in nature, but it didn't matter. Sometimes, pretty was enough.

"*Bon appétit,*" he said, his Cajun accent growing more noticeable. Maybe he spoke French at home. Or in bed. Hastily, she shoved that thought aside. This was dinner, not foreplay. She didn't even know how far she wanted to take this evening, just that, since he was here, getting to know him better seemed like a good idea.

"Where are you from?" She didn't know if the question was rude or not, but learning more about Cole was tempting. He was more than a sexy voice and a hot fantasy now, and that was his fault for showing up uninvited.

"The accent? My *maman* is from the Louisiana bayou. That's where I grew up."

"And now you're out here, working with the Big Bear Rogues."

He shrugged, assembling his burger on his plate. "I go home in the off-season. I have a place out on the bayou."

"Like actually *out* out on the bayou?"

"Sure." He took a big bite of his burger, chewed, and swallowed thoughtfully. "But it's not all Okefenokee Swamp, if that's what you're imaginin'. I do lots of huntin' and fishin' and my houseboat isn't anythin' fancy, but it's mine. When the day comes I can't swing a Pulaski, I've got the place waitin' for me. How about you?"

"Me?" She poked at her burger.

"Yeah. Where do you go when you're not busy being Rapunzel in her tower?"

"Davis." She could feel him looking at her and she loved the way he gave her his undivided attention. "University of California. I'm in the vet school there."

"Wow." He stretched his legs out toward the fire. "So you like animals. And hard work."

"I don't know about liking it." She grinned. "But I want to be a vet, so I've got to do the coursework."

"It must be a real change of pace, coming out here."

"I love it." Had he leaned in a little closer? She could feel the heat coming off his body now. "Sometimes, things get a little too loud and busy. Davis isn't exactly a metropolitan hot spot, but I like to get away and be alone."

He nodded. "I hear you on the space." A shadow passed over his eyes and she wondered what he was remembering. Given the way his fingers stroked the old dog tags hanging around his neck, she had a good guess.

"I don' care for bein' inside," he admitted. "Give me the outdoors any day. Who wants an office with four walls and a door when there's all this? Plus, there are definitely plenty of animals out here," he teased. "For you to practice on."

"Good thing I've got a large animal specialty." She grinned back at him.

He shifted and now he was *definitely* closer. His hip pressed against hers, his legs stretched out close enough to touch.

"This could be our first date." His words were a slow, smoky drawl.

Lost in his accent, it took her a moment to process what he'd just said. "Wow. No pressure."

"Not what you imagined?"

She shrugged. "I like veggie burgers just fine. You—"

"*Oui?*" He took a final bite of his burger, setting the empty plate down on the ground beside his feet, and no man had any right to look so damned sexy.

"I had you pegged for a steak and potatoes guy."

"Sure." He swallowed and grinned at her. "But you made this for me. I'm givin' you points for effort."

She was nervous.

He didn't blame her. They'd had themselves some scorching-hot conversations, but she'd never expected him to actually show up on her doorstep. Frankly, part of him was surprised she hadn't run screaming.

And pleased.

Very, very pleased.

"So," she said, playing with her food. She needed to eat, but he didn't know how to make her feel more comfortable with his being here. Sure, he could go, but he didn't want to do that. Plus, he liked her feminine awareness of him. He wouldn't trade that. "What did you do before you joined the Rogues?"

He pointed to the dog tags he still wore. He should take them off, put them away, but they were a good reminder. "Military."

"Marines?" He could hear the guess in her voice.

"Crash, Fire and Rescue," he admitted. "We responded to air-crash emergencies. Drove the truck to the end of the runway and waited for distressed aircraft to come in. Sprayed a little foam. Hauled a little ass. I did two tours; then I got out."

"Do you miss it?" She sounded more curious than politely interested.

"Honestly? No." *Hell no.*

"Bad memories." She sounded like she understood. "Is it better out here? In the park?" She waved a hand toward the forest surrounding them.

She understood. That was his first thought. His second was that she'd said she also liked getting away. She definitely got it.

"Yeah," he admitted gruffly. "That last tour didn't end so well. A fighter jet came in badly," he said, surprising himself. He didn't talk about what happened. Ever. "The pilot overshot the runway and crashed. My truck was in the way."

The best part about the forest was the lack of fucking walls. He could go any direction he wanted, whenever he wanted. He went to the fire, not the other way round. He'd sat there at the end of the runway, smelling fuel and skin burning, trapped in that damned vehicle for six hours until the boys had managed to cut him free with the Jaws of Life. The scream of the jet fighters coming in overhead hadn't been enough to drown out the moans of dying because, when that first plane had skidded off the runway and plowed into them, they'd been sitting ducks.

"You made it home." Her fingers touched his arm. "I'm glad."

"The other men in my truck weren't so lucky." He didn't tell her more, because she didn't need to hear those things. Bad enough he remembered them every day. How he'd sat there in the truck watching the plane slide closer and there was nothing he could do in that handful of seconds. He'd had his foot on the gas, but fifteen feet wasn't enough with 19,000 pounds of metal and jet fuel barreling his way. Somehow, he'd made it out with just the burn marks down his rib cage and a flat, shiny spot where his dog tags had seared his skin. That wasn't fair and he wasn't even sure it was right. He'd been the driver. He should have gotten them all out of there.

"I'm sorry," she said. Her finger rubbed small circles on the inside of his forearm.

"It's not your fault."

"No," she agreed, "but—"

People always felt the need to say something. To apologize or explain what had happened. He'd been there. He'd gone over the scene a million times in his head, trying to figure out a better outcome. He'd failed; there was no way anyone else could fix it.

Somehow, though, her words helped. "I'm glad you're out here, then. Where you feel better," she said.

Him, too.

She made him feel better.

After his conversational downer, they sat in silence while she finished eating. When she was done, he followed her over to the cistern on the edge of her clearing. As long as it rained during the year, she'd have a steady supply of water during summer months. He passed her the plates. She soaped and rinsed, falling into a quiet, easy rhythm, but it wasn't like they'd had a three-course banquet. The chore was finished quickly.

"So." She chewed on her lower lip. She was working up to something, and it didn't take a genius to figure out what. Here he was. It was dark. They were alone and he was going to have to sleep somewhere. He'd brought a tent and he should probably tell her that.

"Let's sit by the fire for a while," he suggested, and she latched on to the suggestion like it was a lifeline. Definitely nervous.

She hightailed back to the logs set around the fire pit and sat down, her back straight. "You coming?"

"Sure," he said. "But, Hannah . . ."

"Yeah?" She tilted her head to look at him as he sat down beside her.

"I don' bite," he promised.

"Hell." She blew out a breath. "I've never done this before." She moistened her lower lip with her tongue.

"Had sex with a stranger?" He slid an arm around her shoulder and pulled her close. She melted into his side, so that upright posture of hers must have been even more uncomfortable than it looked. Her head hit his chest, bounced up. She was looking at him again and he had no idea what she saw.

He had. Had sex with strangers, that is. He'd been careful and he was clean, but he'd gone home with more than one unfamiliar face. That had never bothered him before. He enjoyed himself. He made damned sure his partner enjoyed herself. As long as his date for the night had been over eighteen, he'd figured no harm, no foul.

This date was different.

This was *Hannah* he was holding. And she was talking again. He'd never met a woman who thought things through this much. Either she wanted to have sex with him or she didn't, right? It didn't have to be complicated.

"Yes. No," she said. "I don't feel like we're strangers."

"Good." He tunneled his fingers into the hair at the back of her neck. Christ, she was tense. He rubbed and she purred. To his surprise, just doing that all night would have been enough.

"I have a tent," he said. Had she fallen asleep? He looked down, but her eyes were open, staring at the dying flames in the fire pit. She was still with him. "I don' have to sleep anywhere else tonight."

"You don't have to sleep outside." She looked up at him and the desire in her eyes woke his erection right back up. "Not unless you want to."

5

"The fantasies we swapped over the radio—were those kind of a bucket list, or were you just makin' stuff up?" His eyes caught and held hers.

She felt like a deer who'd been cornered by a large and hungry predator, despite the ridiculously long lashes shielding his dark eyes.

Outside it got dark and then darker, the stars popping out into the night sky. The crickets sang up a storm and an owl called, swooping in for a midnight snack. She had to figure out something to do with Cole Henry and fast.

"I . . ." She opened her mouth. Closed it. The problem was, she *had* wanted to experience the fantasies she'd shared with him. Sort of. What she hadn't expected, however, was this man sitting beside her, watching her.

"I'm not expectin' you to do anything," he said. "I came up here because you needed a new radio. We could leave it at that. But—" He shrugged casually, although there was nothing casual about his big body. "If you wanted . . ."

"If I wanted, then what?" She flicked on her flashlight, picking out a path back to the tower.

"We could do anythin' you wanted tonight."

"Anything?"

"*Oui.*" His eyes followed the path her beam picked out. "We got maybe eight hours until dawn. Plenty of time."

He set the time limit casually, but he didn't take his eyes off her. She looked at him, and she saw a man who wanted to make sure his own limits were plenty clear. She could have him, no holds barred—but only for the one night. In the morning, he'd get up and go.

He must have read something on her face. "I'm a one-night man, *sha*. You wouldn't wan' me around longer than that anyhow."

"One night?" she asked lightly. "You got a hard and fast limit on sex? When does my clock start ticking?"

"You see me?" he growled. "Do I look like a keeper to you?"

He *looked* damn fine to her. His cotton T-shirt stretched over powerful shoulders and the hard lines of his abdomen. Strong forearms flexed, giving her the occasional flash of the military tattoo on the inside of his wrist. He had plenty of scars, both old and newer. Yeah, she wanted his one night and whatever else he had to offer.

"One night only." His eyes didn't leave hers. "That's my personal rule."

"You have guidelines for one-night stands?" He didn't strike her as the kind of man who let anyone or anything run his life.

"Only this one." A slow grin tugged at the corner of his mouth. "Everything else, *sha*, is fair game. You think that over while I fix this radio of yours. Least I can do since you bought me dinner."

Fixing the radio was just plug and play. Ten minutes of fiddling and then she was up and running. Hannah made a quick test call back to base camp to report in a new smoke that had popped up on the horizon earlier. The smoke wasn't a danger yet, but Hannah would keep an eye on it for the Rogues.

"Widow's Peak to base."

"Base, over. Come in, Widow's Peak. Good to hear your voice." Sam's familiar voice filled the cabin. Probably curious to know what he was up to, Cole acknowledged, toasting the man with his water bottle.

"I'm back in business, thank you."

Standing there, in her cabin, seemed strange. He didn't have to imagine the face that went with the voice. All he had to do was look down and there she was, tucking loose strands of hair behind her ear as she concentrated on her report.

As Sam caught her up on the day's weather report, Hannah bent over the table with her Osborne Fire Finder, the delicious curve of her ass driving Cole crazy. He had to look away from the shorts pulled taut over her rounded cheeks. Otherwise, he'd find himself running his tongue along that crease. Kissing her higher. Longer.

She stretched farther, arms reaching over the topographic map of the forest he'd learned by heart from summers spent hiking every inch. Carefully, she rotated the metal ring with a sighting device that she positioned over the map, determining the directional bearing of the fire.

"I've got a smoke at my azimuth of one hundred fifty degrees and fifteen minutes."

She spoke clearly into the mic, not hesitating. This was her job and she was damn good at it. Here, fires were reduced to technical descriptions: where to find the flames on the map. He used his gut and his senses. When he could see, hear, smell the fire, he was home. She kept the flames at a distance, calling them out by where they fell on a property map.

Yeah, two different worlds.

"I've been thinkin'," he offered when she signed off.

She eyed him suspiciously. "Have you?"

"Uh-huh. I'm thinkin' we could play ourselves some cards. Pass some time that way."

Her face lit up. "Texas Hold 'Em?"

"Sure, *sha.*" Reaching into his pack, he produced a worn pack of cards. The next few moments would set the tone for the night and he needed to choose his words carefully. She liked cards. She liked games. He had big plans for tonight.

"What do you want to play for?"

She played right into his hand. "A kiss?"

She curled up cross-legged on the mattress across from him, flashing bare golden skin beneath the edge of her shorts. When she leaned forward and snagged the deck, the move showcased the shadow between her breasts. She'd skipped a bra, and that was just one more temptation.

With the windows propped open, the air cooled down fast, but that was summertime in the mountains for you. All heat, all day, and then bam, night moved in and the temperature dropped. He had plenty of ideas about how to keep her warm, though—as soon as he won this hand.

"You got yourself a deal. We'll play for our first kiss."

His cards, his deal. He grabbed a baggie of poker chips from his pack, passed her a stack, and dealt each of them two face-down cards. He had two kings. Lady Luck was definitely on his side.

She studied her cards and bet two red chips. Not too conservative, but nothing rash either. She was in this to win. He countered with two black.

"Deal." She gestured impatiently toward the deck.

"Looking forward to collecting?" he teased, dealing three cards onto the mattress. The flop was pretty good for him, too. A king and two clubs. Only a handful of possible combos beat his. From the look on her face, though, she thought she was holding one of them.

She blew him a quick kiss. "Absolutely, hotshot. I hope you're looking forward to paying up."

She had no idea. Chips hit the pot as they both bet. *Come on.* Her kissing him would be damned fine, but he had plans of his own. All sorts of places he wanted to get his mouth tonight.

Turn card was a two of diamonds. Hannah checked.

He flipped over the river card and stifled a grin. Two of clubs. He had her beat for sure.

"I'm all in. Read 'em and weep." Laughing, she shoved the rest of her stack into their pot and flipped over her cards.

She had a good hand. Ace king high flush. He grinned, slowly. "Uh-uh, *sha.* I got you beat."

"Well, hell." She stared at the cards he turned over, chewing on her lower lip.

His honey didn't like losing. He didn't either.

"Kings full of deuces. Time for you to pay up," he drawled. This close, the warmth of her body drew him, her peaches-and-cream scent teasing his senses. Whatever shampoo she'd used in the stream, she smelled good enough to eat.

She leaned forward. "Never let it be said I don't pay my debts."

He was a bastard and he'd undoubtedly roast in hell, because he let her settle her hands on his shoulders. Her lips brushed his. He liked the feel of her, the soft shush of her breath feathering across his mouth. Her tongue traced a naughty path along the closed seam of his lips; then she kissed the hell out of him.

Long minutes later, he caught her shoulders with his hands, curving his fingers over the fragile bones. "You sure know how to kiss a man."

Her eyes widened. *Yeah,* sha, *this big bad wolf is goin' to eat you up.*

"But that wasn't our deal."

"Excuse me?"

"Sure." He smiled, slow and knowing. "I get to kiss you. One kiss wherever I wan'."

Whatever Cole Henry had in mind, he had *no* intention of behaving.

Hannah ran through possible objections in her head and then—damn it—she wasn't going to overthink this. She had one night to make all of her fantasies come true. The clock was ticking and she didn't want to waste another minute.

She eyed the cards discarded on the bed, then the man sitting across from her.

"You cheated," she accused. "If I call your boys at the base, they're going to warn me not to play with you, aren't they?"

"Maybe. It's possible that I've played the World Series of Poker a time or two. But cheat? Never." That familiar bad-boy grin tugged at his mouth. The mouth she'd just kissed. "But we're not settled up yet. You know where I wan' to kiss you, *sha*. I described my kiss for you."

Oh, God. *He had.* More than once, because that had been one of her favorite midnight fantasies.

"You liked what I told you jus' fine." She certainly *liked* the heat and determination in his gaze.

"Those were fantasies." Not a game plan or a road map.

"The stakes were a kiss. I plan on havin' that kiss."

He wouldn't force.

She knew that.

But Cole was Cole, and she also knew he'd push until she flat out told him *no*.

Yes.

That was what she wanted to say. All she needed to do was find the courage.

He put his hand on her knee. "Lie back, *sha*. Open up and let me have my kiss, *oui?*"

He wanted to kiss her *there*. She knew that. He'd told her

exactly how he planned on dragging his tongue through her folds. How wet she'd be and what he'd be doing with his fingers while she rode his mouth like a cowgirl in a very, very naughty rodeo.

Hearing him describe that kiss had been one of the sexiest damn things she'd ever experienced. She'd come so hard, she suspected half the Rogues back at base camp had heard her. Of course, she'd also figured Cole Henry was all talk and a safe distance away.

Her mistake.

His fingers stroked the inner curve of her thigh. "You got a *yes* in you for me?"

God, she did.

"Yes," she said, her voice throaty with nervousness and desire.

"Then lie back."

She didn't want time to think about what she was doing. Big, hard Cole Henry was volunteering to bring all her fantasies to life, and she'd take everything he had to offer. Starting right now. Carefully, she settled back on the mattress, not quite sure what to do with her hands and arms. She settled for leaning back on her elbows. *All the better to see you with.*

He didn't seem to mind.

Dropping to his knees, he slid between her thighs. Big hands latched on to her hips and dragged her to the edge of the mattress. She loved the careful control in those fingers as they moved her around for his pleasure. Tonight, she'd go wherever he wanted her to go.

He pressed her thighs gently open. "Relax."

That was easy for him to say. He knew what was coming next, but she was tense, anticipating his first kiss. The first intimate touch. And excited. God, she was excited. For a long moment, he simply looked. She was still wearing her shorts and panties. Maybe she'd misremembered or he'd meant something else. Then, he smoothed a hand up her calf and over her striped knee socks.

"Cute," he rumbled. "Next time you call me, I'll remember to ask what you're wearin'."

Before she could catch her breath, he lowered his head. She moaned, the sensation of his breath on her pussy, even through two layers of clothing, an electric shock. This was everything she had imagined—and more. Her hands flew to his shoulders and hung on.

His thumbs made the return trip up her thighs, delving into the damp crease where her mound and thighs met. A wash of sweet sensation followed the erotic tickle, so hot and fierce that she cried out.

"*Oui,*" he whispered. His fingers tightened on her hips, lifting her to meet his mouth. No more talking, just the sweetest and simplest of kisses. He nuzzled her through the crotch of her shorts, sweet, light strokes that sent lightning sizzling through her.

A moan, followed by a sigh. "Oh."

The soft brush of his lips was followed by the harder push of air as he exhaled roughly. Inhaled like he loved the scent of her. Once. Twice.

His fingertips teased her entrance through the fabric, while his mouth discovered her clit. She bucked.

Oh. My. God.

His shoulders pressed her thighs wider and she let them fall open, way beyond embarrassment now. This man could kiss.

"You, *sha,* are perfect." He worked his mouth harder against her and she shoved up to meet him, craving the contact.

He rewarded her with more pleasure, his fingertips sweeping beneath the edge of fabric to touch bare skin.

She wanted so much more. "Lose the shorts?"

His answering chuckle should have warned her. "All in good time. This is my kiss, so we're doin' it my way."

Slow. He'd told her he liked to take things slow. To take his time with his woman. She groaned and he laughed.

"Yeah, we got all night."

His fingers explored farther beneath the band of her panties as his mouth covered her clit again, tasting through the clothes she no longer wanted there. She'd imagined this while he'd talked, tried to create in her head the images he'd spun over the midnight airwaves, but nothing, nothing could have prepared her for this.

Thighs tensing, her breathing picking up speed, her fingers curling into his shoulders and dragging his head closer. Making sure he was where she needed him to be. "I'm going to come," she whispered.

He laughed, a rough, low sound. "Not until I tell you you can. I'm not finished with you."

His finger speared her as his tongue discovered the edge of her shorts. Wet heat. An erotic shock that had her shuddering and arching up again. His fingers traced her wet slit beneath her panties, tugging the lacy panel to the side. And his tongue, God, his tongue circled her bare clit. Rubbing over a spot that had her seeing white as pleasure lashed her. *Yes.*

"Come now, *sha.*" The stern command pushed her higher and she let go.

She came hard, squeezing his shoulders and holding on tight.

6

Her hotshot was all done waiting.

When she tried to sit up, he pushed her right back on the mattress. She didn't mind. She'd been wanting his hands on her ever since she'd discovered him sprawled on her steps. She quickly discovered, though, that she might be in a rush—but he wasn't. When she brought her hands up to tug on his shirt, he pressed her palms down into the mattress.

"Don' move, *sha*," he warned as he moved closer. Close enough she could feel the heat and tension radiating off his body. The way he leaned in reminded her that he was bigger. Stronger.

"Or?" Deliberately, she slid her hands off the mattress. She'd make him spell out those consequences. See if his imagination tonight rivaled that of all those other nights they'd spent apart—but swapping fantasies over the airwaves.

His sexy bad-boy grin was answer enough, his brown eyes heating up. "I tie a mean knot. And I bet I'd like your ass pink just fine."

Oh, God. His words sent fire licking through her veins.

"Promises," she whispered hoarsely, licking dry lips. "How about you show me what you can do?"

"I'm waitin'." His gaze dropped to her hands. "Show me you can take orders."

She shouldn't be so turned on by his matter-of-fact command. She shuddered, slapping her hands onto the mattress. He knew all her secret fantasies. Hell, she'd told him.

"That's my girl. I should tie you up anyhow," he continued, his face darkening. "What were you thinkin', Hannah? This tower is nothin' but a lightning rod in a storm. I told you to get out."

"More touching, less talking." She tilted her head back, challenging him.

His thumb raked the side of her jaw. The erotic rasp of the calluses had another, harder shiver racking her body.

"Yeah?"

"Absolutely." She was having Cole Henry tonight.

His teeth nipped her ear. "I did come out here to take care of you. Anything, everything, *sha*. I'm makin' sure you get exactly what you need."

She exhaled. *Yes.* Her choice. To let go and let him take over. She knew he would drive them both toward that sensual height. So good. She'd craved his voice each night, but that was nothing like the ache actually touching him built in her body. She'd never felt like this with any lover before, but Cole Henry was one of a kind. Her big, hot Cajun. The weight of his body held her in place for his sensual touch.

Don't stop.

"Please."

He leaned closer. His hand pushed her thighs apart, making room for himself. "Lie back."

His tone made it clear that she might not have taken his orders about leaving the tower, but she'd be taking these orders. He pushed her tank top up, his fingertips grazing her ribs. "You're not wearin' a bra."

She wished she'd worn one. Something pretty, with lace and satin. Something else for him to peel off, to spin out this moment.

She looked down, unable to help herself. His suntanned hands stroked her paler skin. "Too hot." She grinned at him. "And not enough of me."

He shook his head. "There's plenty of you." His fingertips traced the sensitive curves, exploring her with the rough, hard hands of a man who worked outdoors for months on end, swinging an ax and a shovel. There was nothing easy about him, although he was deliberately careful as he palmed her.

It should have felt awkward, her half-sitting, half-reclining on the mattress, with her shirt shoved up above her breasts. Cole made it hot. Like he really couldn't get enough of her. Like he wasn't waiting for what he wanted.

God, yeah.

His fingers feathered along her ribcage, his touch both soothing and arousing. He refused to rush, even when she wriggled demandingly.

"You're impatient."

"You're making me wait." She was supposed to be done waiting.

"Good things," he promised. "That's what comes to those who wait." His fingers found her nipples and the tender-rough caress made her sigh. He captured the tips, rolling gently, but gentle wasn't what she wanted right now.

"Harder." She only had today. That meant there was no time for him to figure out what she liked, so she'd tell him—or go without. Holding her breath, she waited to see how this big, dominant male would react to a little bedside instruction. *Please.*

"Be careful what you ask for." A harder roll followed close on the heels of his sexy growl.

Better.

"I know what I like." She brought her own hands up, pinching her nipples.

He pulled her into his arms, lifting her ass off the mattress. The sharp sting on her left cheek warned he'd reached his limit. The small tap was just enough to burn, and delicious heat radiated out from the spot.

"You got me to do that."

She did. "So do it."

Cole took charge, his fingers covering her aching nipples. Pinching and rolling, each sensual tug sending her higher.

"You do something for me."

"Sure."

"Shuck those shorts and panties."

Yeah. She popped the button, savoring the sensual brush of the fabric moving down her thighs. Sprawled out on the bed as she was, she could only push her shorts halfway down before his larger body pinned her in place and left her sensually aware of being half-dressed, half-naked.

He'd kissed her before, hard, deep kisses that made her burn. She was wet for him and they both knew it. All she needed now was to get her hands on him. Drag her palms down that muscled back and cup his firm ass. Pull him deeper and harder into the aching space between her thighs. He wasn't rushing, though, damn it.

Her fingers curled into the sheets, waiting for him.

He smiled slowly. "You like bein' bossed around."

She didn't have to tell him everything. "Maybe."

She leaned back on her elbows. She loved watching him work her body, his dark head covering her nipple. The muscles in her forearms bulged as he lowered himself.

And, oh, God, the wet heat of his mouth. His tongue licked and tasted, followed by the sweet sting of his teeth as he caught a sensitive tip. She moaned as the hot rush of pleasure hit her hard.

Cole's fingers curled over her waist, then sank lower. Greedy for his touch, she rubbed her thighs together because she'd never anticipated anything so much. But he skipped her pussy, dragging her panties and shorts to her ankles.

"Toe them off." He rolled to the side, giving her just enough room to do so. "Now."

She was shameless around this man. She reached down and found the bunched fabric. One good tug and she was good and naked.

"That's it." He eased back, dropping between her legs even as one big hand covered her right breast. He flattened the other between her widespread thighs. Every muscle and nerve ending in her belly jumped in anticipation because, God, Cole Henry made this good. Sweet tension built as his fingers stroked lower, teasing sensitive skin.

This was what she wanted. This raw hunger and heated touching with no holds barred.

"Flip."

He guided her down onto her hands and knees, his big hands stroking up her back, canting her ass up. On her elbows, neck arched, she waited eagerly. Sprawled on her sheets, she was hyperaware of him moving behind her and the unmistakable sound of a condom snapping into place, rough and urgent. He didn't want to wait any more than she did. That rough need fed her own excitement, the spice of not knowing what he would do next an erotic encouragement to *feel*. Cole didn't have rules. He'd do her *his* way.

"Please," she whispered. Her head swam with the delicious buzz of wanting him, her fingers curling into the sheet. Her thighs shook with the effort of holding still.

A warm, rough-skinned hand stroked one cheek of her ass. Cupped and shaped her, controlling, but in a good way. "Whatever you wan', *sha*," he growled.

His dick brushed against her swollen folds.

He fisted one hand in her ponytail, using the other to guide himself to her pussy. The rough in and out of his breathing soughed against her ear, his exhalations grazing her neck. Pressing back against him, driving him deep—that was what she needed. That hand stopped her, held her in place. Instead, he pushed himself through her slick folds. Again and again as electric pleasure shot through her.

Cole pinned her, his big body dominating hers in an animalistic display that was perfect. His arms caged her on the bed. *This* was exactly what she wanted. Being in control wasn't part of her plans for tonight. Instead, she had a chance to lose herself in him and the sensations he built in her.

His cock pushed into her tight entrance. No hesitation, no holding back, just a deliberate, steady invasion. She was wet and that made his entrance easier, but his cock was still a tight fit. No part of Cole was small. Fuck holding still. She slapped her hands over his, her nails scoring the sun-browned skin.

He growled, pulling one hand free and reaching between them to stroke her clit, plumping the hard nub until she fought the urge to scream from the delicious sensations. "Open up."

Her visceral response matched his rough, needy demand. *Mine.*

Deliberately, she closed her legs, tightening her ass and forcing him to screw himself deeper one tight, needy inch at a time. She wouldn't last long. She'd come before he was even halfway seated.

She came with a little shriek and he surged deeper, pressing all the way inside her. God. He was so big. And hard. And demanding.

"That's two," he rumbled, pulling out and driving back inside her. He slammed his cock in and out, his hips rising and falling. Sprawled beneath him, she pulled him closer in the only way she could. She canted her hips, taking him deeper and squeezing hard. *Take me.*

In this position, he dominated her and they both knew it.

His hands gripped her ankles and lifted. "Try this for me, *sha.*"

The sensation as he rocked her slowly from side to side was exquisite. The moan slid from her, a throaty sound of satisfaction.

"Yeah." He repeated the motion and she arched up.

"Cole . . ." She wanted more, she wanted him to slow down and speed up at the same time. When she pushed her hips back against him, his hoarse growl said he felt the same way.

He thrust harder and faster, his teasing slo-mo long gone. He pulled his dick back until just the tip was still inside her channel, then slammed back in hard and fast, his skin slapping on hers, his harsh breathing mingling with hers. His mouth covered her neck, pressing kisses against her throat. Her jaw. Her ear. As caught up in the moment as she was.

Another orgasm built inside her. Panting, she rocked on the bed. Braced for each new thrust. Gasping. Taking all of him.

When he pulled out all the way, she whimpered in greedy protest.

"More." She wasn't done with him. He could damn well get back here now.

"Give me a moment, *sha.*" His raspy chuckle sent shivers up and down her spine. "You're goin' to like this just fine. While I get you ready, you do this." His fingers stroked through her slick folds, positioning her fingers on her clit. "Jus' like that."

She wanted his dick, not his instructions. She opened her mouth to tell him so when a tube top popped. She turned, trying to see what he was up to. He'd opened a container of lube, and she had a damned good idea what *that* meant.

"Uh-uh." He replaced her fingers on her clit. "You keep doin' that and I'll do this."

Hands pulled her ass cheeks apart, a slick finger finding the puckered rosette. There was an erotic tug as he separated her farther, coating her back entrance with the lube. Then he was pushing inside slowly until she hissed at the slow burn. God, she loved the pleasure-pain. She'd never tried this before, but tonight she was game. Whatever Cole Henry could dish out, she could take.

He paused a moment, like he was waiting for any protest. "You up for this?"

"More," she demanded. "That's what I'm thinking."

His finger pushed deeper, rotated, and found a spot that had her sucking in her breath. Oh, yeah.

"Uh-huh." His amused chuckle held a darker thread now. From the sounds of things, she was definitely getting *more*.

More sounds of wetness filled the cabin as he rolled on a new condom and lubed up. Placing the slick, blunt head tucked against her rear opening, he asked, "You ready, *sha?*"

Maybe. *Yes.*

"Push out."

She angled her hips, his hands guiding her as he pressed forward. He popped through the tight ring, pushing deep and slow inside her ass. She sucked in her breath at the hot burn as he filled her.

"That hurts." She arched her back, trying to ease the sting and reclaim the pleasure. "Make it better."

He did. Reaching beneath her, his fingers replaced hers. Gently, he captured her folds between his thumb and index finger, massaging her as one big finger speared through her pussy entrance, spreading her moisture over her clit. He circled, pressing and rubbing. Ran his finger up and down her clit.

"Better?"

"Oh, yeah."

Hannah's ass fisted him, hot and tight. He'd wanted to mark her in the most primitive way possible, to take *all* of her. And, Christ, she was letting him.

It was sexy as hell, the way her ass took him. Each thrust

forced her cheeks soft against him. Fingers curled around her hips, he moved her against him. Watched his cock disappear inside her.

Definitely the sexiest damn sight ever.

"Tell me somethin'. You okay?" He hoped she was. He'd pull out, stop if she asked him, but he'd also give just about everything he had to keep right on going.

"Yes. How about you?" She clenched around him, muscles flexing, and he was going to lose it. He knew it. He was going to drive himself in deep and hard, ride her for better or worse. Lose himself in the sensual hitch in her breathing when he hit a sweet spot and then worked his way deeper.

"Never better, *sha*. You have any idea how much I enjoy reamin' this ass of yours?"

"I've got an idea," she said dryly, her fingers curling into the sheets. "But be careful. This is a first for me."

Yeah, he was a primitive bastard, because his reaction to knowing he was first? Possessive. *Victorious.* Nothing he knew made him better than any other lover she'd invited into her bed, but she'd picked him for this. Somehow, he'd won. Come out on top. So he wouldn't be disappointing her.

Plus, he'd bet she knew exactly how she made him feel, how her words fed his frenzy, because there was a little feminine smile tugging at her lips. He moved deeper and then pulled back, working his way inside one slow inch at a time. Pushed in. Pulled out. He kept it slow, waiting for her body to get used to holding him, to his size, because no way he'd leave her behind.

Her breath sped up. She pushed down and took him deeper.

"Yeah, *sha*," he whispered roughly, dropping a kiss on her neck. "You come with me now, okay?"

He thrust, his hips slapping against her ass. In and out. Harder and faster.

His fingers pressed against her hips, holding her to him.

"Now?" The rough little plea in her voice drove him over the edge.

"*Oui, sha.*" Whatever she needed, that's what he'd give her. His fingers covered hers, teasing her clit. Helping her toward the same pleasure. She went first, locking her legs as a low, keening cry tore from her throat. That sound was the most beautiful he'd ever heard. If he could have seen her face, watched her come with him, that would have been perfect. *Next time.*

"There you are." Someone—him—was whispering words against her ear. Pet names and praise. Begging for more as her ass milked his dick in fierce spasms, her clit fluttering against their fingers.

Christ, yes.

He shoved inside her one last time. His balls tightened, the orgasm shooting through him in a white haze of lust and plea-sure. Her fingers stroked his, pinned them to the sheet as she waited for him and held him tight.

Afterward, he cleaned them both up. She spooned against him sleepily while he popped her underneath the covers. He should have found her a clean T-shirt to wear, because the mountain nights got cold, but sleeping naked with her was an-other one of his fantasies. He'd keep her warm. Besides, if the rest of her underwear looked like that wicked white thong, he might not let her sleep.

He had fond memories of her thong.

Say something, he told himself, but she beat him to it.

"That was better, way better than talking on the radio. Thank you." Her voice slurred, sinking into sleep, even as she turned her face into his chest like he was her own personal pil-low. He never spent the night with any of his one-night lovers. He'd always left.

She was right, though. This was better.

He'd had sex before. He liked sex. Liked women. But nothing and no one felt like *her.* Sex with Hannah Green was hotter than any airwave fantasy he'd shared with her. Their chemistry hadn't surprised him. No, the kicker was that, after everything was said and done, he wanted *more* than sex.

More, she'd said earlier. More pleasure, more sensations.

He'd done that, all right. He'd kissed her and touched her and made love to her until he'd worn them both out and now here they were. Tucked up together on her too-small, worn-out mattress. Getting ready to go to sleep.

And then she'd thanked him.

For the first time ever, Cole wanted to break his own one-night rule, because one night with Hannah Green wouldn't be enough. The desire to stay put scared the piss out of him. She was funny and smart and way too damned sexy for his peace of mind.

Dangerous.

Hannah made him happy. With her, he relaxed and let down his guard. Hell, he was smiling against her hair as he wrapped himself around her and drifted toward sleep himself. Leaving tomorrow wouldn't be easy. No, he wasn't kidding himself.

He didn't want to go anywhere but here.

7

Morning brought one more fire.

Smoke curled up from a nearby canyon. The small puff of smoke was almost cheerful, more Santa Claus working his pipe or cotton balls than anything ominous. Looks were deceptive.

"Fresh." She was talking to herself and she probably should have been concerned. Instead, she followed the smoke up, then examined the origin. "No haze yet."

The way that smoke went straight up with no telltale drift up canyon meant the fire hadn't been burning for long. She'd watch for a few and see what happened. Sometimes, after a lightning storm like the ones that had struck Widow's Peak the other night, you got little sleeper fires. This might be a few flames inside an old tree and it might burn itself out quickly.

Twenty minutes later, the column was twice as wide and growing. Her gut screamed this fire was going to be a bitch. And it was close, only four or five miles from Widow's Peak. The smoke drifted over the ridge and hung low over the trees on the edge of the clearing. Cole was out there somewhere.

He'd been gone when she woke up. She'd rolled over and

kept right on going. She'd wanted to snuggle some, put her head on his chest and let her fingers do some walking south and see how fast things heated up between them again. The sex had been amazing, and she'd woken up ready for a repeat. Instead, her ass had hit the floor, although at least the lack of company meant her shame was a private one.

He hadn't gone far. His pack still leaned against the wall next to the door—as ready to make a quick exit as the man— but Cole wasn't there. Maybe he'd slipped outside to take care of some personal business, but she suspected it was more than that. After all, he'd made his rules perfectly clear yesterday. One night. No strings. And now it was the morning after and he was nowhere in sight.

Message received.

She eyed the smoke again and the bastard was even bigger than before. Regardless of what did or didn't happen with Cole, she had a job to do here. She shoved her personal feelings aside and reached for the radio. This couldn't wait for the morning roll call.

"Big Bear Dispatch, Widow's Peak, I've got a visual on a fire."

"Widow's Peak, Dispatch, I copy."

She walked the park ranger on the other end through the fire. After that, all she could do was sit and wait, watching the smoke boiling up on the horizon. Last night had been all kinds of amazing and that meant letting go of Cole wasn't going to be easy. She wasn't ready to go all white picket fence on him, but she did want more than a single night in his arms. Unfortunately for her, it took two to tango.

And Cole had made his position perfectly clear.

It hurt. Sure, he had his reasons for preferring casual sex, but apparently some part of her had been secretly hoping she'd be the woman who convinced him to break his rules.

To stay put and to stick.

Tough shit.

He was a hotshot and she'd known what that meant. He'd

go back to base camp and, from there, head back into danger. Danger like that fire chewing up the ridge five miles away. Already the air was thickly smoky, the forest around her uneasy and on edge. The park was in good hands. Cole was a damned good firefighter. Calm and cool. Hard to rattle and quick to react.

Unlike her. Last night she'd come apart in his arms. She'd been everything but calm. The reality of Cole had been even better than the fantasy—until she'd woken up alone. She hadn't realized that she'd had some dreams about the morning after until it was too late.

Worse, she was pretty sure Cole would feel bad if he knew she was hurting. He was a nice guy, even if he hid that side behind his bad-ass hotshot exterior. He'd hiked all the way out here just to make sure she was okay, and she liked that concern. Hell, she liked the man. Liked his take-charge, take no prisoners attitude. Sure, his confidence made her want to butt heads with him—if only to see what he'd do—but she liked it.

And he was leaving this morning and there was nothing she could do to stop it. If last night hadn't been enough to convince him to stay—if *she* hadn't been enough—he'd go. End of story.

The smoke got darker. Plenty of trouble brewing there.

Booted feet crossed the observation deck. Her hotshot had returned.

He stuck his head inside. "Morning," he drawled, and, God, that sexy rasp got her going all over again. Hopefully, they'd still make those midnight calls when he got back to base camp, although it would be harder to let go now that he wasn't an anonymous virtual hookup.

Now that she had a face and a man to go with the voice.

"Hey yourself." She pointed to the smoke, although he must have spotted it. She had a feeling he hadn't missed the blush heating up her cheeks. Damn it. She wanted to be all cool and casual about what they'd done last night, but he was so far out of her league it wasn't funny.

"Things are heating up out there," she said instead.

He hesitated, but then produced a mug of coffee. He'd done more than walk out, apparently, and she didn't know how she felt about that. She took a tentative sip, blowing on the surface to cool things down just a bit. The coffee was hot and sweet, just the way she liked it. More points for Cole.

"I made it the way I like it." The wry twist of his lips was endearing. "Probably should have checked with you first. Maybe you're a tea person."

And that was classic Cole—looking out for her, but his way. She took another sip and, yeah, still perfect. Who knew they'd drink their coffee the same way? "Coffee's fine," she said, because he was clearly waiting for her to say something.

"About that fire—" He looked out the window and her gaze followed his. "I hiked out and took a closer look. We should call it into base."

"I already did." Again, they were on the same page.

"Good." He moved closer. His denim-clad thigh brushed her shoulder. "I don' think there's any immediate danger to you here, but the fire's sitting right on the trail back to base camp. I'm not gettin' through there today. I'm goin' to need to wait it out."

"Here?" She wasn't holding her breath, was she? Because that would be stupid.

"You wan' me to stay?"

She didn't know what to say. What *he* wanted her to say, which was even more stupid than holding her breath or blushing like a virgin, because this should be about what she wanted. This was her watchtower. He was the guest.

"I . . ." She opened her mouth. Closed it.

"Hell." He scrubbed a hand over his head. "Sorry."

He exhaled hard, but she hadn't got over the shock of his one-word apology. Cole was always sure, confident. On the airwaves or in bed, she'd never seen him hesitate. This was a first.

"Can we pretend I didn't say that?"

"Sure." She still had no idea what was going on here, but the desire to kick his ass down her stairs was growing.

"I shouldn't have put you on the spot like that," he said, prowling closer while she got busy with the coffee cup. "I know we were supposed to be a one-night hookup—"

"That was your rule," she interrupted, setting the mug aside. The brew needed Bailey's. Or whiskey. Anything alcoholic, because *she* needed a lifeline.

"Right." He eyed her. "Would you be open to bending the rules? Just this once?"

She hesitated. "You'd want to do that? Stay longer?"

He sat down on the edge of her desk and pulled her between his legs. His morning-after kiss was every bit as good as his night-before kisses. His hands cupped her head, his fingers threading through her hair and gliding in slow, teasing circles against her scalp. His mouth covered hers and his lips, God, his lips tasted and pressed until her eyes threatened to roll back in her head. His eyes stayed open. He watched her while he kissed her and so she watched him right back.

"*Sha,*" His hoarse groan said it all. "I'm not sure what I said or did to make you think I wouldn't wan' to be stickin' around longer."

"*You* said *you* had rules." She walked her fingers down his chest and looked up at him. The way he'd caged her in, she couldn't see the fire, but that didn't matter. She'd steal these ten minutes. With the fire called in, there was nothing to do now but watch and wait.

"Fuck the rules." He leaned down and captured her mouth in another hard kiss. "One, maybe two days more, and that fire out there will be under control. I wan' that time with you, okay?"

Three. She could think of at least three reasons she should tell him *no*. One, he'd still be going. Two, that still wasn't enough time. And three, well . . . this might be just some hot sex for him, but she had a horrible feeling that she was going to want it to be more.

There were probably a dozen other reasons as well.

"Hannah?" He rubbed a thumb over the side of her jaw. "You got an answer for me?"

To hell with it. She liked looking at him, liked touching him even more. He was stuck out here in the forest until that fire turned or burned out. She could keep him for another day or two. Run her lips and her hands all over the man sprawled on her desk. She'd be crazy not to say yes.

She'd be crazy not to run hard in the other direction, because she wouldn't be able to walk away from this with a whole heart.

She smiled up at him. Slowly. "Convince me."

God, Cole had never been so glad to see a fucking fire in his life. Or to realize that he was trapped behind the line with no way out. He *had* to stay here.

Effortlessly, he scooped her up and switched their places. Now she was the one laid out on the desk. Yeah, exactly where he wanted her.

"You remember that last call?" He knew his voice sounded hoarse. Rough. Jesus. He didn't feel like seduction or playing Prince Charming. No, right now he needed to be balls-deep in her, while she hollered his name and came around him.

Her eyes widened at his question, so, yeah, she remembered all right.

Time to turn those midnight fantasies into fact.

"Turn around. Hands on the desk."

She blinked up at him, dazed, like she was translating his order into some semblance of sense, but then she moved obediently. God, that was a turn-on right there, his Hannah trusting him to make this good for both of them. He hadn't left much room between them. Her ass pushed against his dick as she wriggled around.

"Okay," she said breathlessly, turning her head to look up at him. He wasn't sure whether she was giving him the heads-up that she'd assumed the position or permission to keep on going. Either worked for him.

"Hands on the desk," he whispered roughly against her neck and traced a hand over that vulnerable curve. His hips pinned hers in place. And every time he breathed in, he was surrounded by Hannah. Fuck, she was special.

He'd never get tired of doing this.

"Lean forward." Running his hand down the straight arrow of her spine, he bent her over. The map pinned to the desktop crinkled and she reached instinctively to smooth the little folds out. "Uh-uh."

He gave her a small tap on her ass. Just enough to sting but not enough to hurt. She gave a small squeak of surprise and jumped, bumping her ass against his dick. That was fun, too.

"I wan' all your attention on me," he said roughly. "Can you do that for me?"

Deliberately, he let his fingers toy with the waistband of her shorts, inserting his fingers just beneath the edge in a small caress. Her breathing picked up.

"Yes." She breathed out the word as she stilled.

Waiting for him to touch her some more. He loved that, loved having her spread out beneath him.

"Palms down. Don' move," he warned. Shifting her hair to one side, he kissed her throat. With his other hand, he cupped her ass.

No rush. *We got all sorts of time now.* He kissed his way down her throat, burying his face in the sweet, soft space where her neck and her shoulder met.

"Cole—" Hell if he knew whether she wanted more or something different, or if she just liked saying his name. Any of the three worked for him; seducing Hannah did a number on him.

When he pulled her shorts down her thighs, she went up on tiptoe, pushing into his touch.

"Step out."

Deliberately, he widened her stance with his booted foot. He knew his jeans were biting into her ass, reminding her who was naked here. He had her just where he wanted her. Good thing that sexy moan boiling out of her mouth said she wanted this. Wanted *him.* Luckiest night of his life, the night she'd answered his call and started talking to him.

"I wan' to be able to touch all of you."

She moaned again. This time, when her fingers curled into the map, she didn't smooth the small wrinkles out. She'd never map another fire without being reminded of him.

"Good girl." He rewarded her by pushing his fingers in deep. One finger. Two. Three. Reached for that spot that had her arching back and clawing at the map.

"Let go," he commanded roughly. "Come for me right now, Hannah."

Sweet Jesus.

Cole had her spread out on her desk, one big hand working between her thighs, and she wanted the moment to go on and on forever. White heat spiked through her, and the whole fucking forest could have gone up in flames and she wouldn't have cared. She just wanted more. More pleasure. More Cole. Shamelessly, she rode his fingers, grinding the top of her mound against his palm. Letting go because letting *Cole* happen felt so good.

Yes. She let go of everything but her death grip on the desk. Her body wound tighter with each dark, knowing stroke of his fingers, until something deep inside her snapped and let go.

"Give it to me," he growled, and she had no idea what that

mysterious *it* was, just that she let the tension in her body go, let him sweep her up and away in a sea of pleasure. For a moment, she feared being overwhelmed, but his arms were around her. *So good. So right.* She'd never let any lover control her pleasure, but all Cole wanted was to make her feel good.

Perfect.

His breath hissed through his teeth and she sensed his control going. She wanted him raw and uncontrolled. Slamming in and out of her body while she rose up to meet him. She pressed back hard until his fingers almost slipped from her channel, then drove forward.

His fingers vanished, but then he was canting her hips up, angling her for his penetration. Anticipation filled her. She didn't think he'd take her ass like this, although it would hurt so good, but, with Cole, she simply didn't know. Latex snapped, and then he slid deep inside her pussy with one, smooth thrust.

Deliberately, she squeezed him deep inside, fisting him hard.

"Yeah." He groaned and flexed. The table seemed to rise and fall beneath her, each hard drive of his cock moving her forward. His arms were a heated cage around her, his hips slapping her ass in a raw rhythm. *Harder.*

"Brace," he growled.

Slapping her palms flat on the desk, she pushed out to meet each thrust. Her body shook, raw and on fire. He marked her with each thrust, parting her flesh ruthlessly, and that was exactly what she needed. Gentle was no good. She wanted this white-hot pleasure building fast inside her. Milked him, hanging on when he pulled back. *Mine.*

When she didn't think he could go deeper, he did, pushing farther than anyone else ever had. His dick bumped her cervix, stroked over the sensitive walls. Taking her until there was no hiding from his possession. She loved being dominated by him, loved this animal, possessive, *primitive* side of Cole. His desperate need to tunnel deep into her body and take her.

"Now," he growled, and she let go. His arms banded around her and the next hard thrust pushed her over the edge. She came apart. Came undone. There was nothing but the desk beneath her and the familiar landmarks on the map as his hard ride set off her orgasm and the pleasure rolled through her.

Hannah opened up and let him in. All the way in, no barriers. Nothing held back. *Fuck.* Cole buried his dick to the base before pulling out and driving back in. Her trust was the sexiest goddamn thing ever. Addictive. He loved how his touch set her off, how each stroke drove her higher on the desk, her thighs pinned wide by his. He twisted his head, desperate to see her beautiful face. To watch her as she took him. As she came for him.

The reality of Hannah was so much better than their midnight fantasies. Her body clenched around him, and small sounds spilled from her throat. They had the whole fucking park spread out before them and anyone could be coming up that path right now. It wouldn't matter. He couldn't stop now and she didn't want him to. Primal satisfaction swept through him. Her body trusted him. *Hannah.* She'd opened up all the way and let him in.

With a small shriek, she came and her orgasm triggered his. He pounded deep into her, sealing their hips together.

"Cole." His name was a moan on her lips.

"Yeah, *sha.* I'm right here." He feathered his lips over her jaw.

He pulled out gently, sweeping her up into his arms and heading for their bed. He set her down carefully and spooned himself around her, tucking her sleepy body up against his. She'd let him in, all the way in. No holding back and no going back.

His Hannah.

8

Thirty-six hours. Heaven or hell, depending on who you asked. The air outside was too smoky to make going out for long feasible. If the air quality degenerated much further, Cole had sworn he'd call in a chopper to swing by and pick her up. Somehow, she wasn't surprised he could order park resources around like that. She'd leave if it got any worse, he'd said, and she hadn't argued. She could do that when the chopper actually touched down.

So there was nothing to do but kiss and talk. And fuck. God, Cole was insatiable. He took her hard and deep, touching places inside her no one else had touched. His big hands controlled her effortlessly, driving her to sensual heights she'd never scaled alone.

God, he was like a drug. He touched her and she craved more.

More pleasure.

More Cole.

She shifted in her seat, scanning the smoke-darkened sky. The movement fed the pleasurable ache in her lower body. Sitting, standing, reaching for him—she was pleasantly sore and impossibly aware of where he'd been in her body. "Don' forget me," he'd ordered last night. She didn't need the rough command; he'd branded her intimately.

They'd had sex—all kinds of crazy erotic sex, the kind of stuff she'd fantasized about but never dreamed of trying—until she'd collapsed on the mattress and dragged him down with her. He hadn't complained. Or, she'd passed out before he'd gotten the words out. The fire blocking the trail meant no one could come in or out, the perfect excuse for a long, lazy morning followed by a longer, even lazier afternoon. Every hour, she'd look out, take a new reading, call it in—and then fall back into Cole's arms.

The tankers had shown up late yesterday. She'd heard the rumble of those engines before she'd spotted the planes. There was nothing elegant about the big, lumbering planes, but the park had clearly called in the big guns. Some fires, only the autumn rains could stop. With others, the Rogues could hold the line while the choppers dumped retardant and buckets of water, loading and returning for the next few hours, until the landscape bled red. It brought a whole new meaning to *painting the town red.* Twenty-five hundred gallons of retardant hit the forest below. Mostly water, mixed with an ammonia fertilizer and red dye, so the pilots could see where they hit.

The smoke column hadn't grown since morning. In fact, she was certain it was shrinking. The air was clearer, the chopper unneeded, and Cole would head out in the morning. She felt only desperation.

One more night.

He'd spotted the changes in the smoke much earlier than she, but he was a firefighter, so that was to be expected. That's what he'd said, right before he'd walked out the door to go check on the blaze. He'd popped up from their shared mattress like some kind of demented Energizer Bunny, pulled on his boots, and been gone before she could get any kind of real explanation out of him.

Never mind that she'd had some ideas of her own about how to spend the next few hours, ideas that involved working their way through his stash of condoms. Unfortunately, she hadn't brought any out here, because she'd figured there was just about a snowball's chance in hell of her needing them fifty miles away from base camp.

Alone.

In a watchtower like some kind of modern Rapunzel.

"You're coming back?" She'd hollered the question after his retreating back and immediately felt pathetic. He probably wasn't worried about the future of their thirty-six-hour-old relationship.

"Yeah." He raised a hand that was male shorthand for "Got it," "Whatever you want, dear," and "Now I'm beating feet and getting the hell out of Dodge." Then his head disappeared down the trail, and she was alone.

Again.

She'd done the fire-watch thing every summer for the last four years. She knew the drill and, frankly, she loved it. She liked being alone and she loved the silence. Most people talked too much and, when they weren't talking, made plenty of noise. Phones, iPods, television. Doors slamming, things dropping, chitchatting to fill up the empty space. Coming out to the tower was always a blessed relief after nine months of classes.

Cole wasn't big on talking. He moved silently, at home in the park just as she was. On a surface level, they fit together well. They liked plenty of the same things and they both valued their outdoor time. And in bed? Well, that kind of chemistry didn't happen often—had *never* happened to her before—and she couldn't imagine that either of them didn't want a repeat.

And yet she was fairly certain he'd just run like hell from her. With a promise to come back.

Honestly, she wasn't sure what to make of that. She'd had relationships. She wasn't a virgin, but Cole Henry made her feel like one. He had that effect on her, leaving her breathless and uncertain, but knowing he could open an unfamiliar door and show her sensations she'd barely imagined. Cole wasn't civilized. There was a raw, almost primal quality about the man. She had no problem imagining him as a warrior taking a battlefield. He knew how to fight. To defend. To *take*.

God, she wanted him to take her, which probably meant that, yes, she'd be waiting, all smiles, when he returned from wherever it was he'd gone in such a hurry.

She was twenty-five. In another six months, she'd complete her DVM and take the California licensing exam. She'd be ready to go to work. Her life had no room for this raw, shivering desire. Her breath sped up and her stomach got that shaky, falling-from-four-stories-up sensation just thinking about the man. She didn't need him, but she wanted him.

The radio chats had been a delicious fantasy. Cole, on the other hand, was all reality. Fortunately, every time he opened his mouth, he reminded her why take-charge alphas were bad news. He was bossy. Arrogant. And still so damned sexy that most of her—the part that conveniently forgot about being a modern, independent woman and reverted to a primitive set of nerve endings—welcomed his one-word affirmation that he would be back to stay one more night. Maybe forty-eight hours would be enough to get him out of her system.

Watching the trail where he'd disappeared was pathetic, but, if he stayed on the path, she'd have one more chance to see him before he plunged into the woods. Sure enough, fifteen minutes later, a distant, smaller sized version of Cole popped briefly into view. He was still moving fast, his booted feet chewing up the ground. And because her inner stalker had the upper hand at the moment, she trained her binoculars on him and looked her fill. His face looked deceptively at ease, his gaze moving over the path, first left, then right and straight ahead. She had no idea what he was searching for. He'd brought a change of clothes with him and today's T-shirt was standard-issue Forest Service. The faded cotton pulled over his chest and back as he swung his arms, molding the muscles and reminding her just how good it had felt to hold on to those broad shoulders last night. He'd gone for blue jeans instead of Nomex today, so maybe he was officially off duty. Or just out of clean laundry. Honestly, Cole Henry was a puzzle she couldn't figure out.

But she wanted to.

He was blunt, earthy, and completely forthright. He wouldn't play games, except of the sensual variety, but she loved that. He was also from a completely different world, and the only reason she'd even met him was because their summer jobs had thrown them together. He fought fires. She sat on her ass and watched for fires. Granted, she believed what she did was important—someone needed to keep a weather eye out for smokes—but, at the end of the day, he risked life and limb to put *out* the fires. Cole acted, and that decisiveness and willingness to risk everything was sexy.

It was also one more reason why she could have him for a night, but not for the summer. Or any other month after that. He wasn't a keeper because he didn't want to be kept, and because there would always be one more fire calling him away.

She told herself she didn't mind this—at all—while she stared out at the horizon watching for more smokes. Waiting for something else to happen.

The Big Bear Rogues were on the scene. The hike out to join them cleared Cole's head and gave him space to do a little thinking. Five miles. No big deal, even if his thoughts kept spinning around as out of control as a fighter pilot overshooting the LZ. His time with Hannah wasn't going the way he'd planned. He'd had the sex—the best sex of his life, if he was being honest with himself—but now he seemed to want something else. Damned if he could figure it out.

The fire scene, however, made sense.

As Hannah had noted, the smoke column wasn't as wide anymore as it had been. The fire was probably well under a quarter acre now and low to the ground. The smoke was almost white, a pale, shell gray. There was plenty of brush covering the slopes, though—perfect feeding ground for fire. Plus, a quick visual turned up several pockets of dry and dead fir ready to combust. Right now, the fire was burning in the grass and brush, making quick, short runs toward the surrounding pines. Two-foot-high flames, Cole estimated. A nice little challenge, but nowhere near impossible to knock down quickly.

He pitched in, even though he was technically still on R & R for another twelve hours. The guys could use the help, and he didn't want to pull a Vanna White and stand around watching. Extra hands manning a shovel were always welcome, and the guys had extra safety gear, so no worries.

The hand Sam Clayton eventually clapped on Cole's shoulder was not part of the plan. That hand had no business being where it was, but Sam tightened his grip before Cole could shrug away. *Point taken.*

His eyes met Cole's with a whole lot of steely determination. "R and R or back on team?"

Cole had nothing but respect for Sam, and whatever his team leader was about to say, he undoubtedly deserved. Problem was, everything paled in comparison to spending as much time as he could in Hannah's arms. That made some unfamiliar place inside him ache.

Fuck him if he liked it.

Sam finally cleared his throat. "She doing okay?"

Cole didn't have to ask who the *she* was.

A stand of trees went up on the perimeter, the smoke darkened to almost black. He eyeballed the damage, but two hotshots were already moving in. *All under control.*

"Yeah, I got her radio hooked up." He refused to look at Sam when he answered. Christ. He hoped his plans for the night weren't written across his face. Sam could pull him back.

Sam swore. "Your clock is ticking."

Cole didn't deal with ultimatums. Unfortunately, in this one instance, Sam had a point. Cole just didn't like it. "I'm headed out tomorrow."

Sam's eyes narrowed. "You're headed *back* tomorrow."

He shrugged. "Same thing."

Sam was silent for a moment, watching the rest of the Rogues work. A chainsaw roared as the boys fired her up and chewed through a snag. The fire here was under control, but he didn't need to look at Sam to know that his temporary leave of absence was definitely up. If he wanted to rejoin his team, he did so tomorrow. Not the day after and not next week. No, he did so on Sam's fucking schedule.

Hell.

Maybe Hannah was watching the smoke and thinking about him. He tried the thought on for size and, to his surprise, he liked it. Having Hannah waiting for him, worrying about him—he liked it. A lot. He passed the shovel to Sam. "Tag. You're it."

"Be back tomorrow," Sam said, turning away, the sharp edge of the shovel biting into the hardpack. "I got to hear you say it."

"I'll be there." He forced himself not to look toward the direction where the watchtower was. "I'll pick my gear up at the watchtower and hike out first thing tomorrow. That work for you?"

"Yeah," Sam nodded curtly. There wasn't much left to say after that, so Cole started back down the trail to the watchtower. He'd warned her that he was a one-night stand and she'd agreed.

Nothing happened for hours. Hannah looked for smoke and waited for Cole to come back. She'd already figured out that Cole Henry was no fan of small spaces, nor did he like sitting still.

Eventually, booted feet on the steps announced his return. She went out to meet him on the porch. His hair was wet from a quick dip in her stream, his T-shirt plastered to his broad shoulders, and, God, she couldn't wait to get her hands on him. The clock was ticking and she knew it. She had to get her fill of Cole Henry now or go without. It was that simple, so she'd take everything he'd give her.

As soon as he cleared the trapdoor and had both feet on the observation deck, she hit him with her question. "What's happening out there?"

She couldn't read his face. "Looks like the Incident Commander got the word from the higher-ups. They've got the Big Bear Rogues out here, shutting her down."

"Oh." She hadn't known that disappointment was a sensation she'd feel in the pit of her stomach. She wasn't ready to let go of Cole. For a man who'd been simply a midnight fantasy, he sure was part of her everyday life now. And it wasn't just the out-of-this-world sex, although she definitely appreciated that. She liked the way he fit into her watchtower.

Into her life.

But now that the hotshots had knocked down the fire blocking the trail back to base camp, he'd be on his way. He had a life there, and he'd made his rules plenty clear before he'd so much as kissed her. She'd been lucky to get two nights.

He moved closer, his big hands closing over her shoulders and rubbing. For a long minute, he simply stood there behind her, looking out the window with her.

"You can leave," she said finally, because they both had to be thinking it.

He inhaled. She wondered what he was thinking, what his face looked like, but his fingers stroked softly over her collarbones, dipping into the hollows and tracing a ticklish, erotic path.

"Tomorrow." He bent his head toward her neck, brushing his mouth over the sensitive skin. "I'll go tomorrow."

That meant they still had tonight. She drew a deep breath. "Can we try something different tonight?"

"Sure, *sha.*" She felt rather than saw his smile against her throat. "We can try everythin'."

She leaned into the caress. He had no idea what she really had in mind. She didn't know how he'd react, if he'd be angry or put off or just not interested. Because her idea was probably the antithesis of every alpha cell in his body.

"I want to tie you up," she said quickly, before she could chicken out.

"I think it would be fun. Sexy," she added in a rush.

When he didn't say anything right away, she added, "Please."

He didn't know what to say. Or do. And being at a loss for words was a first for him. He wanted this spelled out. "Because you're worried about what I might do?"

"Not one of your fantasies?"

"Hell no."

The smile she gave him was pure seduction. "I'd love having you at my mercy."

"You really wan' to tie me up right now?" He was in charge of his life and his own damned body. Always. Her slow smile, though, had him rethinking those priorities.

Leaning up, she dropped a kiss on his jaw. "I could be convinced to wait until we were inside."

Well, hell. She knew how to convince a man. "You're not game for ropin' me in on your front porch?"

"You got an exhibitionist streak you're hiding from me, Cole Henry?" Her grin said it all.

"Makin' love to you outside wouldn't be a problem at all." There wasn't much he *hadn't* done and he'd make no bones about it. The bondage thing wasn't entirely new, but he'd always been the one doing the tying. He didn't much like the idea of handing any of his control over to Hannah.

Although, he admitted to himself, as she opened the watchtower door, she already had him tied in knots. Plus, the way she smiled at him, all slow and sexy, said she really, really liked the idea. The sensual curiosity lighting up her eyes was a better lure than any words, so it looked like he'd be giving Hannah's bondage game a try.

Besides, he'd bet she couldn't tie knots worth a damn.

He kicked the door shut and faced her. Curiosity might be a motivator for her, but the nipples pressed against her thin cotton tank betrayed just how much the idea aroused her.

Tilting her head up, he ran a thumb along her jaw. "This means that much to you?"

"It's okay." She shrugged, trying to play her request off all casual. The kicker here was, she'd asked for what she wanted. Part of him—a big part—responded to that. "Not your thing. I get it." She stared at him for so long that he wondered what she saw, what kind of clue she was looking for on his face. "I'd want you to enjoy it."

"Uh-huh." He smiled slowly. "Do I get a safe word? To use while you tie me up and take what you wan'?"

He was doing this for her. Somehow, that made all the difference. He wanted to please her, even if that meant trying something outside of his comfort zone. Once Cole Henry made up his mind, he was all in. His pack hit the floor with a thump and he grabbed the bottom of his T-shirt, stripping the cotton over his head with one smooth move.

She had plans of her own for him tonight. Big plans. She ditched her boots, thinking hard. A quick rummage in her own things produced exactly what she needed. Two bandanas, one red, one blue. His left wrist wouldn't match his right, and the sturdy cotton was no exotic silk tie, but she hadn't planned this out. It would work, she decided, coming back to the mattress.

He'd kicked off his steel toes, the boots discarded by the side of their bed, and he had his hands on the button of his jeans. The way he popped it open was damned sexy. Problem was, he made her want to rush things, to get to the good parts *now*—which included the part of him poking above his waistband. She needed to slow this down.

"Uh-uh. Stand down, cowboy." She stepped in close, running her hands down his arms. The heat radiating off him was something fierce. "I want to do that."

"You wan' to take my clothes off? Be my guest."

Bending his head, he kissed her. That kiss of his was in no rush, no matter how hard his dick was. His lips covered hers, soft and gentle. Sucking her bottom lip between his and then opening her mouth with his tongue. He pushed inside, stroking her tongue, his mouth slanted over hers. He didn't touch her, though. Just his mouth on hers for long minutes, until he finally pulled back.

"Those for me?" He looked down at the bandanas crushed in her fingers. She couldn't tell from his face how he felt about this. Still, she knew Cole. He would never like waiting for orders. He was a take-charge kind of man and, usually, that was exactly what she loved.

"If you've changed your mind, we don't have to do this."

"We don' have to." He shot her a crooked grin. "But we wan' to, so it's okay."

He dropped down onto her mattress and stretched like a big cat. Or a big, bronzed god. The hard, chiseled planes of his abdomen gave her all sorts of ideas. "You come do your wors', *sha.*"

"Hands over your head." She loved being in control of his big body. Sure, the tying-up part was sexy, but that was only part of it. Truth was, she wanted to play this game with Cole. Wanted to tease, to lead him to the sexual edge and hold him there.

His dark eyes didn't leave hers as he stretched his arms over his head. Muscles flexed. "Now what?"

"Hold on to the table," she decided.

With a grunt, he wrapped his fingers around the leg of the table that abutted the mattress. God, he really *was* going to do this. He was all in. She'd have to hope like hell they didn't knock her equipment off, because she wasn't stopping now. Working fast, before her nerves could get the better of her, she tied his wrists in place with the bandanas. One good pull and he'd have the table over, but she'd have a head start. Only thing was, she didn't want to get away from this man.

She ran a finger over her knots. "Not too tight?"

"Jus' fine." His fingers flexed, catching hers. She allowed herself to enjoy the brief caress, before forcing herself to step away.

"You're leavin' now?" He was sprawled on her mattress like some kind of decadent pasha. He might be playing her game, but he was still in control. That, she decided, had to change. Just a little. She wanted to shake him up. Wanted him burning for her.

"I'm not going far."

Hooking her thumbs in the waistband of her shorts, she worked the cotton slowly down her thighs. Cole's eyes heated right up. She shimmied the shorts all the way off, stepping out of them.

"You goin' to pick them up?" His voice was hoarse, but he stayed where she'd put him.

"You think I should?" Smiling mischievously, she turned, giving him a clear view of her ass. A pink, lacy thong separated her cheeks and barely covered her front. She had the most impractical underwear ever for a park employee. She knew that, but there were some things she couldn't compromise on. Decadent panties made her feel feminine and fun.

Of course, the heated look in Cole's eyes made her feel better than any lingerie ever could. The hard ridge of his erection teased her, filling up the front of those blue jeans he filled out so well. Hell, he'd busted out of those jeans, the ripe tip of his dick stretching above the unbuttoned waistband. *Don't rush,* she reminded herself. Sinking down and licking him right now seemed like a good idea, but then things would be over fast. And she wanted this to last.

Bending over, she reached slowly for the shorts. The thong rasped against the sensitive skin of her ass as she moved. The deliberate movement reminded her *exactly* what they'd done last night. A growl escaped from the man behind her. Yeah, he liked his view.

"You better get on over here, *sha.*"

Standing up, she tossed the shorts on the table and stepped closer. Having Cole at her mercy was addictive.

"*Sha . . .*"

Time to give him a little something. She sauntered over to the mattress and stood over him.

"Better?" Pulling the tank top over her head, she tossed it to the ground.

His wicked grin should have warned her. "Two can play this game."

He kicked the mattress and she came down with a shriek, hitting his chest. His hard grunt filled her ear. Legs wrapped around his hips, she straddled him, cradling his erection against her mound. God, he was hot. The feel of him all but seared her skin.

"See?" He whispered the question hoarsely against her throat. "I'm thinkin' this is an improvement. This way, I can kiss you."

Reaching up, he captured her mouth with his own. This kiss was hungry. Hot and raw, his mouth moved over hers, his tongue thrusting past her lips to plunge deep inside. He was taking charge. As she'd suspected, he couldn't shake his alpha nature. This was her turn, however, so she needed to regain control.

"Uh-uh." Pulling her mouth away from his, she sank down his body.

She ran her fingers over the hard planes of his chest, kissing and nipping. When she caught a flat nipple between her teeth and bit lightly, he jumped and cursed. He didn't protest, however, and the thick length trapped between their bodies jerked. Yeah, he liked that. Not satisfied, she ran her fingers along the edge of his waistband, slipping the tips of her fingers beneath in an unhurried, slow tease. Rubbed the slick tip of him.

Deliberately, she pushed down his jeans.

"Toe them off," she said, giving him back the words he'd given her. His eyes darkened, but he did it. Her big hotshot didn't like taking orders. A reward was in order for being so good. Conveniently, she knew just what he liked.

She looked him up and down, trailing a hand down his abdomen. He jerked hard, his dick lifting toward her hand.

"Ask nicely," she said sweetly.

"Fuck." His face tightened. He didn't look nice at all now, but her bandanas held—for the moment—and he was good and hot.

"That's not nice at all," she observed. "But we'll get to that. Later."

Since she'd made her point, she bent her head and licked him. A long, slow drag of her tongue from base to tip. His hips shot off the bed. Yeah, he really, really liked that. And she loved the heady mix of pleasure and power. He was letting her do this—they both knew that—but she wouldn't have passed up on this chance to learn his body for anything.

When her tongue hit the tip of his shaft, she stopped and rested her cheek against him. His crown was slick with precum, the skin satin-soft and hard at the same time. Enjoying the pure pleasure of touching him, she ran the pad of her index finger over him. Every time she breathed out, the small puff of air rushing over the sensitive head forced a sharp exhale from him.

"Hannah—" His eyes promised sweet revenge.

"You've got to say it."

"Please—" he gritted out. "Open up. I wan' to be inside your mouth."

Smiling, she turned her head and opened up. He lifted his head, straining to watch her, the muscles in his abdomen tensing with the effort. So damned sexy and all hers.

She ran her tongue over the fat head, tracing the soft slit. "You taste good, hotshot."

He did, too. She could feel his eyes boring into her head, his body tensing beneath her sensual onslaught, but she was lost. Lost in the taste and feel of this big man. Wrapping one hand around his shaft, she cupped his balls with the other, scratching lightly until she heard his harsh groan. She licked over and around him, swirling her tongue around the crown. The muscles of her jaw burned, stretched wide by Cole, and the raw sounds he made were the biggest turn-on ever.

Slowly, she sank her mouth down, replacing her palms with her mouth. The crown hit the back of her throat and she swallowed. Pulled his dick in, then pushed it back out, swirling her tongue over the hard length the whole time. Once. Twice. Ten seconds later, he was fucking her mouth hard and she was loving each fierce thrust.

"Come back up here," he growled, popping free. "I'm not comin' anywhere but inside you tonight."

She gave him a deliberately impish smile. "Stop topping from the bottom."

Bracing a hand on his shoulder, she pulled herself up his hard body until she was pressed against him, her legs closed and stretched out. Her toes teased his calves and his erection slapped against her belly, hot and slick. She stretched her own arms out, wrapping her hands around his wrists, and slid up and down his body as if he were her own erotic Slip 'n Slide.

Up and down, over his cock. *Yes. God, he was fine.*

He pushed up hard. "Stop teasin'."

"No." Her laughter spilled out as her legs tangled with his. "I think you like this. And, next time, I'll tie your feet."

"Next time it's your turn." The rough warning heated her up more. Ah, hell. Her imagination took off, her body tightening up as one erotic fantasy after another flashed through her head. After all, he'd told her exactly what he was capable of. Even through her panties, she could feel him rubbing against her folds. *I could come just like this.*

The bandanas tore, the harsh sound ripping through her sensual haze. Stuff clattered, falling over on the table overheard. Probably her fire-spotting gear and park equipment, but she'd care later.

Cole's arms closed around her, hard and fierce. "Sorry about the property damage."

He didn't look sorry at all. She had just enough time to register that truth, before one hard tug tore her thong away.

"Shame about those pretty panties," he drawled. "Maybe next time you'll listen a little closer."

She opened her mouth to protest—she *was* on top here, after all, but his hands found her shoulders, guiding her down. Taking her hard and deep, until she didn't know where she ended and he began, just that she came and he followed her over that sensual edge, holding himself deep inside her as he groaned.

He took her down to the mattress, before moving away. She protested, sleep thickening her voice, but he cleaned her up and got her settled. He didn't say much, but that was her Cole. He'd done his talking on the radio and now he was all about showing her how he felt. Desired. Cared for.

Cherished.

9

Waking up in bed with Cole was sexy—even if they didn't quite fit on her mattress. The added layer of closeness was definitely no hardship. At some point during the night, he'd wrapped his arms around her and tugged her head onto his chest. At least, that was her preferred theory and she was sticking to it. The other possibility was that she'd simply assaulted the man in his sleep, crawling right on top of him.

Still, she took full advantage of her current position. Lifting her head, she watched his face. Since he was asleep, he was in no position to complain. Plus, the man had unfairly long lashes. She ran a finger over the stubble on his jaw. Rough and sexy, just the way she liked him.

One minute, he was asleep, eyes closed. The next, he was awake and staring back at her. "Hey," he said. That was all, but his arms tightened around her, his thumb stroking a little circle at the top of her spine.

"Morning, hotshot." Leaning forward, she kissed him.

Long minutes later, he broke off their kiss, framing her face in his hands.

"I got to get goin'." To his credit, he sounded reluctant. "I know that sounds bad, but I got my marchin' orders yesterday from Sam."

"You got five minutes to misbehave?" Hell. That sounded desperate.

"Yeah," he said, but he hesitated. Maybe she'd misread the situation, but the erection stabbing into her hip said he was just as happy to see her this morning as she was him. So, what gave? "I should tell you somethin'. First. Do some confessin' and then see how you feel."

Hell. She pulled back a few inches. "Hit me."

He cupped the side of her jaw, rubbing a thumb over her cheek. "You work ten on, two off, right?"

"That's the schedule." Maybe he just wanted to hook up again. Having some of Cole, however, was better than nothing. "You want me to swing by base camp?"

She held her breath. Putting herself out there sucked, but this was *Cole*. He'd already seen and heard her at her rawest, most vulnerable. How bad could putting her feelings into words be?

"That would be great." He dropped a kiss onto her mouth. A sweet, light kiss. He sucked at her bottom lip, nipping. *Not so sweet.* "But—"

"But?" She couldn't quite keep the hurt out of her voice.

"But I wan' a new rule," he said, rolling her over on their bed. "We get as many nights together as we want."

Were they a "we"?

She stared up at him. His face was fierce and intent—and watching her. When she tried to wriggle away, done with the games, he gave her more of his weight, pressing her down into the mattress. His legs tangled with hers. "What if I want to take the chance, want to see if we could have something more? What if I want more than just the nights?"

"This isn't enough for you, *sha*?" His finger dipped into her wet heat. Stroked. "This is real good, and I've definitely got that five minutes you were askin' about."

"Yeah." She gasped and he drank in the small sound. "Yes, Cole."

She wasn't sure if her hoarse agreement was a plea for more or an acknowledgment that he was right.

"I'll be whatever I can for you," he said fiercely, surprising her. "You wan' a midnight fantasy lover, I'm your man. If you wan' more than just the night—"

Her man. That sounded good.

"Breakfast, lunch, and dinner?" She laughed up at him.

"Uh-huh." He bent his head, catching her mouth in another long, sweet kiss. When he finally released her mouth, she was breathless and his hand was sliding south. "I'd like to spend every hour of the day with you."

She wriggled impatiently. God, his hand was driving her crazy. Just another inch and she'd have him right where she wanted him.

"All day, every day?" she challenged.

"That's what I'm thinkin'." He smiled, slow and easy. "Unless you need convincin'."

He stroked his fingers down her center, parting her and sinking deep into the slick folds. Her breath caught at the pleasure of his touch, even as her heart did some catching of its own. His eyes hadn't moved from her face.

"I need to know what you wan'." His finger pushed inside her channel, moving deeper. He found a spot that made her moan. "How long you want me to stay."

Forever.

She reached up and twined her arms around his neck.

"Break the rules with me." Her eyes held his, but the sweet clench of her pussy on his finger was driving him mad. He had to go. He needed to stay.

"I don' like rules," he acknowledged. That was the truth, right there. Discipline and duty and honor. He liked those. Lived by those. He just didn't need or want a rule book to live his life.

"I think I could love you." Yeah, that was pure challenge in her eyes. Her hands reached up to cup his head, her fingers feathering along his jaw. All that emotion on her beautiful face was for him. He'd done nothing to deserve those feelings, but she had them and she wore them proudly for him to see. Something inside him unlocked, opened up. For *her*. "You want me to love you, Cole Henry?"

"No rules, huh?" He pressed his lips against hers in a quick, hard kiss, but he didn't move his fingers. He loved holding her like this.

"Never." He heard the promise in her voice. Her words were her a gift to him with no strings attached. Come or go, stay or leave, she'd chosen to say what she felt. If he left now, he wouldn't leave those words of hers behind. He'd carry those three simple words with him wherever he went.

He wrapped his arms around her and held on tight.

He didn't want to go anywhere alone.

Never again.

"I love you." He gave the words back to her. "That's the new rule, okay? The only one that counts. Anything else, we can figure out as we go along."

"I can live with that." She smiled at him.

"I've got to go for now. Sam and the Rogues are waitin' for me, but I'll be comin' back for you. You watch for me, okay?"

"I can do that," she smiled slowly. "Fire and you. That's what I do best."

"You've got me all fired up," he agreed. "Best summer of my life. Now, let me make this the best year of your life."

"That's going to be a hard act to follow."

"Well," he grinned at her. "I'll just have to work harder next year and the year after, *oui*? You'll have to stick around to see how things turn out."

Her heart turned over. "The best years of *our* lives," she said firmly.

"That sounds like one hell of a plan," he agreed and kissed her.

Sizzle

LYNN LaFLEUR

A big thank you to Alan for all your help with the firefighter information.

Special thanks to The Sizzling Scribes—Arianna Hart, Cait Miller, Diana Hunter, Ruby Storm, Tara Nina, and Tielle St. Clare—for your support and help with my writing. You gals are the best!

1

———————

Maysen Halliday lowered the window on her SUV and breathed deeply of the sweet air. Springtime in Texas always smelled amazing, especially in the Hill Country of Central Texas. Wildflowers bloomed in abundance on both sides of the county road. Bluebonnets started making their appearance last week, delighting Maysen with their purplish blue color. All too soon the state flower would disappear for another year.

Since her job kept her so busy, Maysen didn't have the chance to take photographs simply for pleasure very often. She planned to remedy that on this assignment and take many pictures of the flowers and scenery around the small town of Lanville. After three years of building her magazine, *Hot Shots,* without any time off, she deserved a vacation.

Thinking of her assignment had her checking the MapQuest directions she'd printed out before she headed north from Houston early this morning. She could've taken a direct route to Lanville but decided to travel some of the county roads instead to enjoy the scenic beauty. She knew little about the small town that would be her final destination, only that Rose River ran through the center and extremely hunky firemen lived there. At least according to the contest she'd run in her magazine.

Brainchild of her assistant, Denyse Wade, the contest had garnered thousands of entries, mostly from women. That didn't surprise Maysen. Women knew what made a man sexy. It wasn't simply his looks, but his whole attitude. Good looks were nice to admire, but selfishness and inconsideration quickly soured a woman on a man, no matter how handsome he might be.

Her rumbling stomach reminded her she'd left her apartment without breakfast. Never able to eat right away, she had to be up and around for at least a couple of hours before she could think about food. A quick glance at her watch showed her she'd been on the road for over four hours. No wonder her stomach yelled at her.

Since Lanville couldn't be more than a few more miles away, according to her MapQuest printout, she decided to tough it out and get to her destination before she ate. Research had shown her the town had some of the typical fast-food places, but also some locally owned restaurants. That's what she wanted to try. Some of the best food she'd ever eaten in her travels had been prepared in family-owned cafés.

Gas for her SUV had to come before food. She pulled into the city limits of Lanville with her gas gauge almost touching the empty mark. Bypassing the quaint courthouse square— which she definitely planned to explore later—she headed for the main highway that passed through town, knowing she'd find gas there.

She saw the Spencer's gas station sign when she stopped at the red light on the highway. Perfect. The man she wanted to talk to would be at that station. Once the light changed to green, Maysen turned left and headed for Spencer's, ready to begin her assignment.

* * *

Clayton Spencer peered at the spreadsheet on his computer. Profits were up at his Dallas/Fort Worth stations and holding steady at the stations in Oklahoma City. His vice president, Silas Hernandez, e-mailed him yesterday about expanding farther north into Kansas. The Spencer's Station and Convenience Store chain now spread across the southern states from the Pacific to the Atlantic. Perhaps going north would be a good idea. He'd bring it up to his board at the next meeting in May.

Clay gazed out the window next to his desk to give his eyes a break from staring at the computer screen for almost two hours. He quickly did a double take when he saw the sandy-haired woman standing at one of his pumps, putting gas into a dark blue Chevy Tahoe. A green T-shirt flowed over breasts the perfect size to fill his hands. When she moved, he saw her faded jeans fit a gorgeous ass and thighs. He could easily imagine those thighs wrapped around his hips.

Lust grabbed his balls and his dick gave an interested twitch, something it hadn't done in quite a while at the sight of the opposite sex. A woman trampling over a guy's heart had the tendency to make him forget about sex. Well, maybe not *forget,* but a few minutes of pleasure wasn't worth the hassle of getting involved with anyone and having his heart stomped on again.

He watched her replace the nozzle on the old-fashioned pump, then screw on her gas cap. Grabbing her keys and wallet, she headed for the store's entrance. She had to be driving through Lanville. As a business owner and the volunteer fire department's chief, he'd met almost everyone who lived here. He would definitely remember her if he'd seen her around town.

Clay allowed himself a few moments of fantasizing about how she looked naked before he returned to his computer. At least he knew his cock would work, should he ever decide to open himself up to another relationship.

Fat chance of *that* happening.

He opened his e-mail when he heard the ding that announced a new message. Another note from Silas, telling him he'd found the perfect station in Kansas City to add to Spencer's chain. Clay chuckled. Silas didn't give up when he got an idea in his head. That's part of what made him such a good vice president.

A gentle knock on the door announced his day clerk, Dolores, before she opened the door.

"Clay, there's someone here to see you." She bobbed her eyebrows. "She's really hot."

Clay swallowed to avoid laughing at Dolores's statement. Sometimes he had a hard time believing some of the things that came out of the sixty-something woman's mouth. "She asked for me specifically or the owner?"

"She asked for you, by name."

Interesting, Clay thought. He minimized the spreadsheet window, rose from his chair, and followed Dolores into the store. His gaze immediately snapped to the woman standing at the drink fountain, the one who had been at the pumps. She looked at him over her shoulder and smiled. "Hi."

"Hello."

She finished drawing her drink and placed the lid on her cup. Hand outstretched, she stepped closer to him. "It's nice to meet you, Mr. Spencer."

"Clay, please," he said automatically. Something about her voice seemed familiar, but he didn't know why. He would've remembered meeting a woman with such beautiful whiskey-colored eyes.

He accepted her hand. Her soft skin tickled nerve endings in his palm that hadn't known the touch of a woman's body in much too long.

Her smile widened. "I'm Maysen Halliday from *Hot Shots* magazine."

His lust faded, even though Clay detected an awareness in

her eyes along with her friendly smile. He wanted nothing to do with the woman and her magazine's stupid contest.

Her gaze passed over his face, shoulders, and chest. The light in her eyes proved she liked what she saw. That didn't matter. Getting involved with a woman who would be in town for only a short time would be incredibly stupid. Been there, done that, had the broken heart to prove it.

Clay released her hand. His irritation must have shown on his face, for Maysen's smile faded. "Is something wrong? I thought you were expecting me."

"I was. Your assistant, Denyse, called yesterday and reminded me you were coming today. I didn't realize you'd come here first."

She shrugged one shoulder. "I figured it would be best to meet the fire chief before I did anything else." Her smile returned, along with a twinkle of humor in her eyes. "Denyse told me you aren't exactly enthused about my article."

"I think that's a vast understatement."

"Why?" She tilted her head, curiosity obvious in her eyes. "It's great publicity for your fire department, and Lanville. *Hot Shots* has a large subscription base; plus, thousands of people look at our online site every month."

"I'm not knocking your magazine, Ms. Halliday—"

"Maysen."

He exhaled quickly at her interruption. "I don't have time to haul you around town while you take beefcake pictures of my firefighters."

"Women love heroes, Clay. And firefighters are very heroic. Plus, according to the pictures that were submitted for the contest, you have some very fine-looking men in your volunteer fire department."

"We have women, too. They work as hard as the men do."

"I understand that. In some cases, they probably work harder than the men. I do plan to feature them in the article."

"But you'll feature more pictures of the men."

She shrugged her shoulder again. "It was a contest for the sexiest *male* firefighters in Texas. Most of the votes came from women. That means more pictures of men because that's what our readers want to see." She picked up her drink and a wrapped straw. "And I don't expect you or anyone else to haul me anywhere, Clay. GPS is a wonderful invention. I can get around just fine on my own."

He didn't doubt that. Maysen Halliday seemed like a very independent woman. He'd researched her when she'd approached him about the article. Single, thirty-two years old, a successful career as a photojournalist before she started her own magazine three years ago. He had no reason not to trust her.

Yet, a tiny part in the back of his brain warned him to stay alert, to not even consider getting involved with her, no matter how much his dick might want to.

She placed one hand over her stomach. "I'm starving. Can you recommend a good place to eat? After that, I'll go to the fire hall and hopefully meet some of your volunteers."

"You will. I made arrangements for them to drop by this afternoon and evening so you can meet them."

Her smile brightened her whole face and sent a shaft of longing straight to his heart. "That's wonderful. Thank you." She unwrapped her straw, then poked it through the opening in the drink's lid. "I probably should check in to my room before I go to the fire hall."

"Where are you staying?"

"The Inn on Crystal Creek."

"You'll like it there. Meals are included for guests, or there's a restaurant right next door. Great food."

"Sounds perfect. Are you free for lunch? We could discuss the article."

His hormones said yes. Luckily, he already had plans for lunch today with the owners of Coleman Construction to discuss a remodel of this station, so he didn't have to listen to his hormones. "I'm meeting some people for lunch."

"Oh." Disappointment filled her eyes. "Maybe another time. I'll be here for several days."

"How many days?"

"I haven't decided yet. This is a combination work assignment and mini vacation for me."

"Surely you can find a more exciting place to vacation than Lanville."

"I don't need excitement, Clay. I'd rather relax and catch up on my reading than hit the club scene."

Something they had in common. Despite having to travel in business, Clay liked to get his business done and return home to his solitude as soon as possible. Although Spencer's headquarters was located in Tempe, Arizona, he could do the majority of his work via computer or telephone. That left him free to choose where he wanted to live. He'd chosen Lanville two years ago and hadn't regretted that choice for one second.

"How about dinner?" Maysen asked. "My treat."

Determination must be Maysen Halliday's middle name. "Sorry, have plans for dinner, too."

"You're a busy man."

"I have a business to run, just like you have a magazine to run."

She pressed her lips together and her eyes narrowed. "You can't avoid me forever, Clay. I want you to be part of my article. You're the fire chief; plus, you're—" She stopped and her gaze passed over his face again. "You're a very attractive man. I want pictures of you in my magazine."

Her compliment warmed him, but he refused to let it go to his head. A woman could easily spout words when she wanted something. "I'll cooperate, Maysen, because I promised I would. But don't expect anything else from me except for your article. No lunches, no dinners, nothing."

She opened her mouth, perhaps to argue with him, then

closed it again before she nodded. "Understood. I'll call you when I get settled so we can set up a good time to meet."

She held his gaze while she sipped her drink through the straw. An image flashed through his mind of those full, soft lips sucking his cock instead of a straw. Clay nodded, hoping she wouldn't notice his burgeoning hard-on. "Fine."

"Bye."

He watched her walk out of his store, admiring the gentle swing of her hips and that amazing ass.

"She's very pretty," Dolores said from behind the counter.

He turned to see the mischievous twinkle in Dolores's eyes. She had worked at this station for over twenty years, first for the former owner, Walt Kinney, and now Clay. Walt had warned Clay that Dolores loved to play matchmaker. Clay had already experienced her attempts in the few months he'd owned this station. He frowned. "Don't play matchmaker."

"Who, me?" She splayed her hand over her generous bosom in mock innocence. "I would never do that."

Clay snorted. "Yeah, right."

"You have to admit she's very pretty."

The quickest way to get her to stop the Cupid attempts would be to agree and get away from her. "Yes, she's very pretty."

Dolores beamed, apparently pleased with his comment. "You could reschedule your appointment with the Coleman triplets and have lunch with her."

"I want to get the remodel started, so I need to keep my appointment with the guys." He shook one finger at her. "Stop trying to find a date for me."

The amusement faded from her eyes, to be replaced with concern. "I worry about you, Clay. You work way too hard. A man has to play. You're too young and virile not to play."

Clay sputtered out a laugh. *"Virile?"*

"Yes, virile." Her little nose rose an inch. "I know a hot man when I see one."

To his surprise, heat flooded his cheeks. He couldn't re-member the last time he'd felt embarrassment. "Thank you. I think."

"What, you think just because I'm a grandmother I don't think about sex?"

His cheeks grew even warmer. "Okay, it's time for me to leave now. I'll be back later."

Clay escaped before Dolores could say anything else to em-barrass him further.

2

Maysen fell in love with The Inn on Crystal Creek the moment she saw it. The three-story Victorian had obviously been remodeled recently, yet retained the charm of the time when it had been originally built. Huge oak trees offered shade; colorful flowers grew in maintained beds surrounding the house and along the walkway to the front door. Another flowered walkway led from the inn to Café Crystal, the restaurant next door. Several cars were parked in the restaurant's lot, proof the lunch rush wasn't over.

Her stomach rumbled, demanding she feed it. As soon as she checked in to her room, food had to be next on her list.

She walked into a foyer rich with history. Maysen could easily imagine all the people who had entered the wide front door in the last century. Polished wood surrounded the windows and gleamed beneath her feet. A cozy sitting area to her left was tucked beneath the stairs, offering guests a comfortable place to sit while waiting for their rooms or simply to talk.

She itched to capture the beautiful furnishings with her camera.

A low moan to her right drew her attention. Maysen stepped

up to a counter with a sign that said "REGISTER HERE" across the front of it. She peered around the corner into a small room when she heard the moan again. A voluptuous redhead and a tall, dark-haired man stood wrapped in an embrace while they kissed.

Obviously lost in their passion, their kiss continued. Maysen watched as the man's hand made a slow journey up and down her back and over her bottom. Her hands gripped his thick hair. The way their mouths moved over each other's proved a lot of tongue must be involved.

Feeling like a voyeur but unable to look away, Maysen kept watching while heat slowly worked its way from the top of her head down to her toes, stopping at interesting places in between. She fought the urge to fan her face. It had been much too long since she'd experienced such a passionate kiss from a man. It'd been a long time since she'd experienced *any* kiss from a man.

An image of Clay flashed through her mind. He had full, well-shaped lips perfect for kissing.

The couple pulled apart after two more short kisses. He touched her cheek with his fingertips, gave her a tender smile. The love flowing between the couple brought a lump to her throat.

The redhead watched him until he walked out a door in the back of the room before she turned toward Maysen. Her smile quickly faded, red rushed to her cheeks. "Oh! I'm sorry. I didn't know anyone was here."

Maysen smiled to hopefully ease the young woman's embarrassment. "No problem. It's nice to see a couple so much in love."

Her smile returned, a little shy and very sweet. "We just got married Saturday."

"Congratulations! Why aren't you on a honeymoon?"

"Too much going on with work. My husband . . ." She stopped and sighed dreamily. "I love calling him that."

Maysen chuckled.

"My husband, Rye, and his brothers are involved in several construction projects around town. I offered to postpone our wedding, but he didn't want to do that. So we decided we'll take our honeymoon in a few months." She stepped behind the counter. "I'm so sorry to rattle like that. I'm Alaina Ma— Alaina Coleman. Sorry. Still getting used to the new last name, too. How can I help you?"

"I'm Maysen Halliday. I have a reservation."

Alaina opened a laptop on the counter and scanned the screen. "Yes, Ms. Halliday. I've put you in the Turret room. It's one of my larger rooms with a gorgeous view of the town and surrounding hillsides."

"Sounds perfect."

"Do you wish to charge the credit card you used to reserve the room?"

"Yes, please."

She pressed a button on the laptop and Maysen heard the gentle whirr of a printer. Alaina reached beneath the counter, then laid a piece of paper, pen, and a key attached to a heavy brass fob on the counter. "Would you sign at the bottom please?"

Maysen scrawled her signature, picked up the fob, and studied it. "An actual key?"

Alaina smiled. "I wanted to keep as much of the original Victorian charm as possible. Putting electronic key readers on the doors seemed . . . wrong."

"It's a beautiful house. Do you own it?"

Alaina nodded. "The Inn officially opened in December after several months of renovation work by my husband and his brothers."

"When was it built?"

"Nineteen oh two."

Maysen itched again to hold her camera and snap photos. "Would you mind if I took some pictures of it? I may feature it in a future article."

Alaina's smile widened. "That would be wonderful. I love your magazine."

"You read *Hot Shots*?"

"Every month. I've subscribed to it for a couple of years. The photos are amazing."

"I'm flattered, and happy you enjoy it."

Maysen's stomach rumbled loudly. Alaina laughed. "Sounds like you need lunch."

"I needed it two hours ago."

"Meals are included with your room. Today's lunch is a hot beef sandwich with green salad and turtle cheesecake for dessert. It's served until two o'clock. Or you can check out Café Crystal next door. Guests get a fifteen percent discount on anything they order. Just show the waitress your room key."

The mention of turtle cheesecake had her mouth watering. But she wanted to see some of the people who lived in Lanville, so going to the restaurant made more sense. "I think I'll check out Café Crystal."

"Your bags will be in your room when you come back."

Maysen smiled. She already liked Alaina very much. "Thanks."

Exiting The Inn the way she'd entered, Maysen followed the walkway to the entrance of Café Crystal. A lovely fifty-something woman greeted her and led her to a table next to a window. Once seated with menu in hand and iced tea ordered, she glanced around the beautiful room. The color scheme from The Inn had been duplicated in the restaurant, along with the old-fashioned charm. While the Victorian had been built in the early 1900s, Maysen had no doubt this building had been built within the last few months. It still had the "new" feeling to it.

Her gaze passed over a table of four men. She quickly glanced back, catching herself before her mouth dropped open at the incredibly attractive men in their early thirties. Other than different hair lengths and facial hair, three of the men appeared identical. They had to be brothers, if not triplets. Clayton Spencer occupied the fourth chair.

He sat so he faced her. As if he felt her gaze on him, he looked her direction. Heat passed through her body again, even more intense than when she'd witnessed Alaina and her husband kissing. Her mind filled with erotic images of Clay's hands roaming over her curves, his naked body pressed to hers. She could almost feel his lips as he kissed her, his tongue dueling with hers in a battle where they both won the prize of ultimate pleasure.

He nodded once in greeting. Taking that as an invitation—whether or not he meant it as one—Maysen rose and walked to their table.

"Hello again," she said to Clay.

"Hello," Clay said. "Guys, this is Maysen Halliday from *Hot Shots* magazine. Maysen, this is Rye, Dax, and Griff Coleman. They own Coleman Construction here in town."

Maysen motioned for them to remain seated when it appeared the three brothers would stand. She didn't often meet men so polite. Or so gorgeous. "Triplets?" she asked Griff.

"Yes."

"Are y'all on the volunteer fire department, too?"

"We were for ten years, but not now."

"That's too bad. Triplets would be unique to feature in my article." She faced Rye, recognizing him from the passionate kiss he'd shared with Alaina. "I met your wife. She's lovely."

His smile lit up his eyes. "I think so, too. Are you staying at The Inn?"

Maysen nodded. "It's beautiful. You and your brothers did a wonderful job. I assume you built this restaurant also?"

"We did."

Which proved the talent of the three brothers. She'd love to see more of their work, perhaps feature them in the article with Alaina's inn.

She noticed the various legal pads and loose papers spread over their table, so she assumed they were having a working lunch. "I don't want to bother you when it's obvious you're busy." She looked at each Coleman. "It was nice to meet all of you." Her gaze landed on Clay and lingered for several seconds. "I'll talk to you later about the article."

He gave her that single nod again, silently dismissing her. Maysen returned to her table. She'd done what she wanted to do—let Clay Spencer know it would be impossible to avoid her.

"She's hot," Dax said once Maysen returned to her table.

Clay glanced at the lovely woman by the window. He couldn't deny what Dax said, although he tried to downplay his body's reaction to Maysen Halliday. "I guess."

Dax snorted. "Like you didn't notice."

He couldn't lie to his friends. The Coleman triplets knew him too well. "Okay, I noticed she's hot. Are you happy?"

"Just trying to help a friend."

"I don't need that kind of help. And you aren't supposed to notice hot women since you have Kelcey."

"I adore Kelcey. That doesn't mean I'm blind." Dax flashed a quick glance at Maysen. "She's looking at you."

Clay couldn't help checking to see if Dax told the truth. He met Maysen's gaze as she sipped from her glass of iced tea.

"I think the lady likes you," Griff said with a grin.

"She wants me to be in the damn article she's doing about Lanville's firefighters."

"You should be," Rye said, "since you're the chief."

"And you're so sexy." Dax batted his eyelashes.

Rye and Griff laughed while Clay shook his head. "I don't know why I put up with this abuse."

"You're just lucky." Dax glanced at Maysen again. "I could think of worse things than being interviewed by Maysen Halliday."

So could Clay. He imagined anything to do with Maysen would be very pleasurable . . . especially if they were both naked.

He'd felt the sizzle between them at his station and a few moments ago when she'd come over to his table. Exploring that sizzle would be a lot of fun, yet Clay knew it couldn't happen. Maysen would be in Lanville for a few days, maybe a week. After that, she'd go back to her life in Houston. He couldn't take the chance on falling for her and ending up with a broken heart. Again.

One look at the three men in their twenties at the fire station and Maysen understood why her subscribers had nominated the Lanville volunteer firefighters as the sexiest in Texas. Tall, tan, and buff, they belonged on the pages of a magazine for women to drool over.

Maysen planned to include many photos of the guys in her article.

She bit the side of her cheek to keep from grinning while Wes showed off the tanker. She recognized the playful flirting mixed in with his serious description of how everything worked on the different trucks. While flattered at his interest, she much preferred dating a man her own age or a bit older so they had things in common.

Like Clay.

She tried to keep her attention on what Wes said, but her mind kept drifting back to the man she planned to prominently feature in her article. She'd done a lot of research on Clay and his family. His grandfather, Trevon Spencer, opened the first

Spencer's gas station in Tempe fifty years ago. With a shrewd business mind and good luck, he turned that one station into a chain of twenty across the southwestern states. His son—Clay's father, Clayton Sr.—took the chain farther east once he became the CEO of the company at his father's retirement. Clayton still sat on the board, but turned over the running of the company to Clay two years ago due to health problems. Now with more than seventy-five stations from coast to coast, Spencer's had the reputation of fair gas prices and clean, well-stocked convenience stores, making them a popular stop for people during their travels.

Her research hadn't shown her the handsome, sexy side of Clay Spencer . . . a side she very much wanted to explore.

3

She made him think of fast, hard sex.

Clay stood at the back of the room, watching Maysen talk to the small group of firefighters who had arrived after lunch. No matter how much he tried to push Maysen to the back of his mind, she kept popping to the front, tempting him with her whiskey eyes, soft voice, and killer body.

He'd dated several of the lovely women in Lanville in the two years he'd lived here. While he'd enjoyed their company, none of them made his heart beat faster or his dick harden with only one look the way Maysen did. His body's lack of response meant he hadn't slept with anyone in town. He hadn't felt that "spark" with a woman that caused him to want to spend more time with her, both in bed and out.

That spark had happened once to him when a woman had breezed into and out of his life a year ago. Clay learned an important lesson from that experience—don't get involved with a woman who didn't live in the area. That meant it would be impossible for anything to develop with Maysen. Once she completed her assignment, she'd head back to Houston and he'd never see her again.

Better to stay alone for now than let his hormones overrule his brain.

Clay chuckled at the starry-eyed look on Wes's face as he talked about one of the fire trucks. He'd probably do backflips if Maysen asked him to. Not that he could blame Wes. Maysen looked beyond hot in those tight jeans.

Escaping from the cloud of testosterone Wes emitted around Maysen, Clay wandered into the meeting room. Emma Keeton continued to add platters of food to the table he'd set up for her. He'd hired the incredible chef from Café Crystal to provide a spread for the firefighters as they came in throughout the afternoon and evening to meet Maysen and make arrangements with her for their interviews and photographs.

The first time Maysen had contacted him about the article, he'd offered to e-mail the list of interview questions to all the firefighters. She'd declined, telling him she'd rather talk to each one in person. It made the interview more personal.

Clay wanted everything over and done with so he could get back to his normal life.

Emma removed a platter of spring rolls from one of the large boxes at her feet. Clay's mouth watered at the rolls' aroma, despite having lunch a short time ago. "May I have one of those?"

She smiled. "Of course. I tried a different combination of spices and would love your honest opinion." She peeled back the plastic wrap covering the rolls and held the platter closer to Clay. "Here."

To say the taste of the spring roll exploded on his tongue would be a vast understatement. Clay stopped himself short of rolling his eyes in bliss. "Wow."

Emma's smile widened. "I take that to mean you approve."

"I definitely approve." He took another bite of the crispy treat before he spoke again. "What kind of spices do you use?"

Eyes twinkling with mischief, she lifted one hand and wiggled her forefinger back and forth. "I can't give away my cooking secrets."

Clay grinned. Not only was Emma a marvelous cook and a good friend, but fun to tease. "Not even a hint?"

"You know the rule. If I tell you, I'll have to kill you."

"Well, since I'm in no hurry to die, I'll pass on you telling me the ingredients."

"Deal." She shifted her attention to a spot past his left shoulder. "Hi."

Clay turned his head to see Maysen walking toward them, carrying a clipboard. His heart took off at a gallop while his cock swelled.

Damn hormones.

"Am I interrupting?" Maysen asked.

Emma smiled at her. "You aren't interrupting anything. I was just setting out a few goodies for the firefighters to nibble on while you talk to them."

Maysen glanced over the items on the table. "Everything looks delicious. I'll have to wait a while before I sample anything. I ate lunch a short time ago and I'm still full."

"Where did you eat?" Emma asked.

"Café Crystal. I had the most amazing chicken Caesar salad. The dressing was . . . Delicious isn't a strong enough word to describe it."

Emma's smile widened. "Thank you."

Maysen's eyebrows wrinkled and confusion spread over her face. It quickly disappeared to be replaced with surprise and delight. "You're the chef at Café Crystal?"

"I am." She held out her hand to shake. "Emma Keeton."

"Maysen Halliday." She accepted Emma's hand, then glanced over the items on the table again. "Maybe I'll change my mind about being too full."

Laughing, Emma picked up a platter and peeled back the plastic wrap. "How about a cheesecake brownie?"

"Ooh, sounds good."

Clay watched Maysen pop the small square into her mouth and slowly chew. Her eyes drifted closed, reminding him of how she would look in the throes of a climax.

His dick twitched in his briefs. He had to get away from Maysen before he developed a full-fledged hard-on. "I'll get out of here so you can start your interviews," he said to Maysen.

"What about *your* interview, Clay?"

He figured if he kept putting Maysen off, she'd get disgusted and forget about including him in the article. That way, he wouldn't have to be around her. "Can't today. Too much to do." He snitched another spring roll and waved it at Emma. "They're great, Emma. Thanks."

Maysen blew out a breath as she watched Clay hurry from the room. "Well, hell," she muttered.

Emma chuckled. "Men. Frustrating, aren't they?"

"And then some." She faced Emma again. "I think Clay is avoiding me."

"Try guilt. That always works for me."

Maysen laughed at Emma's wicked grin. "What do you suggest I do?"

"Tell Clay how much the guys are looking forward to the article, that it's great publicity for Lanville, that as fire chief he should be the first one to volunteer. Stuff like that."

It sounded as if Emma knew exactly how to use guilt on a guy. Maysen didn't want to trick Clay into doing something he didn't want to do. Besides, he'd already agreed to the interview, just not today because he was too busy. That didn't mean she couldn't catch him tomorrow or Friday.

The wicked grin faded from Emma's face. "Clay is a good guy, Maysen. If he agreed to be part of the article, he will be."

Although Maysen had no problem pumping someone for information for an article, she didn't feel comfortable doing the same when it came to personal information. The lovely brunette seemed willing to talk. Perhaps it wouldn't be taking advantage of Emma to ask a few basic questions about the handsome fire chief. "How well do you know Clay?"

"Pretty well. I met him in early October, shortly after I moved here from Dallas. He's good friends with my guy Griff and his brothers."

"Griff Coleman?"

Emma nodded. "Have you met him?"

"At Café Crystal. Clay was having lunch with the Coleman brothers. They had paperwork spread all over the table, so I assume they were discussing business."

"Clay hired the guys to remodel his service station. Which it desperately needs. The former owner, Walt Kinney, hadn't done any upgrades in years."

"I was surprised at the old-fashioned pumps when I got gas there this morning. There wasn't anyplace to put my credit card."

"New pumps are due to be delivered before the end of the month. Clay bought Walt's station in December, but the Colemans have been swamped with work and couldn't get to the remodeling until now." Emma removed another platter from the box at her feet and set it on the table. Despite being full, Maysen's mouth watered at the sight of the bite-sized brownies covered in coconut and chopped nuts. The chocoholic inside her cheered. "To give you an idea of what a good guy Clay is, he plans to pay his employees while the station is closed for the remodel, no matter how long that takes."

Clay sounded like a considerate man, as well as being so nice to look at. "That's very generous of him."

"And he's damned nice on the eyes, too," Emma said with a grin.

"I noticed that right away."

"It's been a long time since he's been involved with anyone. Griff told me the last gal Clay fell for broke his heart." She tilted her head to the side and studied Maysen's face through narrowed eyes. "Are you interested in Clay? Romantically?"

Maysen hadn't known Emma but a few minutes, yet felt deep inside that she could trust her. "Not romantically, but I'm very attracted to him."

"He's attracted to you, too. I saw his eyes heat when he looked at you."

A pleasant warmth spread through her to know Clay might be as interested in her as she was in him. "Really?"

"Yeah. I say go for it. Jump his bones the first chance you get." She peeled back one corner of the plastic wrap covering the brownies. "Go for one of these, too. I can see you drooling."

Unable to resist, Maysen chose two of the chocolate treats. "I'm going to take your advice, Emma . . . on both the brownies and Clay."

Maysen considered her first afternoon in Lanville a huge success. Eleven of the firefighters had come into the fire hall throughout the afternoon and early evening to meet and speak with her. Three of the men agreed to an interview with her right away, so she was able to mark those three guys off her list. She had no idea yet how many quotes she would use in the article, but she wanted to have plenty available.

After munching on Emma's goodies all evening, Maysen had no appetite for dinner. She decided to return to her room at The Inn and dig into the stash of snacks she always carried with her if she got hungry later.

No one occupied the foyer. Maysen planned to speak with Alaina for a few minutes before she went to her room. With no sign of the owner, Maysen headed straight for the stairs. She tugged on her right bra strap where it dug into her shoulder. Ditching the bra had to be the first thing she did when she entered her room. She hated wearing that item of torture. She liked her breasts free, liked to feel that little jiggle when she walked. If she wasn't so busty, she would never wear a bra. Not that she was built like a porn star with implants, but her breasts more than filled the C-cup in her bras.

She found her suitcase on a brass stand at the end of the bed, just as Alaina promised it would be. Maysen smiled. Impeccable service to go along with the lovely room. She couldn't ask for more than that.

Maysen dropped her paperwork and camera case on the deep blue bedspread. Reaching beneath her T-shirt, she unhooked her bra and tugged the straps down her arms. With a relieved sigh, she tossed the piece of lingerie to land on one of the throw pillows.

Cradling her breasts in her hands, she massaged the mounds until they no longer felt as if they were still confined. What started out as relief soon morphed into desire. Her fingertips brushed over her nipples, sending a pleasant zing to her clit. That made her realize how long it'd been since she'd had an orgasm, even one she gave herself. Long hours at work left her little time for pleasure.

She plucked at her hardening nipples through her shirt. Each tug sent another pleasant zing to her clit. Her breathing deepened, her heartbeat increased. Tilting her head back, she closed her eyes and absorbed the sensation of building desire.

Maysen slipped off her sandals and unfastened her jeans. She pushed off her jeans and panties at the same time. A single fingertip slid easily through the moisture along her slit. She circled her clit and moaned softly.

"Mmm, yes."

Maysen placed one knee on the bed, intending to lie down so she could finish what she'd started. Out of the corner of her eye, she noticed the tall, oval mirror standing in the corner. Another glance around the room led her to the antique desk and chair in the bay window. Grasping the back of the chair, she tugged it in front of the mirror. After setting it in the right place, she sat down and draped her legs over the chair's arms. The position left her pussy wide open.

Sandy-colored hair covered her mound, but she kept her labia shaved. The site of the pink, wet folds shot up Maysen's desire. She plucked at her nipples again with one hand and slid the other hand between her legs. Warm cream covered the feminine lips. She spread it over her clit before pushing two fingers into her channel.

Another moan escaped her lips when the walls of her pussy clamped on to her fingers. Her eyes wanted to drift closed again, but she forced them to stay open so she could see everything.

She jerked up her T-shirt. Her nipples looked like hard pink pebbles in the center of the puckered areolae. Maysen withdrew her fingers from her pussy and spread her cream over the firm tips. Her scent drifted up to her nose. Gathering more of her juices on her fingers, she brought them to her face and inhaled deeply, taking the aroma deep into her lungs. She licked her fingers clean. Her flavor flowed over her tongue, making her long for more of the intoxicating taste.

She swiped up more of her juices, licked them off her fingers again. She thought of a man with dark brown eyes and wavy dark brown hair drawing her fingers into his mouth to lick them clean.

Clay.

The image of Clay became even more graphic. She imagined him on his back on that dark blue bedspread, his hard cock lying against his flat belly. Dark hair would swirl over his chest and run down his torso in a thin ribbon. It would widen and form a nest for his hard flesh and tight balls. The same dark hair would sprinkle over his legs, giving that little bit of extra sensation when he rubbed his legs along her smooth ones.

Her clit cried out for more attention. Maysen gave it, spreading her cream over the tight bud of nerves. The image of Clay remained in her mind as she increased the friction on her clit and tugged at her nipples. He would lean over her, hold her wrists next to her head while he kissed her mouth, her neck, her breasts. He'd link their fingers as he moved down her body, dropping kisses along the way. She'd let her thighs fall apart, giving him plenty of room to move between them. His tongue would dive inside her folds, lap up every bit of her essence and return for more.

After she cried out from an intense orgasm, Clay would kiss his way back up her body until his mouth covered hers as he thrust his cock into her pussy. His movements would be slow at first but quickly gain speed as his lust overcame him. Her desire would build again with every stroke of his shaft. She'd throw back her head and wail at the same time that his body trembled from his climax.

"Oh, *yes!*"

Maysen closed her eyes and shoved her fingers into her channel again as the waves of ecstasy washed over her body. The walls pulsed around the digits, trying to draw them deeper into her body, the way they would try to draw Clay's hard flesh deeper inside her.

Several moments passed before Maysen managed to open her eyes. The entrance to her pussy gaped open, needing a cock to fill it. But not just any cock. She wanted it to be Clay's buried inside her.

Once sure her legs would hold her, Maysen slowly lowered them from the arms of the chair and stood. Little zings kept flowing through her body, the delicious aftermath of a strong orgasm. Her gaze drifted over the paperwork on her bed. She should work on it tonight, but that idea didn't appeal to her at all. Crawling into that beautiful bed tempted her more than she could resist.

The long drive combined with the powerful climax had zapped her strength. Deciding the paperwork organization could wait until tomorrow, Maysen transferred everything from the bed to the desk. She turned off the lights, crawled between the sheets that smelled like lavender and sunshine, and closed her eyes.

4

The next two days flew by for Maysen thanks to staying busy with interviewing the rest of the firefighters. In those two days, though, she hadn't seen Clay one time. Curiosity finally got the best of her and she asked one of the firefighters—Tate, a handsome man in his early thirties—why Clay hadn't been around the fire hall. Tate told her Clay had taken off early Thursday morning for Kansas City on Spencer's business. He should be back in Lanville over the weekend.

Maysen couldn't help wondering if Clay really had business that couldn't wait for his attention, or if he'd left to avoid her.

Knowing he ran a successful company, she felt guilty for suspecting him of purposely staying away from her. Yet, she couldn't help feeling this little trip he'd taken hadn't exactly been necessary.

With the last firefighter interview completed, Maysen decided to turn to her camera for the rest of the day. She'd snapped several pictures of the inside of the fire hall and the equipment, yet none of the firefighters in action. Not that she wished anyone to be hurt, but pictures of the men and women actually fighting a fire would be great for her article. Perhaps

Clay could arrange some kind of practice fire so she could take photos of the volunteers putting it out.

She snitched one more donut hole from the box someone had brought in, gathered up her paperwork and camera case, and left the meeting room. Following the sound of hammering and power tools, she walked to the back of the fire hall where volunteers worked on the addition. According to some of the firefighters, thanks to a successful fund-raiser last month, the fire department had the funds to build a larger bay for a new tanker truck. They planned to do another fund-raiser soon to help buy the tanker.

Maysen leaned against the wall and watched the five men and two women working. The men had removed their shirts in the early-afternoon heat. The sun beat down on their skin, turning it shiny with sweat. She couldn't help admiring the muscles and bare skin.

A glance to her right showed her another woman admiring the muscles, too. Even from several feet away, Maysen could see the lust in Talia's eyes when she looked at Dylan. Not that Maysen could blame her. At just over six feet tall with dark brown hair, intense blue eyes, and a muscular body, Dylan fit perfectly into the hunk category.

As if Talia felt Maysen watching her, she glanced her direction. Talia rolled her eyes and fanned her face. Maysen grinned and gave Talia a discreet thumbs-up.

Talia walked over to stand beside Maysen. "I ogle whenever I can."

"I don't blame you." Maysen glanced at the construction, then back at Talia. "Are you here to help with the construction?"

Talia nodded. "I can't stay but a couple of hours today, but want to help as much as I can."

Her gaze drifted back to Dylan. Maysen saw lust flare in Talia's eyes again. "Are you dating Dylan?"

Talia released an unladylike snort of laughter. "Yeah, right. He treats me like his kid sister."

"And you want more."

"I do." She sighed heavily while staring at Dylan with yearning in her eyes. "But I've accepted that it won't happen. I can't make him feel about me the way I feel about him." A touch of pink filled Talia's cheeks. "I'm sorry. I don't know why I'm telling you such personal stuff. I barely know you."

"I've been told I'm easy to talk to. Probably the journalist in me."

"You're definitely easy to talk to." She turned to face Maysen. "Lucia, Paige, and I are having dinner at Café Crystal tonight. Join us."

It would be an opportunity to get better acquainted with the three women on the fire department. In a relaxed setting, she could learn things about the volunteers and Lanville that she wouldn't get in a formal interview.

Maybe even more about Clay.

"I'd love to."

Talia smiled. "Great! I'll let the gals know. The reservation is under Paige's name. Six-thirty."

"I'll be there."

"Hey, King," Dylan called out. "You wanna get your ass over here and help us?"

"No, I wanna get my ass in bed with yours," Talia muttered. Maysen giggled.

In a louder voice, Talia called, "Be right there." She gave Maysen's arm a gentle squeeze. "See you later."

Maysen continued to smile as she watched Talia join the rest of the group. Dylan gave her a friendly punch on her arm. She returned the punch to his stomach. He laughed, but his laughter quickly faded when Talia moved away from him. A look of longing crossed his face before he turned back to the framework.

Perhaps Dylan felt more for Talia than she thought.

Trying to decide whether she should tell Talia what she saw or mind her own business, Maysen began to walk before she turned her head. She ran into a wall of muscle.

"Oh! I'm sor—" Her voice trailed off when she realized the wall of muscle belonged to Clay.

His hands came up to grip her upper arms and steady her. Grateful for the support, Maysen took a breath to calm her racing heart. Inhaling took in the woodsy scent of Clay's aftershave. Instead of slowing her heartbeat, the aroma made it take off at a gallop.

His eyes narrowed, his nostrils flared. She wondered if he noticed her scent, too. "You okay?" he asked.

"Yes, I'm fine. I should've watched where I was walking."

She thought she felt his hands tighten on her arms before he released her. He took a step back. "How are your interviews going?"

"Great. I'm through except for yours. Can we do it today?"

"I'm leaving for Dallas in about an hour. I just came by to check on the construction and see if I need to pick up anything."

Another excuse. Clay must have a complete file cabinet full of them in his brain. "What about tomorrow?"

"You work on Sundays?"

"I work until my job is done."

Respect flashed in his eyes, or so Maysen thought. It quickly disappeared before she could be certain of what she saw. "So do I, which is what I'll be doing in Dallas. I'm staying over tonight, coming back late tomorrow evening."

Maysen considered stomping her foot in frustration. Knowing that would be childish, she tried again to anchor him to a time. "Monday?"

"I might be flying to Tempe Monday. I won't know for sure until tomorrow."

"What's in Tempe?"

"Spencer's headquarters."

She knew that from her research of the Spencer's chain. Maysen had no doubt Clay stayed very busy with the chain's business, but she'd had enough of his excuses. "How can you be fire chief when you're never here?"

"I'm here a lot, Maysen. Lanville is my home, but you caught me at a busy time."

Blowing out an aggravated breath, she straightened her spine. "Clay, I only need an hour for the interview. Two at the most. Is there someone I should call to make an appointment with you?"

He also blew out a breath and looked away from her. "No, you don't need to call anyone." Brows furrowed, he returned his gaze to her. "I can't give you a definite appointment right now, Maysen. Can't you work on the other interviews until we can get together?"

She could do that, but that wouldn't give her more time with Clay. She figured the hour with him for the interview would morph into lunch, or maybe dinner. After that, it would be an easy step to lovemaking. She wanted the sexy fantasies she'd had about Clay the last three nights to come true. "You swear you aren't simply trying to avoid me?"

"No, I told you'd I'd do the interview and I will. Later next week."

"By Friday for sure. I have a job to do, too. Okay?"

"I'll do my best."

Maysen opened her mouth to argue but stopped when Tate called to Clay. "Hey, Chief, got a sec?"

"Sure," he said to the firefighter, but with his gaze still on Maysen. "I have to go."

She watched Clay walk toward the construction area. He wore a black T-shirt and faded jeans that molded perfectly to his butt and thighs. She could easily imagine him wearing nothing but those low-riding jeans, his chest and back shiny with sweat, while he wielded a hammer alongside the other volunteers. His hair would be damp, too, and curl along his nape, almost begging her to run her fingers through it while she kissed him.

Desire curled in her belly. Fantasies helped get Maysen past the gnawing ache of wanting a man's cock buried inside her pussy, but the real thing would be so much better than her imagination. Several of the firefighters had flirted with her. She didn't doubt some of those flirtations could turn into an evening of sex if she wanted them to. Although fit and attractive, the other guys didn't make her long to get naked the way Clay did.

He looked her way, gave a quick jerk of his head, and left through the hole between the studs.

You can't stay away from me forever, Mr. Spencer. I will get my interview from you . . . and a lot more.

The soft patter of rain against the window created the perfect mood for Maysen to work. She wanted to be outside when the sun shone, preferably with her camera. The cool, gloomy day provided the opportunity for her to stay in her room at The Inn and work on her laptop.

Maysen placed the picture of Quade, Shawn, Jose, Wes, and Dylan standing in front of the ladder truck at the top of the page. She added two columns of text below it to check the spacing and tilted her head to the side as she studied it. She hadn't come up with the perfect title yet, but she liked the way this picture looked as the first one leading in to her story.

She hadn't completed her article yet, but she did have the introduction finished. Maysen had written and rewritten it at least six times. She read over the four paragraphs of the introduction while she munched on Chex Mix. Denyse would go over the entire article when Maysen finished it, but Maysen wanted it as perfect as possible before she turned it over to her assistant. Finally satisfied with the beginning, she dusted the crumbs off her fingertips and opened a new page in her desktop publishing program, prepared to continue with the next part of the article.

Giggles and footsteps preceded the pounding on her door. "Open up, Maysen," Emma called out. "We know you're in there."

Maysen rose from her chair at the desk and opened the door. Emma stood on the other side, Alaina and Kelcey behind her. All three women held boxes. "What are you doing here?"

"Have you had supper?" Emma asked.

"Kinda. I had a snack—"

"A snack isn't good enough." She passed Maysen, followed by the other two women. "Café Crystal is closed today so I've been experimenting with some new recipes. Alaina and Kelcey offered to be official tasters. I thought you might want to help, too."

Maysen closed the door, then leaned against it. She gazed from one woman to the other—all different in looks and personalities, yet the best of friends along with being involved with the Coleman triplets. Maysen had met Kelcey Ewing over the weekend. She'd had trouble at first believing the soft-spoken blonde could be involved with an outrageous flirt like Dax Coleman. Seeing them together, so obviously in love, quickly changed her mind. They complemented each other perfectly.

The ladies set their boxes on Maysen's bed. "I always feature prime rib Friday and Saturday nights," Emma said, removing foil-covered plates from the boxes, "but I'm thinking about starting a chef's special on Thursday night, too."

Alaina unpacked her box of silverware, napkins, wineglasses, and a bottle of Bordeaux. Kelcey's box held what Maysen recognized as four thin slices of cheesecake, all different varieties.

"I made these last night and popped them in the microwave before we came up here." Emma uncovered one plate. "Beef tenderloin with creamy garlic sauce."

Maysen's mouth began to water as the food's aroma drifted to her nostrils. Despite the snack she'd recently devoured, her stomach released a loud gurgle. Emma grinned and uncovered the other plates. "Honey citrus pork chops. Zucchini parmesan casserole. Pecan-crusted salmon. I thought we could each sample all of them, unless there's something you don't think you'd like."

"What's not to like?" She wiggled her fingers at Alaina. "Give me a fork."

She crawled on the bed, followed by the other three women. They sat in a circle, the four plates of food between them. Maysen tasted three of the dishes before she spoke. "These are amazing."

Emma smiled. "Thanks. I like experimenting with different recipes."

Maysen forked a bite of the beef tenderloin, the last dish to try. She rolled her eyes in pleasure at the taste of the tender meat. "Oh, God, that's better than sex."

"Then you've obviously had sex with the wrong men," Emma said with a grin.

Maysen snorted. "I haven't had sex in so long I've forgotten how to do it."

"Trust me," Alaina said, topping off her wineglass, "it'll come right back to you with the right man."

Sipping her Bordeaux, Maysen studied each of the three women. She'd immediately felt a kinship with Emma, Alaina, and Kelcey, something that hadn't happened to her with any other woman except Denyse. She felt as if she could ask these women anything and they'd be honest with her. "Okay, true confessions time. Y'all are involved with the Coleman triplets, which happen to be three of the most gorgeous and sexy men I've ever seen. Are they as good in bed as they look?"

The three women exchanged a glance, a grin, then looked back at Maysen. "*Yes,*" they said at the same time.

Maysen forked another bite of beef. "I'm insanely jealous and hate all of you right now."

Alaina laughed along with Emma and Kelcey. "I know some of the firefighters must have flirted with you. Why don't you ask one of them out?"

"Because none of them interest me, and the firefighter I want isn't interested in *me.*"

"Clay?" Emma asked.

Maysen nodded. "I know I'm being silly. I mean, I'll only be in Lanville a couple of weeks, tops. I should go out with Quade or Wes—who've both asked me—and forget about Clay. He certainly wants nothing to do with me. I finally got him to promise I could do the interview with him by Friday. I hope he's back from Tempe by then."

"Clay isn't in Tempe," Kelcey said.

Maysen slowly lowered her fork to the empty plate in front of her. "He didn't go to Tempe today? Are you sure?"

Kelcey nodded. "He met with our guys this morning to finalize the remodeling plans."

A slow burn started in Maysen's stomach and spread throughout her body. Clay had lied to her. She'd asked him for an hour of his time and he'd made up an excuse about going to Tempe instead of allowing her to interview him.

She'd had enough of his stalling.

"Ladies, will one of you give me Clay's address? I need to pay him a visit."

5

Clay settled on the couch, propped his sock-clad feet on the coffee table, and stared into the fireplace. Rain and a cold front had dropped the temperature fifteen degrees, making it cool enough for a fire. The only thing that would add more to the fire would be having a woman sitting next to him.

As it had many times since he'd met her, Maysen's image flashed through his mind. He recognized the attraction in her eyes whenever she looked at him. He could have her right here beside him if he'd stop being a coward.

Clay took a sip of his white wine, then rested his head on the back of the couch. He'd fallen in love with a woman a year ago who'd come to Lanville for only a short time. When she left, she took pieces of his heart with him . . . pieces that still seemed to be missing. He couldn't take the chance of falling in love with another woman who would be here for a week or two and then go back to her life 300 miles away from him.

He wondered—not for the first time—why none of the lovely women he'd dated who lived in Lanville and the surrounding towns affected him as strongly as Maysen. She traveled in her job and had insane work hours, just like he did. She remained single at thirty-two, perhaps because of her job. Or perhaps she hadn't yet met the man who made her body sing when he touched her.

He would love the chance to make her body sing.

All that soft, ivory skin that would tan easily when exposed to the sun. Her short sandy hair with so many shades of gold and brown in it. Pink lips that curved so easily into a smile. Enticing whiskey-brown eyes that could see all the way into a man's soul. A body more voluptuous than slim with full breasts and shapely hips. He guessed her height to be around five-seven with legs that would fit perfectly around his waist.

He wondered what little sounds she made when she came.

Clay pressed his hand over his burgeoning cock behind the fly of his jeans. He could find out. As long as he didn't let his feelings get involved, he and Maysen could have a great time in bed for her remaining days—and nights—in Lanville. Once she left, he'd go back to his life and keep searching for "the one."

The doorbell intruded on his thoughts. Clay frowned. He couldn't imagine someone coming to see him in the rain, especially without calling first. The sun wouldn't set for another hour, but rainclouds had turned the sky dark hours ago. Someone must really need to talk to him to brave the stormy weather.

Setting his wineglass on the coffee table, Clay rose and walked to the front door. He blinked in surprise when he saw Maysen on the other side, complete with light jacket, umbrella, camera bag, and leather satchel.

"What are you doing here?" he asked.

Maysen's gaze dropped to his chest. He'd drawn on a pair of very faded jeans and left his shirt unbuttoned after his shower. He thought he saw her swallow before she spoke.

"I've come to do your interview."

She pushed past him without giving him a chance to comment. He had no choice but to close the door and follow her into the house. She stood in the center of the living room, looking at her surroundings. The awe on her face pleased him. He'd been working his ass off every spare moment for the last eight months remodeling his home.

"Clay, this is a beautiful room." Stepping closer to the rock fireplace, she held out her hands toward the flames. "It's a perfect night for a fire." She straightened her shoulders and turned to face him. Determination replaced the awe. "And it's a perfect night to do your interview. You've put me off long enough. The phony excuse you gave me about going to Tempe was silly, Clay."

"Hey, wait a minute." He moved closer until he stood two feet away from her. "That wasn't a phony excuse. I did plan to go to Tempe but decided not to fly in the stormy weather."

"Planes fly in stormy weather all the time."

"I'm smarter than to take my plane up when there's lightning."

"*Your* plane?" Her eyebrows shot up into her bangs in obvious surprise. "You have a plane?"

Clay nodded. "It belongs to the company. I travel a lot in my job. It's easier for me to fly my own plane than try to coordinate with an airline's schedule."

"You're a pilot?"

"I am. Sometimes I fly myself, sometimes I have another pilot fly the plane if I want to work or have people with me."

"Where do you keep it?"

"Here, on my property. I have a private hangar and small airfield."

"You do?" Her eyes lit up like a child's with a new puppy. "May I see them?"

Clay couldn't help chuckling at her eagerness. "Seeing them in daylight and without the rain would be better."

"Oh," she said, the light fading from her eyes.

The disappointment in her voice made him want to change

his mind and take her out to the plane's hangar, even in the rain. Since that would be stupid, he decided to change the subject. "You came all the way out here in this storm to interview me?"

"I'll admit I came here on impulse and without thinking." He thought a hint of pink filled her cheeks, but he couldn't tell for sure in the dim firelight. "But when Kelcey Ewing told me you didn't go to Tempe, I saw red. It pissed me off that you lied to me."

"Why would Kelcey tell you I didn't go to Tempe?"

Maysen waved one hand, as if to erase his question. "That doesn't matter. What *does* matter is you didn't tell me you didn't go out of town. So no more excuses. We're doing your interview now." She removed her jacket, sat on the couch, placed her satchel on the coffee table, and motioned toward his wineglass. "I'll take one of those."

Hands on hips, Clay watched Maysen remove a legal pad, clipboard, file folder, and pen from her satchel. He didn't know whether to be angry or amused at her bossy attitude.

When she had all the items on the table, she looked up at him. One eyebrow arched. "Wine please?"

The chuckle threatening to escape proved to Clay that amusement beat out anger. "White or red?"

She glanced at his glass of Chardonnay. "Whatever you're having is fine."

Maysen waited until Clay left the room before she closed her eyes and fanned her face. She hadn't expected to find him in an unbuttoned shirt that showed off his broad, tan chest with its light sprinkling of dark hair. She'd gotten only a glimpse, but long enough to see the hair trailed down the center of his stomach, tempting her to follow it with her fingertips, then her tongue.

His clean scent had enveloped her, evidence that he'd showered recently. His damp, wavy hair swirled around his ears and covered his nape, practically begging her to run her fingers through it.

She wanted to touch him so much, she ached with it.

A dimly lit room, a fire in the fireplace, rain falling outside, a glass of wine . . . they all combined to set a romantic scene. Maysen wished her visit here could be attributed to Clay's invitation and not work.

But it is work, that's all. Clay has made it very plain he wants nothing to do with me.

Sighing softly, she removed her camera from its bag and took off the lens cover. She stood and slowly turned in a circle, taking in the entire room. The ranch-style décor screamed masculine, yet soft touches toned down the testosterone level. She noticed the throw pillows with splashes of jewel tones on the couch and two arm chairs. Framed artwork graced the walls, some oil, some pencil drawings. Fat pillar candles in various heights sat in holders along the fireplace mantle and on some of the bookshelves. A thick rug with more splashes of jewel tones covered the wooden floor in front of the hearth.

Everything in the room said home.

She snapped pictures of the fireplace, the mantel, the rug. Focusing upward, she took pictures of the heavy wooden beams that crisscrossed the ceiling. She couldn't claim to be an expert at construction, but they looked like real wood.

"The rest of the house doesn't look as good as this room," Clay said behind her.

She lowered her camera and turned. He held a glass of wine in one hand, a plate of cheese, crackers, and green grapes in the other. It pleased her to see he hadn't buttoned his shirt. She'd take every opportunity she could to look at his torso.

"I'm remodeling when I get the time." He set the plate on the coffee table, then picked up his wineglass. "I'm slow and meticulous, so it takes me a long time to get something done. So far I've finished this room and the kitchen, with help from the Colemans."

"I've heard great things about them and their company. Why don't you hire them to do everything?"

"They are great, but I want to do the majority of the work. I've called on them to help with the heavy lifting, like getting those ceiling beams in place. That would've been a bitch all alone. Other than that, it's just been me." He shrugged. "It's important to me to do it myself."

Warmth and respect flowed through her at his statement. Maysen understood exactly what Clay meant, for she felt the same way. She liked the sense of accomplishment when she learned how to do something new.

Clay held out a wineglass to her. She accepted it, took a sip of the cold liquid. "Mmm, good."

"Where do you want me?"

Oh, such a question! She wondered if he'd chase her off if she told him the truth . . . that she wanted him naked on the rug in front of the fireplace. "The couch is good."

He sat in the corner, his body turned toward her, one arm along the back. She could feel him watching her as she set down her camera, picked up her pen and paperwork. She sat on the couch facing him, legs folded in front of her, leaving a foot of space between her legs and his. After taking a sip of wine, she set the glass on the coffee table and uncapped her pen.

"Some of my questions for you are different from the other firefighters since you're the chief. I have a lot of great information for my article from the interviews I've already done." She grinned at him. "You're getting off easy."

His lips twitched before he sipped his wine. "A question for you first."

A little leery but intrigued at what he wanted to ask her, she nodded. "Okay."

"Why were you taking pictures of my living room?"

Maysen relaxed. That question she could easily answer. "I take a lot of photos of houses, plus tear pictures out of magazines of interiors and exteriors. I live in an apartment now, but I hope to build a house soon. I have a thick file folder full of decorating ideas."

"What type of house do you want?"

She'd asked herself that dozens of times. "Something roomy and airy with lots of windows. I like light." She gazed around the room. "There's quite a bit of wood in here, but the walls are white and you have huge windows to let in the sunlight. Your drapes are heavy, but they're also light colored. The room will still seem airy even with them closed." She looked back at Clay. "Lots of closets and storage, too. There can never be too many closets."

"You'll want your own office."

"Definitely. One with lots of storage, too. I do everything digitally now, so I don't store negatives, but I like to print out many of my photos for future reference. It takes a lot of cabinets to file thousands of photos."

"Kitchen?"

"There has to be cabinets everywhere and a walk-in pantry. And an island in the middle with three or four stools on one side to sit for eating or so friends can visit with me while I cook."

"Do you like to cook?"

"I *love* to cook but don't get much time to do it."

"Are you any good?"

She lifted her chin an inch. "I'm an excellent cook, thank you very much."

His eyes twinkled with humor while he took another sip of wine. "How about master bedroom?"

"Huge walk-in closet. That's a must."

Clay chuckled. "I'm sensing a theme here."

Maysen grinned. "I pretty much want a gigantic storage space with some furniture here and there."

"And lots of windows."

"And lots of windows," she echoed.

He shifted his arm on the back of the couch, until his hand rested no more than an inch from her shoulder. "This house was built in the 1940s. Very few closets, very little space, and not nearly enough insulation or windows. I'm gutting a room at a time, putting in more insulation, new and bigger windows, building larger closets. I added on to the kitchen and built a breakfast nook with a bay window. I like to watch the sunrise while I eat breakfast."

It sounded perfect. "Will you show it to me?"

"I'll give you the grand tour." He set his wineglass on the end table next to him. "But remember, the house is a work in progress."

Camera in hand, Maysen followed Clay through what she assumed would be a dining room someday and into the kitchen. One step inside the spacious room and she fell in love with it. He'd left the light burning above the stove, giving her enough illumination to see. She could almost believe Clay had reached inside her mind and withdrawn all the different fantasies she'd had about her dream kitchen and built it.

He flipped a switch on the wall. Recessed lighting filled the room. Two walls of cabinets, the island in the middle with three tall, padded chairs, extra-wide refrigerator-freezer, stove with six burners, and double oven made the room a cook's dream come true.

"You did all this work yourself?" Maysen asked, running her hand over the granite-topped island.

"Not the cabinets. George McGettis built those. He does all the cabinetry work for Coleman Construction. But I did the majority of the rest of it."

"It's wonderful." She lifted her camera to take a shot but

paused before she pressed the shutter button and looked at Clay. "May I?"

"Sure."

She snapped several pictures of the room—some from a distance, some using the zoom feature. Clay followed her as she wandered into the breakfast nook to take photos there also. She would love to capture the rising sun through the bay window, especially if Clay sat at the table with coffee mug in hand. She imagined half his face lit by sunlight, half still in shadow.

That would be a magnificent picture.

"Laundry room's through there," Clay said, pointing to a closed door. "I haven't gotten to it yet, so there's nothing in it but the washer and dryer. I'm going to build on to the room and install a new back door. There will be a new garage, too. I haven't decided yet if I'm going to attempt it or hire the Colemans to build it."

It didn't matter to Maysen what Clay decided to do about the garage, or any other part of his house, as long as he kept talking. The sound of his voice sent pleasure to every nerve ending. She didn't dare look down at her nipples, for she had no doubt they poked against her T-shirt.

"Bedrooms are this way," Clay said, his hand on the small of her back to guide her. "I'll warn you right now, they're a mess."

Maysen decided mess described the rest of Clay's house perfectly. He'd removed all the drywall so only studs remained. She counted three small rooms and one larger one.

"There were originally five bedrooms." He stepped through a doorway into the larger room. "I tore out the wall between one of those rooms and this one to make my bedroom bigger. I'll do the same with two of the other bedrooms and use that room for an office. The remaining bedroom will be a guest room."

She couldn't help being impressed by everything he'd done so far. "How long have you been working on your house?"

"Eight months, off and on. Mostly off. I've had to travel a lot for the company lately. I plan to start on this room by the weekend."

Maysen stared into his eyes, aware of how close they stood. Out of the corner of her eye, she saw a pile of rumpled covers in the next room. It must be where Clay slept. With only a few steps, she could be on those covers with him.

He hooked his thumbs in the front pockets of his jeans, which opened his shirt to expose more of his torso. Unable to look away, she stared at the masculine perfection before her. If she reached out her hand just a few inches, she could touch him. . . .

His finger lifting her chin dragged her gaze to his face. "You look at me like you want to devour me," he said, low and husky.

She wouldn't lie to him about the way she felt. "I do."

"That's handy, since I want to devour you, too."

Maysen blinked, surprised at his comment. "You do?"

"Is that so hard to believe?"

"You told me there can't be anything between us, not even a lunch date."

His thumb swept across her lower lip. "Maybe I changed my mind."

"Oh." Maysen swallowed, trying to put moisture back into her dry throat. "Then what should we do about this . . . thing between us?"

"Maybe we should start with this."

6

Clay pressed his lips to Maysen's in a gentle kiss of hello. It would be easy to sweep her into his arms, carry her to his sleeping palette, and ravish her. That wouldn't do. He wanted to make love to Maysen—slowly, gently, completely.

He almost changed his mind about ravishment when Maysen's lips softened beneath his in surrender. Needing to touch her, he ran one hand into her hair, cradled the back of her head. A low moan came from her throat before she tilted her head and parted her lips. Clay deepened the kiss, moving his mouth over hers while he tickled the corners of her mouth with his tongue.

She answered his tickling with her tongue, sliding it between his lips to caress his. One hand gripped his shoulder, her fingernails digging into the muscle. Clay accepted the bite of pain as her request for more. He gave it, holding her head in place while he plundered her mouth with his tongue.

The camera in her hands kept him from pulling her close to his body. Probably a good thing, since he didn't know how much control he would have if he felt her curves against him right now. His cock swelled, hardened, until he wondered if the zipper on his jeans might pop open.

"Your bed," she whispered against his lips.

Maysen deserved more than a pile of messy covers. She deserved wine, candlelight, romance. Clay shook his head. "I have a better idea."

Taking her hand, he led her back to the living room. He didn't have a big bed, but he did have a thick, soft rug in front of the fireplace. He couldn't imagine anything more beautiful than the firelight shining on Maysen's skin.

He removed the camera from her hands and set it on the coffee table. With a gentle tug on her fingers, he guided her to the middle of the rug. He dropped to his knees and looked up at her, giving her the option to join him or not.

It took her no more than two seconds before she sank to her knees in front of him.

Clay raised his hands, palms toward her. Maysen touched his palms with hers, entwined their fingers. She didn't say a word, simply leaned closer to him. Clay met her halfway with a bare whisper of a kiss.

He could feel her warm breath against his cheek, absorbed the faint taste of wine clinging to her lips. Far more intoxicating than any kind of liquor, her kiss made his mind spin with fantasies of having her naked body beneath his . . . skin against skin, hands roaming over slick flesh, her softness yielding to his hardness.

He shifted his mouth on hers, touched his tongue to the seam of her lips. She immediately opened for him, swept her tongue across his. Clay released his hold on her fingers, ran his palms up her arms to her shoulders. A gentle tug and Maysen scooted closer to him. Her arms wrapped around him beneath his shirt, hands spread wide over his back.

Her whimper shot straight to his balls, drawing them up tighter to his body.

With her lips still pressed to his, she drew his shirt down his arms. Clay had no choice but to release Maysen long enough for her to remove his shirt and toss it aside. Fingernails slid up and down his bare back, not scratching, but in a caress that drove him closer and closer to losing control.

He couldn't allow that to happen. Maysen had to be satisfied before he ever thought about his own pleasure.

Ending their kiss, Clay reached for the hem of Maysen's T-shirt. She lifted her arms as he tugged it over her head. His gaze snapped to her breasts spilling out of a low-cut, lacy, ivory bra.

He let his fingertips coast over the velvety skin above the lace. "Pretty bra," he managed to rasp. One finger dipped into her cleavage, earning him another whimper from Maysen. "Do your panties match it?"

"Yes."

"Thong? Bikini? Granny panties?"

She arched one eyebrow, which for some reason made his balls draw up even tighter. "I don't do granny panties."

"What *do* you do?"

Her lids narrowed, her eyes turned sultry. "I guess you'll have to find out."

Clay kissed her again, pouring all the desire he felt for her into the kiss. He cradled the back of her head with one hand, caressed one firm breast with the other. She continued grazing his back with her fingernails. Each journey took her a little lower. On her final trip, she slipped her fingers inside the waistband of his jeans.

"Mmmm," she mumbled against his mouth. She kissed his chin, his jaw, the sensitive spot beneath his ear. "I don't feel any underwear."

"That's because I'm not wearing any."

"Commando is very sexy." She nipped the pulsing vein in his neck. "You smell good."

So did she. The aroma of flowers drifted up from her hair, a different scent than her skin. She smelled fresh, like springtime. He didn't think he'd ever get enough of her scent.

"Unfasten your jeans for me." She nipped the vein again, sending a shiver up and down his spine. "I don't want to let go of my prize."

Clay chuckled. The woman had him crazy with wanting her, but could still make him laugh. "I certainly wouldn't want you to lose your prize."

She grinned before kissing him again. Clay reluctantly released her to unfasten his jeans. As soon as he lowered the zipper, Maysen slid her hands all the way inside the denim and cradled his butt.

Maysen moaned, rested her forehead against his neck. "God, Clay, you feel as good as you smell."

He growled when she dug her fingernails into his ass. "Hey, easy with the nails."

Her siren's smile proved she could be a very wicked woman. "I like to scratch."

Clay enjoyed learning these little tidbits about Maysen. "What else do you like to do?"

"I think"—she glided her hands over his hips, taking his jeans with her—"it would be better"—his jeans fell to the top of his thighs—"if I showed you."

With his jeans no longer covering his dick, it sprang forward, as if searching for that warm, wet place between Maysen's thighs. Flashing him an impish grin, she fondled his cock and balls. "It's better if I show you, don't you think?"

Oh, yeah, definitely better. But if he continued to let her "show" him, this would be over long before he wanted it to be. He pulled her hands away from him, ignoring her frown of disappointment. "It's my turn to show you some things."

Her gaze dropped to his cock. She licked her lips. "I want to touch you."

"I want to touch you, too. Let me?"

She looked back into his eyes and nodded.

Clay reached behind Maysen and unhooked her bra. Slipping his fingers beneath the straps, he tugged them down her arms and dropped the bra to the floor. He swallowed as he cupped her breasts in his hands, rasped his thumbs over her hard nipples.

Maysen's low moan dragged his attention from the firm globes in his hands to her face. Head tilted back, eyes closed, lips parted, she appeared to be a woman ready to surrender to the passion building inside her. To urge along that surrender, he leaned over and swiped his tongue across one nipple.

"Clay," she whispered. She tunneled her fingers into his hair and arched her back. He obeyed her silent request by licking her nipple again before moving to the other one and giving it the same treatment. They both beaded beneath his tongue, begging him for more.

He would gladly give it.

Clay lowered her to the rug. Remaining on his knees, he bent over and lavished her nipples again . . . back and forth between the two, giving both equal attention with his tongue and teeth.

Maysen ran her hands over his ass, his hips, his cock. She wrapped one around his shaft, began a slow, milking motion. Clay wanted to pleasure her before she pleasured him. He unfastened the snap on her jeans, clasped the zipper's tab.

Her hand over his stopped him from lowering the zipper. "Take off your jeans first. I want to see all of you."

Clay stood, shucked off his jeans and socks. He would've returned to the rug, but Maysen lifted one hand to stop him.

"Turn around. I want to see *all* of you."

He did as she requested, turning in a slow circle. He could feel her gaze on him, as warm as the fire that burned a few feet from them. When he completed the circle, he started to kneel again. A quick shake of Maysen's head stopped him.

"I'm not through looking."

Clay stood still, his arms at his sides, while Maysen rose to her knees again. She scooted closer until only six inches separated her mouth from his cock. Reaching out, she ran a single fingertip around the head, over the prominent veins, and down to his balls.

"You're magnificent, Clay. Long and thick and straight. And so hard." Her thumb tickled the slit. "I love how hard you are." A pearl of moisture beaded the tip. She wiped it off with her thumb, brought the digit to her mouth, and sucked off the drop of pre-cum.

With a loud moan, Clay leaned over, clasped her face, and kissed her. No longer soft or gentle, he kissed her with passion, with heat, with desire. She continued to caress his shaft and balls, squeezing both while her hands roamed over them.

Before Clay had the chance to stop her, she ended their kiss and engulfed the head of his dick in her mouth.

This isn't what Clay planned. He'd planned to make love to Maysen, bring her to a climax over and over, before he ever thought about his own orgasm. He should pull away from her. The warmth and wetness of her mouth made that impossible.

She dragged her tongue down to his balls, licking both orbs as she caressed the sensitive skin between them and his anus. He wouldn't be able to hold off a climax for long if she kept . . .

Clay drew in a sharp breath when she pushed one finger inside his ass.

"Do you like this?" Maysen looked up at him while she circled her tongue around the head again.

"Yeah." His voice sounded choked and Clay cleared his throat. "Oh, yeah."

She took him even farther in her mouth, until her lips

touched his groin. Clay had to pump. Gently holding her head, he slowly fucked her mouth.

Clay loved the intimacy of oral sex, both giving and receiving. To find a woman who apparently enjoyed it as much as he did made the act even more intimate, more special. He caressed her face as he moved, telling her without words how good her mouth felt on his cock.

The pleasure built and built, until Clay worried he wouldn't be able to hold back his orgasm much longer. "Maysen, you have to stop."

Ignoring his comment, she continued to lick and suck.

"Maysen, I mean it. I'm close to coming."

She pushed another finger into his ass.

"Aw, *fuck!*"

The climax crested, galloping up and down his spine, his limbs, his shaft. Clay's body trembled as every nerve ending in his body flared to life. His dick jerked and his balls emptied into Maysen's warm mouth. Closing his eyes, he threw back his head and groaned loudly.

When he could think clearly again, he opened his eyes and looked into Maysen's face. She sat on her heels, gazing up at him. The firelight turned her ivory skin golden. His chest tightened, as if something squeezed his heart.

No. He wouldn't fall in love with her. He *couldn't*. They could have fantastic sex, but that had to be all.

Leaning over, he kissed her tenderly. "You weren't supposed to do that."

"Why not?"

"Because I didn't get the chance to pleasure you."

That siren's smile returned to her lips. "The evening is young."

"That's true. So what should I do first? Maybe I should"— he lifted her hands, laved her left palm—"play with your nipples until they get nice and hard again. Then I could"—he kissed the back of her right hand—"suck on them. Gently. I wouldn't want to hurt you."

"Of course not," she said, her voice sounding strangled.

He liked that simple touches and words could affect her so strongly. His cock, starting to relax a moment ago, began to harden again. "There'd be some biting in there, too, in case you're curious."

"I think I can handle some biting."

He trailed his tongue across her palm and down to her wrist. "And a lot of caressing. I really like"—he nipped the pounding pulse in her wrist—"Caressing."

Her breasts rose and fell faster with her increased breathing. "Caressing is good, too."

"How about"—his mouth moved up her arm to the bend of her elbow—"licking?"

"Oh, yes. Licking is *definitely* good."

He tickled the inside of her elbow with the tip of his tongue. "Any particular place on your body you want licked?"

"I'm sure I can think of a few—Oh!" she gasped when he moved farther up her body and bit the spot where her shoulder met her neck.

"I told you there'd be some biting," he whispered in her ear.

Clay smiled to himself when she shivered. He continued to gently nibble his way up her neck while he cradled her breasts in his hands. He lifted and squeezed them, flicking the nipples with his thumbs until they felt as hard as diamonds.

Maysen grabbed his head and brought his lips to hers for a voracious kiss. "I want your mouth on me."

"I had my mouth on you."

She frowned. "You know what I mean."

He suspected what she meant, but she needed to say the words, to tell him exactly what she wanted him to do. "Sometimes a guy needs a little help in knowing what a woman wants."

Instead of saying anything else, Maysen stood, unzipped her

jeans, and pushed them and her panties down her legs. She stepped out of them and kicked them aside.

Perfection. That word popped into Clay's head at the sight of her body. The firelight played over her skin, highlighting curves and dipping into valleys. Sandy-colored hair covered her mound, but he couldn't see any on the feminine lips. His gaze swept all the way to her feet and back up to her face.

Utter perfection.

She moved to within inches of him. "On your knees, Clay."

7

He dropped to his knees before her. Maysen drove her fingers into his hair, guided his mouth to her breast. Clay latched on to her nipple and suckled. Every pull of his lips made her pussy clench with the need to be filled. She tightened her hold on his head. "More."

He continued worshipping her nipples while he clasped her ass with one hand, sliding the other between her thighs. Maysen gasped at his touch.

"You're so wet," he growled against her breast. Fingers slid over her labia, gathering her cream to spread over her clit. "I have to taste you. Lie down."

Maysen stretched out on the rug, her legs spread. She expected Clay to immediately start licking her pussy. He surprised her by moving between her legs instead. Still on his knees, he cupped her breasts and kneaded them. He'd stop long enough to tweak her nipples between his fingers before kneading her breasts again. Maysen's eyes drifted closed in complete bliss. She felt his lips brush each nipple, then the valley between her breasts. He kissed his way down the center of her stomach. The tip of his tongue dipped into her navel.

A jolt to her clit caused Maysen to jerk. She'd never realized her navel could be so sensitive.

"Your skin is so soft." Clay continued down her body. He dropped kisses all over the nest of curls on her mound, nuzzled her with his nose. "I love the way you smell." One swipe of his tongue across her clit and Maysen quivered. "I love the way you taste."

Maysen grabbed his head and tried to push him closer to her. He pulled back, removed her hands, and pushed her arms up to lie beside her head.

"Leave your arms there. Don't move them."

Maysen had never been into demanding men, but a thrill coursed down her spine at the command in Clay's voice. She nodded, silently letting him know she would obey him.

Lowering his head, Clay circled her clit with his tongue, glided it over her feminine lips. Over, around, back and forth . . . he covered every part of the moist, velvety flesh between her legs. Unable to lie still with ecstasy so close, she began to shift her hips in rhythm with his stroking tongue. "That feels so good, Clay."

"That's what I want—to make you feel good." He parted her folds with his thumbs and delved between them. "Mmmm."

The gentle vibration of his moan made Maysen purr. She curled her hands into fists, fighting the urge to clasp his head instead of leaving her arms in place as he'd told her to do. She could easily disobey him. That thought lasted only a moment. The anticipation of what he would do next outweighed her desire to disobey.

His tongue glided up and down her slit several more times before darting around her anus. He pushed her legs farther apart, slipped his hands beneath her ass, and lifted it higher. Maysen closed her eyes, concentrated on the feel of Clay's wet tongue, the scrape of his teeth, the suction of his lips. He didn't leave one tiny part of her pussy untouched with his mouth.

When he started sucking on her clit, Maysen lost it. She

grabbed the edge of the rug above her head, needing something to hang on to while bliss engulfed her. Lights flashed behind her eyelids, tingles shot out into her limbs and back to her pussy. Her internal walls pulsed, searching for Clay's cock to milk.

She opened her eyes when she sensed he rose over her. His nostrils flared, desire burned in his eyes. She managed to lift one hand enough to motion toward her camera bag. "Condoms. Side pocket."

Both his eyebrows arched. "You carry condoms in your camera bag?"

"A gal's gotta be ready."

Humor flashed through his eyes before he kissed her, deeply and thoroughly. "Don't need one yet. I'm not through making you come."

Although she desperately wanted to feel Clay's cock moving inside her, she couldn't argue with his unselfish reason for not fucking her yet. She stretched her arms higher over her head. "Go for it."

She loved the way Clay's eyes sparked when he looked at her breasts, now lifted because of her new position. Straddling her hips, he cradled the firm globes in his hands once more. All the attention to her breasts and nipples soon raised her desire again, despite the intense orgasm she'd experienced. Clay plucked at her nipples, twisted them, sucked them. Maysen arched her back, pressed her breasts into his hands.

"You like all this attention to your nipples?" Clay asked.

"Yesssss."

He drew one into his mouth, wiggled it between his teeth. "Can you come this way?"

"Sometimes."

"How? Tell me what to do. Let me help you come again."

Maysen had to kiss him because of his unselfish desire to

please her. "Suck one nipple hard while you twist the other one."

He proceeded to do as she said, lavishing all his attention to the hard tips. He moved from one breast to the other one, suckling one nipple while he tugged and twisted the other. Maysen clutched the rug over her head again. She had to do that or she would jerk out every hair on Clay's head from grabbing it as the sensations galloped through her body. Every nerve ending, every pleasure point seemed to be focused in her nipples. Her heart thundered in her ears, her lungs struggled to draw in enough oxygen. So close. Another orgasm was *so close. . . .*

It crested when Clay bit her nipple. No longer able to hold back, Maysen grabbed handfuls of Clay's hair as the climax rolled over her, through her.

Her head still spun from the intense pleasure when Clay moved away from her and searched the outside pockets of her camera case. He located the three condoms she carried, then tossed them on the rug beside her.

"Do you think we'll need all three?" she asked.

"Yeah, no doubt about that." Quickly tearing open one of the packets, he rolled the latex down his hard cock, then stretched out on top of her. She inhaled sharply when she felt his erection pressing against her stomach. "I have more in the bathroom when we need them."

When, not *if.* Before she had the chance to respond to his comment, he entered her with a long, lazy glide.

Clay buried his face against Maysen's neck, fighting to stay in control and not come too quickly. He thought with the powerful orgasm he'd had a few minutes ago in Maysen's mouth, he wouldn't be able to come again so soon. His hormones had other ideas.

The feel of her warm, wet sheath surrounding his cock urged him to move. He did, slowly, wanting to savor being inside Maysen as long as possible. Her breath caressed his ear each time she exhaled, sending tiny shivers up and down his spine.

He slipped his hands beneath her ass; she clutched his shoulders and wrapped her legs around his waist. Clay pulled back until only the head of his cock remained inside her. Another long glide and she gloved him completely again.

"That feels so good," she whispered.

Clay lifted his head so he could see her face. Her eyes appeared slumbrous and heavy-lidded, her lips deep pink from his kisses. She shifted beneath him and her breasts slid across his chest. His dick gave an interested twitch.

Maysen moaned in her throat. "Mmm, I like what you did."

"Maybe you'll like this, too."

One more unhurried movement and then Clay couldn't remain slow any longer. Holding tight to her ass, he increased the speed of his thrusts. Maysen gripped his waist tighter with her legs, continued to caress his back while he moved. Apparently, that wasn't enough for her. She lowered her feet to the floor, arched her hips to meet him each time he pumped.

The firelight picked up the sheen of perspiration on her skin, turning it even more golden. Needing a deeper connection with her, Clay pushed her arms over her head again and linked their hands together. He stared into her eyes while they moved together in perfect rhythm. The urge to pound his dick into her pussy faded, to be replaced with a desire for tenderness, a need to feel every part of her instead of hurrying toward an orgasm.

After her eyes slid closed, her head tilted back, and pulsations surrounded his cock, Clay sped up his thrusts and flew into the heavens with her. With a loud groan, he collapsed on top of her.

Slowly, he floated back to earth. His hands remained linked with Maysen's so he could feel every bit of her body beneath his. The beat of her heart matched his, as did her heavy breathing. He garnered enough strength to lift his head from her shoulder and peer at her face. Her eyes remained closed, her lips parted. The lure to taste her again called to him. He covered her lips with his in a gentle, unhurried kiss.

With a long moan, Maysen's mouth softened beneath his. He released her hands and placed some of his weight on his elbows so she could breathe easier. As soon as he let go of her hands, she wrapped her arms around his neck and hooked her ankles around the back of his thighs. It seemed as if she didn't want to let him go.

Which worked perfectly for him.

One kiss led to two, then three. Clay shifted on top of Maysen so he could move one hand to her breast. He squeezed the firm mound, flicked her nipple with his thumb. She gasped, but not in pleasure.

Clay ended their kiss. "Nipples sore?"

Maysen nodded. "A little."

"I'm sorry."

"Don't be." A small smile turned up her lips while she buried her fingers in his hair. "It's worth being a little sore now for feeling so good a few minutes ago."

Her positive attitude deserved another kiss. "I think I'd better take care of something in the bathroom."

"Okay."

He gave her one more kiss before he rose and headed for the bathroom to take care of the condom. It pleased him to see Maysen hadn't bothered to get dressed when he returned to the living room. She sat next to the coffee table, glass of wine in one hand, cracker piled with cheese in the other.

She flashed him a sheepish smile. "I'm hungry."

"Go for it." He dropped down beside her and popped a grape into his mouth. "I could fix you something more substantial than cheese and crackers."

"This is fine." She washed down her bite with a sip of wine.

"Actually, I ate shortly before I came over, but sex makes me hungry." Another sip and she drained her wineglass. "And thirsty."

"I'll go get the bottle."

Halfway to the kitchen, Maysen spoke again. "Do you have any chocolate in there?"

Clay stopped, then looked at her over his shoulder. "Oreos. Will those do?"

She grinned. "Perfect."

Chuckling, Clay continued on to the kitchen. He'd expected the sex to be hot with Maysen. He hadn't expected to like her so much.

His smile faded. He had to remember she'd be in Lanville temporarily, would leave as soon as she finished her article. They could have a few more nights of hot sex; then she would go back to Houston. As long as he remembered that and didn't let his heart get involved, he wouldn't have any problems.

He grabbed the bottle of wine and package of cookies and returned to the living room. Maysen had exchanged her wineglass for his half-full one. She sat with her knees drawn up to her chest, sipping on the cold liquid, while she stared into the fire. A fist squeezed his heart at the sensual picture she presented with her golden skin and tousled hair. Right now, he wished he mastered a camera the way she did. He'd love to capture the image of her bathed in firelight for all eternity.

"You okay?" he asked as he sat beside her.

"Sure." Smiling, she held out her glass so he could add more wine. "Just enjoying the fire. It'll be too hot soon to have one."

"That's for sure. I'm not looking forward to the hot summer."

"Aren't you from Tempe? It gets hot in the summer there, too."

"Yeah, but it's a dry heat."

He grinned when Maysen laughed. "I know, hot is hot." He picked up the empty wineglass from the coffee table and poured the cold Chardonnay into it. "But I'd rather have one hundred degrees and dry than one hundred degrees and humid."

Maysen took one of the cookies from its package. "How did you end up in Lanville from Tempe?"

Clay waited until she'd bitten off half the cookie. Taking her wrist, he snatched the other half with his teeth. She glared at him, but he could see the humor in her eyes. "Never steal a woman's chocolate, Clay."

"Hey, the package is almost full. There are plenty of cookies."

"For now."

She picked up another Oreo and bit into it. Clay leaned closer to her and opened his mouth. Maysen hesitated a moment, the laughter still shining in her eyes, before she pressed the other half of the cookie into his mouth. Holding her gaze with his, he chewed as she did. Once he swallowed, he kissed her softly.

"Just getting the last crumbs from your lips."

Maysen touched his mouth with her fingertips. "You're a very good kisser, Clay."

"I'm glad you think so." He cradled her nape in his palm. "You're an *amazing* kisser."

He proceeded to prove to her how much he enjoyed her kisses. He didn't stop showing her until she lay on top of him on the rug, both of them fighting for breath after mind-blowing orgasms.

"I think . . ." She inhaled deeply and blew out the breath. "I think you were trying to distract me."

He kissed the top of her head. "From what?"

"Telling me how you ended up in Lanville."

"Is that what I was doing?" He slowly glided his hands up and down her back. "I thought I was making love to a beautiful woman."

Maysen lifted her head from his chest. "You did that very well. Every time."

It pleased him to know he'd satisfied her. Clay had never believed in wham-bam-thank-you-ma'am sex. He much preferred lovemaking where both he and his partner found fulfillment. "I'm glad you enjoyed it."

"Maybe . . ." She circled his mouth with a single fingertip. "I could stick around for an hour or so and enjoy it again?"

Or all night, if he had his way. Smiling, Clay squeezed her butt. "Sounds like a great plan."

8

A raging hard-on and the need to pee woke Clay the next morning. He decided he could hold off on a trip to the bathroom to take care of the hard-on first. Although after making love with Maysen five times last night, it surprised him his cock could still get hard.

With a smile on his lips, he rolled toward the fire and reached for Maysen. His smile faded when he found an empty place beside him. He first thought that she'd left, but a quick glance around showed him her clothes scattered across the floor. He saw his jeans, but not his shirt.

The scent of bacon and coffee registered in his brain. His smile returned. He didn't often awaken to someone preparing breakfast.

Deciding on the trip to the bathroom after all, Clay threw off the blanket he'd spread over them last night and rose. He took care of nature's call before he grabbed his robe from the master bedroom, or what would someday be the master bedroom. He traveled the back hallway to the kitchen and found Maysen transferring scrambled eggs from a skillet to two plates that already held bacon and toast.

She wore the shirt he'd donned after his shower last night. Her toned legs looked incredible beneath the shirt's hem.

Clay walked up behind her, slipped his arms around her waist, and kissed the side of her neck. "Good morning."

Maysen smiled at him over her shoulder. "Good morning."

"I like you in my shirt." He spread his fingers wide over her stomach. "Are you wearing anything under it?"

"Not a stitch."

His hard-on that had dissipated a short time ago came roaring back. He rubbed his dick back and forth across Maysen's ass while he cradled her breasts in his palms. "Mmm, nice."

He liked the little sound of pleasure in her throat when he plucked at her nipples. She still held the skillet and wooden spoon in her hands, so she couldn't stop him from exploring her body. Not that he believed she would stop something that felt so good to both of them.

Her head fell back to his shoulder. "Breakfast will get cold."

"I have a microwave."

Her laugh made him grin. "Clay, eat first, nooky later."

"God, you're mean."

"I know." She set down the skillet, picked up both plates, and held them out to him. "Take these to the table. I'll get the coffee."

He had no choice but to obey her. Plates in hand, he walked to the breakfast nook. Maysen had already set silverware and cloth napkins on the table, along with two glasses of orange juice. "You're lucky."

"Why am I lucky?" she asked as she walked to the table, two large ceramic mugs in her hands.

"Because I went to the grocery store yesterday. If you'd stayed over Sunday night, you wouldn't have found anything to cook."

"Then I guess my timing was perfect." She placed the mugs

on the table and sat in the chair across from him. "In more ways than one."

He laughed when she bobbed her eyebrows in a playful leer, then watched her fork up a bite of the fluffy eggs and place them in her mouth. Her eyes closed while she chewed, obviously enjoying their flavor. One thing he'd noticed about Maysen—she didn't hide her feelings. Whether happy, angry, or aroused, he never doubted how she felt.

Her gaze rose to meet his. She stopped chewing. "What?"

"I enjoy looking at you."

A pleased smile spread over her lips. She glanced at his chest, exposed by the gap in his robe. "I enjoy looking at you, too."

Clay picked up a piece of bacon from his plate, bit off half of it. She'd cooked it more chewy than crispy, exactly how he liked it. "Good."

"I'm glad you think so. I didn't know if you like crispy bacon or not-so-crispy bacon. I also didn't know how you like your eggs, so I went with scrambled."

"Scrambled is fine. I'm not picky when it comes to food."

"Me either. Except for olives." She shuddered. "Can't stand olives."

"Green or black?"

"Either." She pointed her fork at him. "If you ever want to share a pizza with me, do *not* order olives on it."

"I'll remember that."

Sharing a pizza with Maysen sounded good. Sharing *anything* with Maysen sounded good to him. He'd decided last night before she ever arrived that they could have fun together without hearts and emotions getting involved. He didn't know how long she planned to be in Lanville, but he saw no reason why they couldn't continue seeing each other. Just for fun.

"You like pizza?" Clay asked.

"Is there anyone who doesn't?"

"Probably someone somewhere, but I love it." He popped

the last bite of toast in his mouth and wiped his hands on his napkin. "I was in Kansas City over the weekend. My VP took me to this dumpy-looking place that had the best pizza I've ever eaten. Want to go?"

Maysen froze with her coffee mug lifted halfway to her mouth. "Excuse me?"

"I asked if you want to go to Kansas City for pizza."

She set her mug back on the table without drinking any of the hot liquid. Clay struggled not to laugh at the deer-in-the-headlights look in her eyes. "We can't go to Kansas City."

"Why not? My schedule's my own. So's yours. I have a plane. It's less than a two-hour flight. There's no reason why we can't go."

"You aren't serious."

"I *am* serious. I promise we'll order a pizza without olives."

A slow smile spread over her lips. "You're really serious?"

Clay held up one hand, palm toward her. "I swear I'm really serious."

"I love doing spontaneous things, and that would definitely be spontaneous."

"So let's do it."

She looked down at his shirt she wore. "I need to shower and get some clean clothes."

He laid his napkin in his empty plate. "Go back to The Inn and do whatever you need to do. I'll clean up the kitchen and file a flight plan. We can be eating pizza by one o'clock."

The joy that lit up her face warmed his heart. She jumped up from her chair, gave him a quick kiss, and ran from the room.

Chuckling, Clay cleared off the table and set the dishes on the counter by the sink. He'd finished refilling his coffee mug when Maysen came back into the kitchen, dressed and with all her paraphernalia in her arms.

"I'll be back as soon as I can."

"Don't rush. We can take as much time as we need."

"We're going to Kansas City? On your plane? Just like that?"

"Just like that."

She threw one arm around his neck and gave him a much longer kiss than the one a few minutes ago. Clay laid his hands on her waist, but she skittered away before he could let them travel to more interesting places on her body.

"Be back soon!" she called out as she hurried from the room.

Clay chuckled again. This would be a fun day.

Maysen had pictured Clay's plane as a little two-seater, only big enough to get him to his destination without any fuss. She never expected to stand in the hangar on his property and look up at a small jet.

She should've known better. After all, the plane belonged to a very successful company. And Clay had mentioned last night that other people sometimes traveled with him. "People" indicated more than would fit in a two-seater.

Her gaze swept it from nose to tail. "How big is it?"

"Ninety feet long with a wing span of seventy-eight feet."

"You know how to fly it?"

His lips quirked as if he tried not to laugh. "I do. Want to see my pilot's license?"

"No, I believe you."

"Then let's go." He held out his hand to her. "Ready to board?"

She laid her hand in his. "I'm ready."

The luxurious cabin didn't surprise her after seeing the sleek outside of the plane. Done in shades of ivory, brown, and green, it screamed comfort and style. Maysen counted eight padded chairs and a long couch that would easily seat four people, or could be used to take a nap. "Twelve people can fly on this?"

"Fourteen, counting the pilot and copilot." He tapped the end of her nose. "You get to be my copilot."

Maysen set her camera case and portfolio on one of the chairs. "I'd like that."

"Want to see the rest of the plane first?"

She nodded.

He motioned to the seating area. "Obviously, this is where people sit. There are pullout tables if someone needs one." He pointed to a long cabinet beneath the windows. "There's wireless for laptops, and satellite for phones and music. There are several DVDs in here if someone wants to watch one on the TV across from the couch or on their laptop." Taking her hand again, he led her toward the back of the plane. "Galley's back here, and the restroom. There's a smaller galley and lavatory behind the cockpit."

More luxury greeted Maysen when they stepped into the galley. Spacious and well-lit, it held all the major appliances, only in smaller sizes than a house. She opened the door to the restroom and her mouth dropped open. Accustomed to tiny lavatories on commercial jets where a person could barely turn around, this generous room even had a shower stall. "Wow."

"This isn't the best part of the plane."

She wondered at the mischievous gleam in Clay's eyes, until he opened a door at the end of the galley. He led her into a bedroom complete with a queen-sized bed. The walls didn't have any porthole, but a large skylight occupied the ceiling above the bed.

"I gave up some seats to have this room instead."

"How do you fly the plane and sleep at the same time?"

"I don't. I told you sometimes I hire a pilot." He glanced at the bed. "I probably should've kept the extra seating. I'll bet I haven't used this bed more than five times in a year."

His comment made an idea pop into her head. This whole trip came about from a spontaneous suggestion by Clay. Maysen saw no reason why everything they did today shouldn't be done on a spur-of-the-moment thought. The bedspread, with its swirly pattern of earth tones and forest green, looked very inviting.

"Do you just sleep in this bed or use it for other activities, too?"

The gleam in his eyes returned when he looked back at her. "Just sleep."

She ran her fingertip down his cheek. "It's a shame such a beautiful room has been used only for sleeping."

Clay laid his hands on her waist and pulled her against him. Maysen could feel his cock hardening inside his jeans. "You're right. That is a shame. But I'd be willing to rectify that oversight."

He leaned closer as if to kiss her. Before their lips met, Maysen gave his chest a hard shove. Wide-eyed and mouth open, Clay fell on his back on the bed. She quickly followed him, straddling his hips and propping her hands next to his head.

His eyes twinkled with humor and a grin tugged at his lips. "What was that?"

"I'm being spontaneous."

"Mmm, I like that." Gripping her waist, he gently tugged until she lay on top of him. He ran his hands beneath her T-shirt and unhooked her bra. "I really like spontaneous."

Maysen didn't have time to take a breath when he flipped their positions. He palmed her bare breast as his lips covered hers.

Instant heat.

He shifted between her legs and pressed his cock against her mound. Maysen answered by placing her feet on the bed and spreading her thighs so that enticing column of hard flesh rubbed her clit.

Clay's mouth wandered down her neck, dropping kisses along the way. "Did you restock your camera bag?"

Despite desire streaking through her veins, she grinned at

his question. "You don't have any condoms on this fancy plane?"

He lifted his head and gave her a sheepish look. "I told you, I only sleep on this plane."

"Then it's a good thing I made a stop at the drug store before I came back to your house."

"I knew you were a smart woman." He kissed the tip of her nose. "Be right back."

Knowing it would take Clay less than a minute to return with the condoms, Maysen jumped up and quickly shed her clothing. She reclined on the bed, one knee bent in invitation, mere seconds before Clay came back in the room.

9

Maysen smiled to herself when Clay stopped in mid-step. Heat flared in his eyes as his gaze swept her body. He dropped the condoms on the end of the bed and whipped off his T-shirt. He stared at her face while the rest of his clothes and shoes soon landed on the floor next to hers. She had only a moment to admire his body before he joined her.

"I wanted to undress you," he said before gently nipping her chin. "I still don't know what kind of panties you wear."

"I wanted to surprise you."

"I do love surprises."

Maysen tilted her head back to give Clay more room when he kissed her neck. He didn't stop this time but continued kissing his way down her chest and over to one firm nipple. She sighed when he kissed it.

"Still sore?" he asked.

"No."

Clay drew the tip into his mouth. He sucked and licked and nibbled, sending delicious zings to her clit. Her pussy clenched with every pull of his lips. A nice, long lovemaking session would be wonderful. Later. Now, she longed to feel him pounding into her. "I want you inside me."

If possible, the heat in his eyes flared even hotter. "You're tempting me."

"Good." Sliding a hand between them, she wrapped it around his shaft. It pulsed in her palm. "Fuck me, Clay."

He shook his head, pulled her hand off his cock. "Not yet. I have to lick your pussy first."

Okay, that worked, too. Maysen stretched her arms over her head, then spread her thighs wider. Clay kissed each nipple, then worked his way to her mound. He touched her folds gently, almost reverently, with his tongue.

"You're so wet. I love that." He lifted his head and looked into her eyes as he pushed two fingers inside her. Maysen moaned when he wiggled his fingertips over her G-spot. "Like this?"

"Oh, yessss."

"How about this?"

He placed his lips directly over her clit and suckled. The direct stimulation to the bundle of nerves shot pleasure through her body faster than lightning. Her heart took off at a fast gallop; perspiration dotted her skin. The waves of bliss went on and on, flowing to the top of her head, the tips of her fingers, the ends of her toes.

She hadn't floated all the way back to earth yet when Clay flipped her to her stomach. Before she could take a breath to ask him what he planned to do, he drove his tongue into her ass.

"God!" Maysen arched her upper back off the bed but couldn't move her lower body since Clay held her down with one arm across her hips. His other hand stayed busy between her legs, two fingers pumping in and out of her pussy as his tongue continued to flash across her anus.

It should be illegal how good his mouth felt on the sensitive area.

He took his time nibbling, licking, fucking her ass with his tongue while his fingers continued their magic inside her. Maysen buried her face against the pillow and raised her hips as high as she could to get even closer to his mouth. She'd never had an orgasm from anal stimulation, but none of her lovers had ever taken so much time there. Clay worshipped her as if he didn't care whether or not he ever had an orgasm, as long as she did.

That type of unselfishness aroused her even more.

Sparks flashed behind her closed eyelids. The waves started rolling over her again, but much faster than her last climax. They grabbed her, making her body tremble and jerk. "Ohgodohgodohgod."

Clay pushed his thumb into her ass. Her anus pulsed around the digit; her pussy walls clamped his fingers. His fingertips continued to caress her G-spot, slowly bringing her back to reality.

He kissed each buttock, the small of her back, the spot between her shoulder blades. "You okay?"

Maysen couldn't stop the bark of laughter. "No, all of my bones dissolved."

She would've swatted him for chuckling at her if she had any strength in her arms. "You make some very sexy moves for a woman with no bones."

A whimper escaped past her lips when he slowly pulled his fingers from her. The mattress shifted with his movement; then she heard a condom package tearing. Maysen lay still, trying to catch her breath and get her mind to stop spinning.

Clay's knees pushed her legs farther apart. The head of his cock slid into her pussy. Maysen moaned at the delicious stretch. He didn't move, but stayed still until she lifted her hips to drive him deeper.

"Don't do that, sweetheart. I'm trying not to come yet. Listening to those sounds you make, feeling how responsive you are . . . God, it's sexy." He nuzzled behind her ear, bit her ear-lobe. "*You're* sexy."

His cock slid in another inch. Despite Clay telling her not to lift her hips, she couldn't help herself. She needed to feel him all the way inside her. She rose to her knees, her face still buried in the pillow.

"Oh, yeah," Clay said in a strangled voice. "You have an amazing ass." He ran his hands over it while he slid in another two inches. "I want to go slow, but I don't know if I can."

"Don't." Maysen reached back with one hand and dug her fingernails into his thigh. "I want it hard and fast."

"Whatever my lady wants."

Maysen groaned when Clay shoved in his shaft and began to pump. Every few moments, he would stop pumping and circle his hips, brush his balls harder against her clit. It should be sensitive after two orgasms, yet she arched her back more to heighten the contact.

The brush of his balls not quite enough to come, Maysen rubbed her clit with her fingertips. She touched his shaft thrusting between her folds, wishing she could feel his skin instead of the latex covering it.

"Come again for me, Maysen. I want to feel your pussy squeeze my cock."

His words, along with his hard thrusts and her fingers, pushed her over the top. Pleasure peaked, sending Maysen flying again. This time, Clay made the journey with her. A low growl came from his throat. He muttered a soft "Shit!" as his cock jerked inside her and he collapsed on her back.

Clay's weight made Maysen fall to the bed. She couldn't breathe, but she didn't care. She'd take ecstasy over oxygen any day.

"You're . . . dangerous, do you . . . know that?" Clay rasped in her ear.

His warm breath sent goose bumps scattering across her flesh. "I like being dangerous."

She moaned at the loss of him inside her when Clay withdrew. He fell to his back on the bed. Maysen turned her head toward him. He lay with his eyes closed, one arm thrown over his head. The position made his biceps bulge. He didn't have the puffed-out muscles of a bodybuilder, but ones of a man who didn't mind doing physical labor. The fact that he wanted to do most of the work in his house's remodel proved that.

She let her gaze wander down his body, noting the light dusting of dark hair on his chest and stomach, the sheen of perspiration on his skin. His cock, encased in the flesh-colored condom, had softened, but still remained impressive.

She had to take a picture of him.

"I'll be right back," she said, easing toward the edge of the bed.

"Okay," he responded without opening his eyes.

Maysen removed her camera from its bag and returned to the bedroom. Clay still lay where she left him. She adjusted the camera settings to allow for the dimness in the room, brought the camera to her eye, and pressed the shutter button.

Clay must have heard the click. He rolled his head toward her and opened his eyes. "What are you doing?"

"Taking your picture." *Snap.*

"Hey!" He covered his cock with his hands.

"Don't do that. I'm not taking X-rated pictures, just from your navel up. Although I wouldn't mind taking a few below your navel, too."

"Maysen—"

"Don't be a prude, Clay. Put your arm back by your head and give me a sexy look."

Laughter sputtered through his lips. "I don't believe this."

"This is only for me." *Snap.* "Take off the condom please."

He hesitated for several seconds before asking, "You swear the pictures are only for you?"

She lowered the camera and lifted one hand, palm toward him. "I swear."

Maysen could almost see the wheels turning in his head, trying to decide whether or not to trust her. She could understand that. Despite two rounds of incredible sex, they barely knew each other.

She began to think he wouldn't comply when he rolled to his side and opened a drawer in the stand next to the bed. He withdrew a tissue, wrapped the condom in it, and tossed it in the wastebasket fastened to the wall. Reclining on the bed again, he bent one knee and laid his arm by his head. "Snap away."

Maysen smiled. "Really?"

"I figure if you're going to be naked while taking pictures, I can pose for them."

Although she normally didn't make a habit of walking around without clothes in front of a lover, she felt so comfortable in Clay's presence that she hadn't thought about being nude. "Do you want me to get dressed?"

"You're kidding, right?" His gaze stroked over her body. "I'm enjoying the view."

Grinning, Maysen snapped another picture. She turned her camera to a ninety-degree angle and snapped again, this time getting Clay's body from his thighs to his head. She moved around the bed, shooting from different angles and with different zoom settings.

"I thought you use a digital," Clay said.

"I do." *Snap.*

"Then why don't you look at the display screen on the back?"

"I'd rather use the viewfinder." *Snap.* "I feel like I have better control over my shots that way." *Snap.*

She leaned over to get closer to him. Apparently Clay liked what her new position did to her breasts, for his nostrils flared when he looked at them. He peered into the lens again, this time with eyes heated with desire.

"Right there. Don't move." Maysen zoomed in for a close-up of his face so she could capture those amazing eyes. "You are so gorgeous, Clay. You should be in a magazine, or in a calendar."

He snorted. "Yeah, right."

"I'm serious." Maysen lowered her camera. "You should be in a calendar. A firefighters calendar." The light bulb went off in her mind, a way to capture Clay's image forever and help the Lanville fire department at the same time. "Oh! What a great idea."

"Now, wait—"

"No, listen." She set her camera on a small table, crawled on the bed, and sat back on her heels. "It could be a fund-raiser for your new tanker." Now that the idea had formed in her brain, Maysen flew with it. "I have a lot of contacts and can get the calendars printed for practically nothing. I'll do a full-page ad in the magazine to go along with the article, no charge to your department. It'll be on our Web site, too."

"Maysen—"

"I could take pictures of the guys in their fire gear, but with the jacket open and no shirt. And some with no jacket. There are major hunks on your fire department."

"Maysen, will you—"

"You could charge eighteen to twenty dollars each and sell a ton. You'll be on the cover, of course, and—"

"Maysen!" Clay sat up and grabbed her upper arms. "I'm not going to be on the cover of a calendar. Or anywhere in it."

His adamant statement deflated her excitement. "Why not?"

"Because I'm not a model."

"You don't have to be a model, Clay. None of the firefighters are models, but they're hot and sexy, and women would drool over their pictures in a calendar." She laid her hands on his thighs. "Your department needs a new tanker. This will be a great way to raise money."

"You honestly think women would buy a calendar of the Lanville Fire Department?"

Maysen nodded. "I do. I'll make the pictures tastefully sexy, like the ones I just took of you. Not even any bare butts, although women would love those."

Clay released her arms and ran his hands down his face. "I don't know, Maysen. Lanville is a small town and old-fashioned in a lot of ways. I bet we wouldn't sell ten calendars total."

"Clay, you're thinking too small. I told you I'll run an ad in my magazine. It has circulation across the country. Our Web site gets hits from all over the world. We could do an online calendar for people outside the U.S. Shipping would be expensive for a regular calendar, but they could purchase a PDF copy and print off the pages."

"The guys won't want to pose for a calendar any more than I do."

She laughed at his naïve statement. "Clay, you can't be serious. You don't think Dylan would be first in line to pose?"

Clay chuckled. "Okay, you got me there. Dylan would definitely pose."

"I'll bet most of the guys would. And the three gals could be in the pictures, too." Maysen clapped her hands in glee. "Oh, Clay, this will be such fun!"

The humor faded from his face. "Maysen, there are thirty-five firefighters, most of them men. You don't need me for the calendar."

"Yes, I do." She cradled his face in her hands. "You're the fire chief. You're also the most handsome man of the bunch. I want you in the calendar." She gave him a quick kiss. "Please?"

His eyes narrowed, leaving Maysen with the sinking feeling that he would say no. Then his lips quirked and his gaze flashed to her breasts again. "Maybe there's something you can do to convince me to be part of the calendar."

His devilish expression told her exactly what he wanted her to do, but she pretended she didn't understand. "And what would that be?"

"Well . . . I kinda have a problem."

One quick glance at his cock showed her his "problem" in full, glorious detail. "Really? You think I can help you?"

He palmed her breast, rubbed the nipple with his thumb. "I'm willing to let you try."

"How generous of you."

"That's me. Mr. Generous."

Maysen placed her hands on his chest and gently pushed, following him as he reclined. "There is a condition to me helping you."

"Oh?" He cradled her ass and squeezed. "And what would that be?"

"You have to help me, too."

She loved the cocky grin that crossed his lips. "I like the way you think."

10

It shouldn't be so difficult to get men to take off their clothes.

The younger guys didn't seem to have a problem posing however Maysen wanted them to. They thought being in a calendar would be cool. The men in their late thirties to early forties, not so much. She especially had to coax Manny, who didn't think his wife, Cathleen, would appreciate him appearing shirtless in a calendar. Cathleen surprised him by showing up in the park where Maysen had set up the photo shoot and urging Manny to participate. She even stayed to watch and offered suggestions on how he should pose. She kept telling him what an amazing body he had, which always made Manny blush.

Maysen thought they were so cute together.

She'd spent the last week setting up shoots for the firefighters. On rainy days, she shot inside the fire hall next to the equipment. On sunny days, she took them outside to the riverbank, a house, a tree-filled pasture. She hadn't taken pictures at a fire yet, but planned to do that this week. Clay had told her last night the firefighters would fight a practice fire Saturday at an old house the owner wanted to demolish before building a new one. Action shots would add so much to the article and calendar.

She'd already taken hundreds of shots, wanting a lot of pictures from which to choose. Denyse would help her with that. Her assistant had a great eye when it came to photos. And sexy men.

Thinking of sexy men made the vision of Clay pop into her head. She smiled as she began to gather up her equipment to load into her Tahoe. They'd seen each other every night for the last week, either at his house or her room at The Inn. She coaxed him into letting her take sexy pictures of him in front of his fireplace . . . including some where he had a full-blown hard-on.

No one else would see those pictures. She planned to make a screensaver for her laptop with all the sexy pictures she'd taken of Clay. It would be something she could look at and remind her of the wonderful man she'd spent time with while here in Lanville.

She hadn't discussed any future plans with him, nor had he discussed them with her. Other than calling her "sweetheart" on his plane once, there'd been no other terms of affection.

Maysen originally thought she could enjoy time with Clay and his body while she finished her assignment, then go on her merry way and forget about him. That didn't seem to be working out as she'd planned. She enjoyed his company more and more, and longed to be with him when they were apart.

For the first time in her life, she wondered if she could be falling in love.

She'd longed to make her magazine a success, learn to be the best photographer ever. She'd accomplished both those things. Along the way of building her career, she'd pushed her personal life aside, deciding she could worry about it once she'd established herself.

Now she wanted more than simply a career.

Believing it too soon to tell Clay of her developing feelings, Maysen kept them locked away in her heart, waiting for the right time to talk to him about a future together.

"Hey," Clay said from behind her.

She'd been so involved in her thoughts she hadn't heard Clay's approach. She turned to him and smiled. "Hey."

He slipped the bag from her shoulder that held her lens filters and laid it in the back of her Tahoe. "Through for the day?"

"For now. Kory and Kirk are supposed to meet me at the fire hall after three."

"You're shooting them together?"

"I think the twins angle will be very sexy."

Clay closed the rear door, leaned against it, and crossed his arms over his chest. "You have a thing for twins?"

She liked the teasing in his eyes and decided to play along. "Maybe. Kory and Kirk are really cute."

"And young."

"They're twenty-five. That isn't too young."

He studied her face for a moment before speaking again. "You ever been with two guys at the same time?"

Even though they'd been naked together every one of the last eight days, it surprised her that he would ask such a personal question. Yet, she had no problem telling him the truth. "No."

Having answered his question, she thought it fair he do the same. "How about you? Have you ever been with two women at the same time?"

Clay scratched behind his ear and Maysen thought a hint of pink touched his cheeks. "Yeah, once. I got completely plastered on my twenty-first birthday and my buddies arranged to have two gals visit me. I hope I had a good time. I barely remember it."

Maysen laughed, happy to know something about Clay's past. They'd talked freely about their jobs and Lanville and places they'd both visited, but little about their families or past. Maysen considered this a step to them becoming closer.

A loud *beep-beep* came from the pager at Clay's waist. His

expression turned serious as he pulled it from his belt and looked at the display.

"That's the signal for a brush fire. I have to get to the fire hall."

"May I come, too? I want shots for the article."

"If you'll stay back and follow my every instruction."

"No problem."

Heart pounding from both fear and excitement, Maysen climbed behind the steering wheel in her Tahoe and followed Clay from the park.

Maysen parked where Clay indicated and watched as the equipment arrived to fight the fire. The ambulance came first, quickly followed by two attack trucks, a pickup with a skid unit, an engine, and a tanker. She'd learned during the interviews that the tanker held 3,000 gallons of water. The firefighters could get more from a nearby cattle tank if necessary, or they'd call to have more brought to them. Luckily, they didn't have to do either this time as they managed to extinguish the three-acre blaze in under two hours, and before it reached any homes.

Using her long-range zoom lens, Maysen snapped picture after picture of the brave volunteers who risked their lives for no compensation—nothing but the satisfaction of helping others. A lump formed in her throat as she watched the weary men with their smoke-smudged faces trudge to the vehicles for the trip back to the fire hall.

So brave and daring. Heroes, every one of them.

Maysen pushed her hair back from her face. She wrinkled her nose at the smell of smoke. Although not directly in the path of the fire, smoke had drifted her way from the light breeze. It would definitely be shower time once she got to her room at The Inn.

Clay walked in her direction, removing his turnout coat. She snapped several pictures of him while he shrugged it from his shoulders and tossed it and his helmet on the seat of a pickup. The black T-shirt beneath the coat stretched over his shoulders and back. There was nothing flattering about the turnout pants or black boots, yet Maysen thought Clay the sexiest man she'd ever seen.

He approached her, reeking of smoke and sweat. Instead of disgusting her, the scent of his labor caused desire to curl in her stomach . . . and lower.

"Did you get enough pictures?" he asked.

A tendril of his dark hair curled over his forehead. Maysen reached up to push it back. "I did."

He leaned against the side of her Tahoe, weariness showing in the slump of his shoulders, the lines bracketing his mouth. "I have to go back to the fire hall and help with the equipment, then write up a report. And shower. Do you want to meet later for dinner?"

"I'd like that." She looked down at her clothes that smelled as smoky as his. "I need to clean up, too, and download my photos. And I want to call Denyse and see if she's proofed my article yet."

"How do you feel about Mexican food?"

Maysen smiled. "Love it."

Clay glanced at his watch. "I'll need at least a couple of hours. How about if I pick you up at six?"

"Perfect."

He kissed her softly, touched her cheek with his knuckle, then turned and headed for his pickup.

Maysen sighed. There was no falling in love involved. She'd already fallen.

"I'll take care of it," Luis said to Clay.

Clay barely had time to remove his boots and turnout pants when Luis, Dylan, and Quade had cornered him in the locker room. He looked from one man to the other, ending up on

Luis. His assistant chief hated to do any kind of paperwork. The fact that he volunteered to take care of the report on the fire made Clay suspicious. "*You're* offering to write up the report?"

"I am. So take advantage of me before I change my mind."

"And we'll take care of the equipment," Quade said. "So there's no reason why you need to stay."

The wicked looks in the men's eyes also made Clay suspicious. "What's going on? Why are you trying to get rid of me?"

"We aren't." Dylan flashed his famous dimpled smile, which didn't charm Clay a bit. "We're just being nice, Chief."

"Yeah, well, you three don't do 'nice.' So what are you *really* doing?"

A subtle nod from Quade to Dylan must have been some kind of signal. Dylan clapped Clay on the shoulder. "Manny heard you invite Maysen out for Mexican food. You've been a lot more relaxed and happy since she came to town. We want you to go and have a good time with her. We'll take care of everything here."

He looked at the men again and saw nothing but sincerity in their eyes. It touched him that they wanted to do something nice for him and Maysen. "Thanks, guys."

"Get out of here," Quade said with a grin. "You might be able to catch Maysen in time to shower with her."

Sounded like a hell of an idea to Clay. He waved at the guys over his shoulder as he jogged toward his pickup.

Eager to see Maysen, Clay took the stairs at The Inn two at a time. Maybe Quade was right and Clay could shower with her. They'd done that this morning at his house, but he wouldn't mind watching soap suds run over her body twice in one day.

It surprised him to find her door open a crack. She must not have closed it all the way when she arrived. He'd have to reprimand her for that with a good tongue lashing.

Clay grinned at his own joke. He loved to lash Maysen with his tongue . . . all over her body.

He laid his hand on the door to push it open when he heard her voice.

"It was incredible. Scary, but incredible. Firefighters are so brave and heroic."

Her assistant must be on the phone with her. He doubted if Maysen would mind if he went in her room and waited until she finished her phone call.

Her next words stopped him.

"The photos are amazing. I can't wait to get back to Houston and finish my article."

He'd known Maysen would go back to Houston eventually, but she hadn't seemed in any hurry to do so. He'd asked her more than once how long she planned to be in Lanville. She'd always told him she planned to stay until she was ready to go.

Apparently, that time had come.

"Soon," Maysen continued. "I have a ton of things to do."

Clay didn't need to hear anymore. He turned and headed back downstairs.

You're an idiot, Spencer. You promised yourself after Karen that you would never fall for a woman who didn't live in the area. And what do you do? You fall in love with a woman who lives 300 miles from here.

It didn't matter that he had a plane. With them living in different parts of the state, they would have to arrange their schedules to see each other. Spontaneity wouldn't be a possibility. He traveled a lot in his job. So did Maysen. A relationship couldn't work with too much time apart. Clay had never believed in the absence-makes-the-heart-grow-fonder bullshit.

He couldn't see her tonight knowing she'd soon be leaving. He had to end things with her now.

Halfway home, Clay's cell phone rang with the ringtone he'd assigned to Silas. Not wanting his vice president to go to voice mail, Clay pulled over to the side of the road to answer the call.

"Hey, Silas."

"Clay, we're ready to sign contracts for buying those five stations in Kansas and Missouri. I'm going to FedEx them to you first thing tomorrow morning."

Although Clay's family owned the company, he had vice presidents who did a superb job of running Spencer's, which let Clay live in Lanville instead of Tempe. E-mail, faxes, and FedEx helped keep Clay notified of anything that required his specific attention. He'd signed a lot of paperwork that had been sent via FedEx.

Not this time.

"I'll fly out there and take care of it, Silas. It'll give me the chance to see my parents and grandfather."

"Sounds like a plan to me. We can talk about those two stations in Tulsa while you're here. I think the owners are almost ready to sign on the dotted line. Maybe you can take care of that, since they're close to you."

"I can do that."

"Great. Let me know your flight plan after you file it. I'll pick you up at the airport."

"Will do."

Clay pressed the button to end the call. He continued to hold the phone while he wondered what to do about Maysen. Decision made, he dialed her cell number.

"Hi," she purred into his ear.

Clay closed his eyes. Ending things with her over the phone made him feel like a coward, but if he saw her again, he'd probably drop to his knees and beg her to stay. "I have to cancel dinner. I just got a call from my VP, Silas. I'll be heading to Tempe in the morning."

"Oh."

The disappointment in her voice tugged at his guilt. He

couldn't let that change his mind. Although he and Maysen burned up the sheets, she'd never indicated she wanted anything more from him than a good time. She'd often referred to her life in Houston. Now she could go back to it.

"You could still come over," she said. "I'll go pick up the food for us."

"I'm really wiped, Maysen. I'm gonna shower and go to sleep so I can get up early tomorrow."

She didn't say anything for several moments. When she spoke again, he could hear disappointment in her voice once more, along with pain. "Did I do something wrong, Clay?"

"No, I just have to take care of business. So do you. Now that you have your fire pictures, you can finish the article, right?"

"Yes."

"So you'll be going back to Houston. I understand that. We both knew from the start that our . . . affair wouldn't last."

"Yes, I guess we did." She cleared her throat. "So, is this good-bye? Over the phone?"

"I may have to fly to Tulsa from Tempe, so I don't know when I'll be back to Lanville. We may as well say good-bye now."

That comment sounded so unfeeling. He couldn't let her go with such a cold statement. "You're a special woman, Maysen. I enjoyed our time together."

"I did, too."

"Take care of yourself."

"You, too. Good-bye, Clay," she whispered.

Clay ended the call, then tossed the phone on the passenger seat. Closing his eyes again, he pinched the bridge of his nose while his throat burned. His chest felt as if his heart had crumbled into dust. He'd fallen hard and fast for Maysen, even harder and faster than he had for Karen. He'd never felt so empty and alone as when Karen left him.

Until now.

Sitting around his house would only make him feel more alone. Clay decided he'd take a shower, throw some clothes into a bag, and file his flight plan for Tempe. His bedroom would be waiting for him in his parents' house. With the station closed and in the middle of the remodel, he didn't have to hurry back to Lanville. He could visit with his parents and grandfather for a few days before he went to Tulsa.

His plans made, Clay pulled back onto the road. He'd survived a broken heart once. He'd learn how to survive another one.

11

Maysen stared down at the legal pad on her desk while she drew little squiggles over the page. She had so many things on her to-do list, she didn't know where to start. None of them mattered. She hadn't been able to concentrate on anything since she returned to Houston on Tuesday.

Otherwise known as the day after Clay broke her heart.

Disgusted with herself for the self-pity, Maysen threw her pen on top of the pad. So he hadn't fallen in love with her the way she'd fallen in love with him. It happened all the time. She'd had relationships in the past where she and her guy didn't click. There hadn't been that special something between them that Maysen knew would let their relationship last.

That special something called love.

"Okay, I've had enough of this." Maysen's assistant, Denyse, stood before Maysen's desk, hands on her hips and a scowl on her face. "You've done nothing but mope for three days. I refuse to let it be a fourth." She pointed toward the door to Maysen's office. "Get off your ass, get back to Lanville, and get your man."

" 'Get my man'? You sound like something from a B-rated Western."

"I don't care how I sound. What I *do* care about is you." Denyse rounded Maysen's desk, pulled herself up, and sat on top of it. "I can't believe you left Clay without fighting for him."

"What was I supposed to fight?" Maysen swiveled her chair toward Denyse and leaned back. "Clay and I never made promises to each other. It's like he told me, we went into our affair knowing it wouldn't last. It ended before I thought it would, or wanted it to, but it's over. End of article, close the magazine."

"Bullshit."

Maysen chuckled and shook her head. She could always depend on her friend to say whatever she thought.

Denyse pointed a finger in Maysen's face. "You love Clay. I could hear it in your voice when you talked about him over the phone. This"—she picked up the legal pad and waved it before Maysen—"is proof your heart is broken." She tossed the pad back on the desk. "What I don't understand is why you left him without talking to him. You should've told him how you feel."

"What good would that have done if he doesn't feel the same way?"

"How do you know he doesn't feel the same way? Did you ask him?" She leaned closer until their noses almost touched. "It's called *communication*, Maysen. You have no problem saying what you mean with your employees. Why not with the man you love?"

Denyse slid off the desk and walked to the doorway. Before she left the room, she looked at Maysen over her shoulder. "It's a five-hour drive to Lanville. If you leave now, you can be there by two."

After Denyse left, Maysen sighed and picked up her pen to resume her doodling. She'd drawn no more than thirty seconds when she threw down her pen again. Denyse was right. Maysen had let Clay decide when their relationship ended without any input from her. Maybe he didn't love her, but she should've given him the chance to tell her that.

She loved him and she wanted him in her life. She refused to give up before they had the chance to give their relationship a try.

Maysen shut down her computer, grabbed her purse and camera case, and hurried from her office. She didn't stop at Denyse's desk, but waved to her friend and kept walking.

Denyse grinned. "You go, girl!"

Maysen's shoulders sagged in disappointment and fatigue. The long drive from Houston, combined with anxiety over what would happen with Clay, left her drained. "He isn't here?" she asked Dylan over the noise of hammers and power tools in the fire hall.

She'd driven straight to Lanville from Houston, stopping one time for gas, to use the restroom, and grab a snack. Once she decided to talk to Clay, nothing short of a tornado could have stopped her. Unless it was Clay being out of town.

"I haven't seen him all week," Dylan said, wiping the perspiration from his face with the hem of his T-shirt.

"He's your fire chief. How can you not know where he is?"

"Luis is in charge when Clay has to be out of town."

Maysen should have thought of that. She knew as assistant fire chief, Luis ran the fire department in Clay's absence. "Where's Luis?"

Dylan shrugged. "Don't know."

Beyond frustrated at Dylan's lack of help, Maysen grabbed a handful of his sweaty T-shirt and tugged him closer. "Then I suggest you find out. Now."

If she hadn't been so upset, she would've laughed at the way Dylan's eyes bugged out. "Yes, ma'am."

Ignoring the urge to pace, Maysen leaned against a wall and watched the volunteers working on the tanker bay. Kory and Kirk finished putting up the last sheet of drywall. She assumed the next step would be to tape the seams and fill the nail holes before painting began. Then the bay would be ready whenever the department could afford the new tanker.

Hot Shots would help with that. The layout for the calendar should be finished soon. Maysen had sketched out some ideas and handed them over to her two best graphic artists. She could hardly wait to see the draft.

"I called Luis," Dylan said after joining her again. "He said Clay was supposed to go to Tempe and then Tulsa, but he doesn't know for sure where Clay is."

Hearing the name of those two cities triggered a memory in Maysen's brain of Clay telling her he had business in both places. Damn it.

Dylan tilted his head to the side, studying her through narrowed eyes. "How come *you* don't know where he is? I thought y'all were hot for each other."

She waved aside his question. "It's a long story. I really need to see Clay. Do you have Luis's phone number?"

"Why don't you just call Clay? He always has his cell on."

Apparently, Clay hadn't said anything to the firefighters about breaking up with her, which she appreciated. "I want to surprise him." She pulled her cell phone from her pocket. "Luis's number, please?"

She dialed as Dylan spouted off the numbers. Mouthing a "thank you" to Dylan, she stepped outside to place the call in private.

Fifteen minutes later, after convincing Luis to do some detective work for her, she had an address for the hotel in Tulsa where she could find Clay. She bought a hamburger and Coke from a fast-food drive-through and headed northeast.

Clay glanced toward the windows when he saw the flash of lightning out of the corner of his eye. Thunder boomed a few seconds later. He'd left Tempe early to beat the line of thunderstorms moving into Tulsa, which left him stuck here on a Friday night with the whole weekend ahead of him before his Monday morning meeting.

Nothing on TV appealed to him. He'd tried reading, but stopped when he got to the sex scene since it made him think of Maysen.

Who am I kidding? Everything *makes me think of Maysen.*

He hated the way he'd ended things with her over the phone, like a coward. He should've driven straight to The Inn and talked to her face-to-face. Maybe they could've worked out some kind of schedule, if she'd still wanted to see him.

A loud knock on the door surprised him. Since he wasn't expecting anyone, he assumed someone had gotten the wrong room. He fastened the two bottom buttons on his shirt as he walked toward the door.

Seeing Maysen on the other side stole his breath and his ability to speak. Mouth slack, he stared at the raindrops sparkling in her hair and spotting her jacket.

He finally found his voice enough to say "Maysen" before she brushed past him. She stopped by the end of the bed. He shut the door and turned toward her. "What—"

"I came here to say something to you and you're going to listen without interrupting. Understand?"

Not interrupting wouldn't be a problem since he still couldn't get his tongue to work. He made a motion with his hand, indicating she should continue.

She peeled off her damp jacket, tossed it over the back of the couch, and set her camera case on the floor. "I don't like the way things ended with us." She crossed her arms beneath her breasts, which drew his attention to her hard nipples visible through her T-shirt. "You just threw me aside without giving me the chance to make a decision about seeing you again."

"Maysen, I—"

"I said no interrupting."

Having never seen her in this kind of mood, Clay decided it would be a good idea to obey her. He snapped his mouth shut.

"I know we never talked about our feelings or anything beyond the moment. I didn't expect to come to Lanville and fall in love, but that's exactly what I did."

Clay shook his head, certain he hadn't heard her right. "Wait. You love me?"

She frowned. "I *told* you not to interrupt. We both have crazy schedules, but I'm willing to compromise so I can be with you. I need to know if you're willing to compromise, too."

When she said nothing else, he gently prompted, "May I talk now?"

She lifted her chin an inch. "You may."

Instead of speaking, he used his mouth for a much more pleasurable activity. He took the few steps necessary to be right in front of Maysen, cradled her face in his hands, and devoured her mouth.

Her lips immediately softened beneath his. She wrapped her arms around his back, dug her fingernails into his flesh. He deepened the kiss when he felt the brush of her tongue over his lips. She whimpered.

That sound of surrender spurred him to kiss her even more passionately. He nipped at her lips, slid his tongue over the soft bites, and pushed his tongue past her lips. She tasted of heat, of desire.

Of love.

Sliding his hands beneath her buttocks, Clay lifted her and laid her on the bed. He followed her down, lying between her spread legs. He pumped his hips, pressing his hard shaft firmly against her pussy. He could feel her warmth through his jeans.

"I've missed you," he whispered against her lips.

"I've missed you, too."

Clay pushed up her T-shirt and bra, baring her breasts. Her

nipples were hard, the areolae puckered. Clay licked both peaks until they were nice and wet, then began to suckle.

Maysen tunneled her fingers into his hair and arched her back. "You're so very good at that."

He raised her arms over her head, which lifted her breasts. "Good enough for you to come?"

"I think you have a thing about making me come by sucking my nipples."

"I do. I love sucking them." He flicked her nipple with his tongue. "Licking them." The flat of his tongue caressed the other tip. "Biting them." A gentle nip with his teeth and she squirmed beneath him. "Rubbing them." He circled both nipples with his thumbs. "But especially sucking them."

He rose to his knees, watching Maysen's face as he caressed both breasts. He released them only long enough for her to jerk off his shirt and pitch it to the floor. She attacked the fastening on his jeans next, tugged the denim to his thighs . . . and sighed.

"I love it when you don't wear briefs."

"I love it when you don't wear anything."

The wicked smile he cherished turned up her lips. "Then maybe you should help me get out of my clothes."

"Be happy to."

He helped her to a sitting position so he could remove her T-shirt and bra. She lay back against the pillows as he climbed off the bed and quickly jerked off his jeans. He returned to her, naked and ready to love her.

Maysen lifted her hips so he could tug off her shoes and the rest of her clothing. Starting at her ankles, Clay slid his hands up her smooth legs. His tongue followed his fingers, leaving a wet trail on her skin. Right leg, left leg, right, left, until he reached her mound. He spread her labia with his thumbs, gave her one slow stroke of his tongue.

"Mmm, delicious." The tip of his tongue danced over her wet folds. "I could spend hours licking your pussy."

"I'll let you. Tomorrow. Now I need you to fuck me."

He'd obeyed her so far this evening. He knew no reason to stop obeying her now. "Did you restock your camera case again?"

She pushed his hair back from his face. "I haven't been with anyone in a long time and I'm on birth control. I don't want anything separating us, Clay, not even a condom."

"I haven't been with anyone either. And I feel the same way you do."

With one thrust, he buried his cock inside her pussy.

So tight and wet and warm. Clay growled low in his throat. Her walls clasped his dick as if she didn't want to ever let him go. That normally worked for him, but he didn't want this to be over too quickly. Holding her tightly to him, he flipped them so he lay on his back with her on top of him.

"Ride me," he said in a husky voice.

She rose to straddle his hips, looking like a goddess rising from the sea. He watched the gentle sway of her breasts as she moved on top of him. The swaying changed to bouncing when she started moving faster. Clay cradled them in his palms, kneading them while she rode him.

"That's the way, sweetheart. Ride my cock. Fuck me hard."

"Clay, I'm coming!"

What a glorious sight she made in the throes of climax with her head thrown back and her back arched. Clay managed to hold his orgasm until he felt her channel milking his cock. After that, he couldn't stop it. He gripped her hips as the pleasure flowed down his spine, through his balls, and out the end of his shaft.

Maysen wilted on top of him. Her sweaty skin stuck to his. He didn't care. Now that he held her in his arms again, he had no intention of ever letting her go.

"I love you, Maysen."

She lifted her head. Tears filled her eyes, but he knew they weren't tears of sadness. "I love you, too."

He brushed a falling drop away with his thumb. "I'm sorry I hurt you."

"It was worth a few days of pain to be with you now."

He touched her hair; so happy to have her with him, he had to fight back his own tears. "We have a lot to talk about."

She pushed herself to a sitting position again, his softening cock still buried inside her. "I had ten hours to think while I drove here. I love running the magazine, but I love photography more. I could turn over the daily operations to Denyse. I'd still travel to take pictures for the articles, but I wouldn't have to worry about the day-by-day stuff. It would give me more time with you. I want to help you with your house."

"*Our* house."

She smiled tenderly. "Our house."

"You sure you want to live in Lanville? Because I'm willing to move to Houston if you want to keep things the way they are at your magazine."

Maysen shook her head. "I love Lanville. And trust me, you don't want to move to Houston. It's too big and spread out, and the traffic is a nightmare. Plus the humidity is at least 394% all the time."

"Spencer's has a refinery south of Houston, so I'm familiar with the area. Luckily, I get to fly into a small airport and don't have to mess with Houston's traffic."

"That *is* lucky." She stretched out on top of him again and rested her chin on her stacked hands. "Speaking of your plane, there's something I want to do."

The look in her eyes proved whatever she wanted to do, it would be naughty. That worked for Clay. "What?"

"I want to make love with you in the bedroom while we're in the air."

"I'll have to hire a pilot for that. He'll know what we're doing."

She shrugged one shoulder. "He can imagine, but he won't know for sure."

"True." He tightened his arms around her waist. "Well, if we're going to do that, we should make the trip someplace worthwhile. Where would you like to go?"

"Surprise me. Remember, I like spontaneity."

He remembered. And he couldn't think of anything better than to keep surprising Maysen for the rest of their lives.

Five-Alarm Masquerade

STACEY KENNEDY

*For all those sexy firefighters who inspire me to
write stories about them*

Acknowledgments

To my editor, Peter Senftleben, thank you for all that you do!

To my agent, Jessica Alvarez, who encouraged me to write a firefighter novella, thank you. I wouldn't have gotten here without you!

Kerry Vail, thanks for being such an amazing friend and supporter. The time you spend to make my work shine is greatly appreciated and the shoulder to lean on means the world to me.

A big shout-out to Dawn McGarry Lima for letting me pick her brain about all things firefighter. You never turned me away when I asked endless questions, and your input gave me a great look into a firefighter's life.

And to everyone at Kensington, thank you for giving me a new home. I'm very grateful.

1

On her tulip-lined pathway, Abby Hill stood, unable to move, barely able to breathe. She stared in horror as harsh smoke drifted through the air and fire licked out of the bedroom window of her Federal-style row house.

Firefighters passed by in a blur, portraying a sense of calm in the chaos. Though she'd heard things like possible electrical fire discussed among the men, the voices around her were distant. She wrapped her arms around herself, tears dampening her cheeks.

"Miss, you need to back up," a low, smooth voice said.

"This can't be happening," Abby managed through her tight throat.

Firm hands gripped her arms and turned her to face warm green eyes with hints of brown around the irises. The firefighter, decked out in full work uniform with a *4* on his black hat, had dark soot on the right side of his squared jaw. His brows drew together with his frown. "Is this your house?"

Abby never thought of herself as a person who showed emotions to a stranger. Now, she could hide nothing. "Oh,

God . . ." Hot sickness rolled through her and the world got dizzy, real fast.

His grip on her arms tightened. "I'm taking that as a yes."

Before she could drop to the cement below, she found those firm hands belonged to strong arms as the fireman tugged her into his powerful body. He lowered her to the ground, settling her between his legs.

Abby pressed her head against his rough coat, which smelled richer with smoke than what lingered in the air. She held on tight to the coarse material, unable to let go.

Quick minutes passed, and soon the wooziness faded. All but sitting in his lap, she noticed the smoke wasn't nearly as thick. When her spun-around thoughts centered, that's when she realized something didn't make sense. "Why is my bedroom window broken?"

The firefighter's thick thighs pressed against her, as did his arms. "We needed to break the window to evacuate the heat and smoke before we put out the fire."

Somehow, being in his arms made facing what happened easier, or maybe the shock had worn off and she could process better. She noticed that no other windows were broken in her house. "Was the fire only in my bedroom?"

"Yes, you got lucky." He shifted on his knees, yet didn't move away. "The fire was contained to the master bedroom."

She gulped. "Lucky?"

He hesitated, and all the pressure around her faded before he squeezed his arms. "I'm afraid you can't enter your house until the chief gives you the all clear. Do you have someone you can stay with?"

She gripped his coat, resting her head against his arm, tears trailing over her hot face. Though she noticed the firefighters coming in and out of house, and heard the loud conversations going on around her, she didn't care she sobbed in front of strangers. "It's gone."

He leaned away and his gentle eyes held hers. "Abby Hill? Is that what I heard the police say?" She nodded, and he waited for the car with the loud muffler to pass before he added, "What you have is a partial loss, Abby. Yes, your bedroom is gone. The rest of your upstairs might have smoke and water damage, but your insurance will cover it."

She understood why he looked to her as if she was over-reacting. In the scheme of things, this didn't seem all that bad. "I don't care about the rest of the house." Her voice cracked. "The photos of my family were in my bedroom." Ten years ago, a car accident had stolen away her parents, younger brother, and older sister. "It's all I had of them. There's nothing left."

He rubbed her back, giving an understanding nod. "I'm sorry."

Somehow, his response was better than, *At least you weren't hurt, or it could've been worse.* Though there were positives in her current hell, it didn't change the fact that every picture she had of her family was likely destroyed. Nothing else remained that proved they'd ever existed, except for their gravestones.

A moment passed as his eyes searched hers. "You have no other family that would have some photos?"

"Both my parents didn't have siblings. There are a few friends of the family . . ." Her chest ached. "Possibly they have some, but it's not . . ."

"Not the special pictures of you and your family," he offered.

Her chin quivered. "Exactly."

His lips pinched with his regard of her. The firefighter excelled at serving the public; she actually believed he felt bad for her. While she knew she should let him go, being a complete stranger and all, she couldn't find it in herself to tear herself away.

Staring into his piercing eyes, she had the oddest sense that he didn't want her to either. Something so sweet and pure passed in the air between them. A sensation of understanding that at this moment she needed more than anything. And how did that make any sense?

Why was being in a stranger's arms providing her with such warmth and familiarity, and more than anything making her feel this safe?

"Where is she?" a familiar feminine voice snapped. "And if you dare tell me again that I can't see Abby, I'll remove your manly bits, you giant ass!"

Abby glanced over her shoulder, catching sight of Sierra, dressed in her typical black skirt and red blouse. Abby didn't know how Sierra found out about the fire, but she didn't care; she needed her best friend.

Sierra's blue eyes were narrowed, and her bright red lipstick covered her frown as she gave the firefighter a glare promising a painful death. After a good stare down, the man gestured in Abby's direction, then Sierra rushed forward. She yanked Abby into her arms. "Jesus, sweetie. Can you believe they wouldn't let me through to see you?"

"It's all gone." Abby rested her head against Sierra's shoulder, hugging her tight. "They're gone."

Sierra paused, then heaved a sigh. "Shit, this is awful. I'm so sorry, Abby."

Of course, Sierra understood the depth of Abby's despair. Sierra had been there the night they worked on their high-school assignment together. That fateful night Abby didn't go for her brother's special dinner to celebrate his touchdown at the football game, and the night where the car carrying her entire family collided with the transport truck.

Leaning away from Sierra, Abby looked into her best friend's teary eyes. "That's all I had of them."

Sierra gathered Abby's hands. "You don't have any pictures in your attic or storage?"

Abby shook her head. "I kept everything in my bedroom in a memory box. I wanted to scan them all, keep them safe, but—"

"Don't do that to yourself," Sierra interjected with a soft voice. "You're not to blame for this. It's a horrible accident."

Abby remembered hearing something similar from her therapist. Not that she thought she could've prevented the car accident that killed her family, but her guilt for not being with them that night had stayed with her for a long time.

With her therapist's voice in her head reminding her she couldn't stay in the past and mourn things she couldn't change, she pushed off the cement pathway. She glanced around, seeing that the entire neighborhood was watching from the other side of the street, and she didn't want to process the loss of photos under the scrutiny of onlookers.

Sierra must've read Abby's thoughts, since she reached up and fixed Abby's hair. There wasn't a day that Sierra had let Abby walk out the door with a strand of hair out of place. She ran her fingers under Abby's eyes, clearing away her mascara. "Let's get out of here." She gave a small smile, wiggling her eyebrows. "Unless you'd rather stay in the arms of that sexy firefighter."

Abby blinked. "Who's sexy?"

Sierra snorted. "Seriously?" She grasped Abby's shoulders. "When I found you, you were in the arms of that."

Abby spun to face the house and she discovered a man whom she suspected was the fire marshal, dressed in a blue uniform. "Am I missing something, or are you suddenly digging older guys?"

"Older guys?" Sierra stepped in next to Abby, then she frowned. "Ew, not that guy." She gestured to the garden off to the right. "*That* guy."

Abby followed Sierra's direction, and her mouth dropped open. Though the firefighter's attire made the man look bulky, she wondered how much of that was the gear, or if his thickness was due to a muscular body.

Standing near her front window, he chatted to another firefighter, who was slightly shorter than him. The height difference made the taller firefighter look masculine. He'd clearly noticed them ogling, since he caught her gaze.

Under his direct stare, funny things happened low in her belly. Odd, strange happenings, considering seconds ago, a soul-crippling despair had overwhelmed her. The fireman's features portrayed more than confidence, more than strength, but she thought that came from the sexy, arrogant twinkle in his eye.

The firefighter broke the connection, and Abby exhaled. He turned to the other man and exchanged words. Then hotness packaged in firefighter gear approached. Similar to when she watched her bedroom burn, she froze.

She knew, with total certainty, her reaction was absurd. Her bedroom was destroyed, along with precious pictures, but her body flared with a heat so addictive and intoxicating.

Over Abby's shoulder, Sierra whistled. "Holy hell—all he needs is the fire burning behind him and we'd have one of those perfect calendar shots."

"No kidding," Abby agreed.

On his way down the pathway, Abby scanned over his black boots, to the thick pants she knew had suspenders, and images of a shirtless man filled her mind. She swallowed, forced herself to stop thinking in the gutter, and focused on appropriate places, like his face.

That didn't help much—he had a chiseled face with masculine features, all making him way too noticeable. Lifting her gaze, she looked past his kissable lips that held a slight arch in the corners, and when his piercing eyes captured hers, she finally released the breath she'd be holding.

Whoa . . .

He was drop-dead gorgeous.

Once the firefighter reached her, he smiled. "You look like you're feeling better."

Abby blinked.

Sierra elbowed her in the side. "She's much better, thank you."

"Glad to hear it." His voice wasn't too deep, but low enough to sound smooth. "Do you have somewhere to stay, Abby?"

Her mind stuttered under how he said her name. As if he wasn't stating a name, but the one word held powers making her feel like he noticed her, too. A hot shiver slid right down to her toes. "Um . . ."

"She can stay with me," Sierra interjected with a laugh. "Unless you're offering—"

Abby jabbed Sierra hard in the side and Sierra cursed.

The firefighter chuckled, focusing on Abby. "Please give the chief the address and telephone number where you'll be staying so he can get in touch with you. You'll also want to contact your insurance company right away."

She parted her lips to respond, yet closed them a second later.

Eyes squinting, lit with a twinkle of mischief, he said, "All right, Abby, you're good to go." His eyebrows creased. "Again, I'm sorry about your home." He hesitated. "And your pictures."

He turned, walking down her pathway.

Abby stared after him, her mind snapping into focus. On a gasp, she hurried to reach him. Just as he neared her front door, she grasped his bicep, giving his coat a tug. "Wait!"

Glancing over his shoulder, he looked at her hand before his gaze lifted. She nearly melted into a puddle of goo right there on her front porch. "Thank you for holding me like that. I know it's not in the job description."

He tipped his hat, giving a soft smile. "Maybe it should be."

*   *   *

Engine Company 4 arrived on location to the first-alarm fire, bringing Gavin Morgan and his fellow firefighters to the Beacon Hill neighborhood in Boston, known for its gas-lit streets and brick sidewalks. Ladder 24 showed up a minute later. Within minutes, he and his crew extinguished the blaze.

Watching Abby's gorgeous honey-colored hair sway in the wind as she approached the chief near the street sign, Gavin experienced déjà vu. Something about her seemed familiar, yet he couldn't place why. With her soft blue eyes and freckled-covered cheeks, she reminded him of sunshine.

Her warm, sweet scent of sugar and cinnamon lingered in his nostrils. The sensation of her wrapped in his arms was now burned into his flesh. He clenched his fists before he stretched out his fingers, shaking off his entire body buzz.

"Morgan, get in here."

He turned and headed up the tulip-lined pathway toward the front steps. Standing in the mocha-colored hallway, fellow firefighter Jett had a smart-ass grin planted on his scruffy face. "Aw, wasn't that the sweetest thing."

Gavin entered the house and thumped Jett's shoulder. "Shut up."

Jett baked a laugh. "Come on, man"—he offered Gavin a plastic hook—"it's not every day I see you hugging a stranger."

Gavin could've spat out a lie explaining his actions, but Jett would read him. He was close with all his crew, but with Jett, the friendship exceeded the brotherhood between firefighters.

"Felt bad for her." He swiped at the bead of sweat on his cheek. "What could I do—push her off when she's crying?" Even he heard the weakness in his argument. Why had he held her?

In his six years with the department, he'd never consoled a victim. Christ, when Abby first dropped to the ground, he'd waved off the EMT who had approached. But his job wasn't to comfort her. He'd been there to fight the fire at her house.

Jett rested his plastic hook over his shoulder. "Did you see her friend nearly castrate me?"

Gavin pushed Jett forward. "Looked good on you."

Jett's laughter led Gavin down the hallway. He moved through her living room and by what he saw, Abby appeared to be a neat and simple woman. There weren't any expensive-looking items decorating the lower floor. She had enough furniture to decorate the room, but not too much that it looked cluttered.

From the living room, he spotted the kitchen at the end of the hallway, with multicolored ceramic floor and white cabinets. As he neared the staircase by the entrance to the kitchen, he noticed paintings of nature. Nothing abstract, or art he never understood, but simple sunrises.

Gavin smiled, thinking that appropriate for a woman who radiated sunshine herself, which he thought was remarkable considering her sadness. He couldn't help wonder how beautiful she'd look wearing a smile.

Hurrying up her staircase, he took two at a time, then he entered the first door on the left. Her spacious master bedroom now resembled a sight he'd seen many times; nothing was salvageable, and all that remained were burned walls and charred furniture.

Though the room had been ventilated and no smoke lingered in the air, Gavin drew in a deep breathing, searching out further smoke, but none remained. While the bedroom wasn't burned beyond recognition, Abby wouldn't recover anything. He scanned over the destroyed area and noticed that her desk, with the mirror over it, had a lot of damage.

Gavin approached the desk, placing his plastic hook on top. With his gloved hand, he brushed some of the debris away, noticing the remnants of a wooden box and burned pictures within.

As he shifted more of the burned rubble away, his chest con-

216 / *Stacey Kennedy*

stricted when he spotted one photo, seeing Abby smiling with nameless faces around her. While the bottom half of the picture was burned, and even the part that wasn't destroyed had been damaged with water, the faces were recognizable. He assumed the other people were her deceased family.

Damn sad.

Turning away, he found Jett near the far wall. "Got something?"

"Looks like the fire sparked here," Jett muttered.

Gavin approached, settling in next to her queen-sized bed that had no mattress anymore, but still contained the metal bed frame. He noticed a charred V above the electrical outlet. "Fucking old houses."

He'd seen it before, and he knew this wouldn't be the last time a fire in one of these historic homes had malfunctioning wiring. Part of him was glad that this happened while Abby wasn't home, and not sleeping when the fire had started. She could've been in the bed right next to the blaze.

A surge of heat stormed into his muscles as he pictured the danger she would've been put in. Yet, at the intensity washing over him, he told himself how ridiculous his reaction was. She wasn't his to worry about.

Once again, he pushed away the thoughts that shouldn't be on his mind, and he removed his glove. Using the back of his hand, he touched the torched wall, sensing heat behind it. "Hot spot."

"Yeah, some here, too," Jett added, from across the room.

Feeling as he always did while searching a home, a stranger in someone else's private space, he examined the walls. By the time he reached her walk-in closet, Gavin concluded the hot spots were contained on the wall where the fire had started.

Entering the closet, he discovered it slightly intact. Her clothes hanging on the railing were either partly burned with fabric strands dangling off melted plastic, or had been affected by either smoke or water damage.

He figured that was the only positive that came out of bedroom fires. Getting a new wardrobe on their insurance company's bill had to be a fun day out. Yet, in regard to Abby, he suspected she'd rather have her family's pictures than new clothes.

Running the back of his hand over the walls, he tried to imagine what that'd be like—to lose people he loved tragically. His family, with generations of cops and firefighters, was a tight-knit group. He never had a sister, but he had two older brothers, and Gavin couldn't imagine what Abby had suffered.

Perhaps that's why her pain bothered him. He was close to his family and they spent as much time together as possible. What would he do if he lost that connection? He shook his head, not even wanting to consider it.

Besides, he figured his pain would mirror what he'd spotted in Abby's eyes, and that wasn't a dark place he wanted to travel down. He needed his friends. He needed his family. Both mattered to him.

After he finished searching her closet, he didn't feel any hot spots on the walls, but he noticed stickers on the back wall. From radio stations to a vanilla mocha sticker, and stickers of her favorite television shows, she had covered the entire wall. Above the stickers, written in bold letters was, *Things that make me . . . ME!*

Gavin smiled. She'd likely look at her stickers every day before she dressed. *Cute.*

Turning to exit the closet, something else caught his eye. Behind a row of thick sweaters, he discovered at least twenty lingerie outfits—from sexy-as-hell teddies to bras with matching panties, and a whole slew of garter belts.

"Christ," he murmured.

Running his fingers down the black lace bra, heat slid into his groin at the silky, sensual fabric. Grasping one of the teddies, he noticed Abby was a size ten. "Perfect." He loved curves and, more importantly, a soft, warm woman.

The images in his mind of Abby, a woman made of sunshine, in this lingerie sent a heady desire within to see it for himself. His cock twitched, throbbing in his work pants, and he dropped his hand.

Fucking pervert, Morgan.

He clearly needed to get laid. It'd been a month too long. Not only was he hugging a stranger on her front lawn, but the sight of lingerie made him rock hard. Shaking his head, he took a step forward to exit her closet, but then he caught sight of the books on the shelf by the floor.

He squatted and picked up a book. The books themselves didn't interest him, the subject matter did. He glanced over the cover page, *A Sexual Power Exchange.* At a quick glance, Gavin found that Abby's bookshelf was filled with books about being sexually dominated in the bedroom.

The realization dawned on him that his reaction to her wasn't an odd response, but came down to the simplicity of a man protecting a woman. Something had flared between them, of that he was sure. Now he knew why—they had chemistry, as it appeared they had shared interests.

A slow, dominant heat rushed through his veins with his building smile. Though Abby didn't know him and he didn't know her, one thing was certain. Gavin didn't run when facing down a fiery inferno; he charged forward and took control of that blaze.

2

The ringing of the phone blaring through Sierra's house had Abby hurrying down the long, thin hallway. Her watery footsteps followed her. She had ignored the first three phone calls while she showered, but figured on the fourth call she'd better answer it, in case it was an emergency.

Rushing into the guest room, she held the towel tight around her and jumped onto the double bed with the flower-patterned duvet. She reached for the phone on the nightstand table and pressed it to her ear. "Hello."

"Oh, thank God, you're not dead," Sierra gasped.

"Dead?" Abby laughed. "Why would I be dead?"

Sierra's tight voice relaxed a smidgen. "I've called three times and you never answered."

"You know, there is this thing, it's called a shower." Leaning up against the fluffy pillows, Abby stared at the abstract art against the chocolate-painted wall. "You always think the worst. Let me guess, ax murderer, right?"

"Nope, crazed kitchen knife murderer." Sierra heaved a sigh. "Okay, now that I know you're not being hacked to death, have you looked at the time? It's eight o'clock in the morning."

Abby glanced at the clock next to her on the dark oak night-stand. "Yeah, so?"

"Well, missy-moo, you haven't been out of bed before eleven since you started staying at my house. So, yeah, I kinda freaked out!"

Sierra watched too many reality crime shows. More than once, she panicked when Abby didn't return her phone call right away, thinking the worst. Besides that silly business, shame settled inside Abby.

She'd never missed a day at the bookstore she owned. Luckily, she had two dependable employees who had taken over the majority of the responsibility at the store for the past couple weeks. Abby had put in half days instead of her usual full days. "I thought it was time I get back into my routine."

"Great," Sierra said with a firm tone. "Moping around isn't good for anyone." Her voice lightened. "Especially for me, since you stank up my house."

"I did not!" Abby exclaimed. Okay, maybe she hadn't gotten all fancied up, but still . . . "I showered every day."

"Just kiddin'." Sierra snickered. "Heard any word from the insurance company?"

Abby glanced out the window with the white lace curtains, watching a tree sway in the wind. "Nothing further to tell you, except they're being incredibly slow about processing the claim." She paused, a heady sense of guilt tightening her chest. "Are you sure I'm not putting you out? I could go home and stay in my guest room."

"No way," Sierra bit off. "I didn't ask that to kick you out—I asked to check in. Your house stinks of mold, smoke, and other shit I don't want to mention. You're staying with me until your life is back to normal. No more asking that question, okay? The first gazillion times were enough."

Abby smiled. "I just want to be sure that I'm not *that* person—you know, the unwanted guest."

"You'll never be, so get that out of your pretty little head." Abby could practically see Sierra flicking her hair over her shoulder as Sierra added, "Moving on, I'm still in New York, dealing with a total asshat of a broker."

Abby laughed, sending droplets of water sliding down her arm. "You think all brokers are asshats."

"Because most of them are complete, arrogant jerks." Sierra sighed, sounding more tired than annoyed, as she usually did when she traveled for work. "Anyways, I should be home on Monday."

"Crappy." Abby followed the path of the droplet on her arm with her index finger. "I wanted to go into Back Bay tomorrow to do some shopping—your too-small jeans are giving me a complex."

"Oh, please," Sierra retorted with another snort. "We're practically the same size."

The sudden ringing of the doorbell had Abby groaning. Seriously, was this the day of interruptions? Perhaps she should've stayed in bed until eleven o'clock. "Okay, babe, gotta go. That's the doorbell, and I'm naked."

"It's probably the courier delivering a package from work," Sierra said with an obvious smile. "I vote for you to answer the door in your towel, then take a picture of the dude's face when you do."

Abby rolled her eyes. "Only you would be perverted enough to do that."

"Of course I would," Sierra said with no shame. "A girl needs to have fun any way she can. Anyways, if it's a package for me, open it. I'm waiting for a report from a jerk-face in Atlanta. Call me if it's anything important."

"Can do." Abby jumped off the bed. "Enjoy New York."

"Won't happen, but you have fun shocking the courier boy

with your sexy body." She paused, then chuckled. "Or maybe it's your dream come true and it's that smokin'-hot firefighter."

"I never should have told you about my dreams." The nameless man had haunted her dreams ever since the day of her house fire.

Who was she kidding?

Even wide-awake, he haunted her. Though she wished she had the life she had in her dream, she didn't really care. Dream firefighter was better than no man at all, and her dreams had been vivid and exciting.

"Of course you should have told me, that juicy stuff is too good not to share," Sierra mused. "Talk to you later, I'm off like a prom dress."

Abby shook her head with a laugh, and hung up the phone. While Sierra would be daring enough to answer the door in a towel, Abby wasn't nearly as bold. Sure, she liked being sexy in the confines of her bedroom, but her bravery stopped there.

Sierra had more guts to go after what and *who* she wanted. Abby held the same type of strength with a boyfriend, but she'd been single a year now. Her last boyfriend moved to Houston for employment, and he wanted an in-town girlfriend, not a long-distance relationship. For Abby, the breakup hadn't produced a single tear.

At the second ring of the doorbell, she dropped her towel, and the cool air raised goose bumps along her flesh. Going against Sierra's suggestion, she grabbed the oversized—not sexy—housecoat off the hook behind the door.

Rushing out of the bedroom, she wrapped the housecoat around herself and trotted down the staircase. She opened the front door and discovered Sierra had been right—someone from the courier service stood on the other side. But Sierra had also been wrong—a woman in a brown uniform smiled at her, not a young hottie.

Abby smiled, imaging the disappointment Sierra would've

had to see a woman standing there instead of man she could tease. Maybe Abby was just a wee bit disappointed, too, not to see that sexy-as-hell firefighter.

She needed to get him out of her head.

Only problem?

He seemed permanently stuck there.

"Package for you, ma'am," the pretty blond woman said.

Abby accepted the silver box that looked too fancy coming from a courier service. It had a black bow around it, and at closer examination, the ribbon had glitter. "Do you need a signature?"

The woman shook her head with a twinkle in her eye. "No name required." She turned and headed down the front steps. "Have a nice day."

"You, too," Abby called.

With a wave good-bye, the woman got into her big truck and drove off. Abby drew in a big deep breath, catching a whiff of freshly cut grass. She glanced up into the clear blue sky, watching the birds flying by before she shut the door behind her.

She entered Sierra's modern living room, which was a much colder space than she preferred. Abby liked warm colors, soft couches, not modern things that seemed so straight-edged and lacked that squishy feeling of a big, comfy couch.

Dropping down into the rounded black leather chair in the corner of the room, she eyed the box in her hands. She couldn't believe anyone would send such a fancy package for business. "Sierra, girl, you have a weird job."

More than intrigued to find out the contents, Abby undid the black bow and took off the silver top. When she peered inside the box, she was damn sure her eyes were betraying her. "What in the holy frickin' hell."

Reaching into the box, she pulled out a black masquerade mask. The front of the mask was covered with jet-black lace, as well as sparkling gems and stones. The back of the mask had a long black silk ribbon to secure it to a head.

She placed the mask next to her on the chair; then she took out the gorgeous black lace shelf bra. After which she discovered a teeny-tiny matching thong, and garter belt with black stockings that had lace on the tops, too. At the very bottom of the box, she noticed sleek black high-heeled shoes.

Dropping the shoes on the floor, she looked at the lingerie again and noticed it was her size. That didn't surprise her. Sierra was her size, but her friend preferred her clothing tight. Though what shocked Abby, she couldn't believe her best friend—whom she'd known since they were five years old— had never told her about her crazy sex life.

Who in the hell was sending Sierra fancy lingerie?

As far as Abby knew, Sierra wasn't dating—or having sex— with anyone. Even more shocking was that Sierra would wear the lingerie. That was more of Abby's thing. She'd accepted long ago she had a little fetish where it came to lacy things.

Abby liked how it made her feel when she wore it beneath her clothes—her dirty little secret. She loved the reaction she received from ex-boyfriends when she dressed up, or how it turned them on to find naughty undergarments beneath her jeans and T-shirt.

Men liked her in it.

She liked how they looked at her when she wore it.

Everyone won, as far as she was concerned.

Running her fingers over the lace, heat pooled low in her belly, as it always did when she reminded herself of sexy moments in lingerie. She shifted on the chair, noticing dampness between her thighs, and she laughed softly.

Apparently, she needed to get laid.

It'd been almost a year since her ex-boyfriend dumped her over the telephone. Maybe she needed a good ole one-night stand to kick the edge. Clearly, fantasizing over some firefighter she didn't know was intensifying her ridiculously horny state.

Putting a night out on the town on her mental to-do list, she placed the beautiful lingerie next to her on the chair and reached into the box. She pulled out an invitation on black thick paper with silver calligraphy writing on the front.

The Five-Alarm Masquerade requests
the pleasure of your company . . .
Hotel Commonwealth's Presidential Suite
Friday, the tenth of August at seven o'clock in the evening
Invitation-only event (No RSVP required)
Rules of The Five-Alarm Masquerade on reverse.

Abby blinked, stunned to her bones. It didn't take much to derive a conclusion that Sierra was invited to some type of sex party. "Holy shit!" What in the hell had Sierra gotten involved in? Ménage à trois? Orgies?

Daring herself to keep reading, Abby flipped the invitation over . . .

The Five-Alarm Masquerade Rules

1. Attendance means that you, as a consenting adult, agree to partake in sexual acts with other consenting adults. All members may refuse an offer for a sexual encounter and are freely able to choose their partner or partners for the evening.

2. While in the Presidential Suite, women must wear the lingerie provided to them. Men are to wear pants, but must remain topless.

3. Condoms are provided in each available hotel room. Unprotected sex will revoke further invitations to the masquerade.

4. No cameras, videotaping, or cell phones are allowed, and may be left at the front desk for safekeeping.

5. "No" or "Stop" are considered safe words. Any member who disregards the safe words will be ousted to the authorities, regardless of the privacy clause.

Rules are nonnegotiable. Any members who do not follow the rules above will be escorted from the hotel and will lose their membership to *The Five-Alarm Masquerade*.

Abby shifted against the chair, staring at the invitation. "Good Lord, Sierra, what kind of kinky shit are you into?" She had no idea that Sierra was so wild, and beneath the shock, Abby was hurt Sierra never told her. Abby told Sierra everything about her life—even the not-so-good things she'd done over the years.

Past all that, what was horrifying her more than the hurt of there being secrets between her and her best friend, she noticed a sense of underlying jealously. When had Sierra's life become so exciting? Had she met someone on her work trips who brought her into this type of sexual adventure?

Abby had always been reserved, and didn't act bold like answering the door in her towel—just in case a hunk waited for her on the other side. Sierra was courageous, and apparently, she experienced thrilling nights of hot sex because of it.

Glancing over the stunning lingerie, Abby shivered, her sex clenching with a desire to be wicked. How would that be to wear something so beautiful, be entirely mysterious, and act as brave as Sierra?

Exhilarating.

She reached for the mask again and traced the diamond-like

jewels that adorned the sides. Sensual images of her dressed in this lingerie, the mask, and partaking in such a sinful event filled her mind.

Heat ripped through her like wildfire, settling between her thighs with a fierce throb. As the need inside threatened to envelope her, she dropped the mask and reminded herself, "Not yours to love."

"*But it could be...*" a naughty little voice in her head argued.

3

Hotel Commonwealth, located in the grand boulevard of Boston's Back Bay, had once impressed Gavin. He hadn't come from money. He'd grown up in a middle-income family and had always been okay with that.

After attending the monthly event for nearly a year, the shock of the luxurious hotel had faded. He didn't need fancy things to impress him. Even if coming to such a lavish place for the private sex parties had once increased the fantasy.

Moving through the Presidential Suite, soft instrumental music poured out from hidden speakers, creating the typical romantic setting. He scanned the grand living room decorated with all the fancy fixings. From lavish curtains to the crystal chandelier, the room exuded wealth. Though in this rich space, the people mingling within the room held Gavin's interest.

As per the rules of the masquerade, all the men were topless, wearing black dress pants or jeans. The women were beautifully dressed in all types of lingerie, from corsets to teddies to bra and panty sets. Everyone in the suite wore masks, hiding their true identities, as did he.

"Are you available tonight?"

Recognizing the soft voice, Gavin smiled, turning to face a stunning bleach-blonde dressed in a string thong and push-up bra he'd played with a few times at the parties. Her icy blue eyes stood out against her jet-black mask. She had a great mouth and a tight body he had enjoyed.

"Tonight, luv, I'm not," he told her.

For him, the view wasn't tempting enough—only one woman mattered tonight. Gavin had only lasted one week before he set his plan in motion. He'd spent a few days ignoring his thoughts of Abby. Then he'd spent a few more days fighting against his impulse to see her again. After that, he gave up.

Truth of the matter, he could check in on her and try to meet her that way, but he didn't want to date Abby. He wanted to land himself between her killer thighs. He needed to feel the warmth that exuded from her, while she shuddered around him.

His previous lover smiled her saucy grin that had caught his attention when he'd first met her at the party. "Very well. Enjoy your night." She swayed her hips as she strutted away, her round bare bottom giving him one helluva view.

Not tempting enough . . .

The images of Abby in her lingerie had haunted him, both in his dreams and during his workday at the fire station. Now he had a plan—ridding himself of Abby's hold over him. He didn't like thinking about any woman so much. He liked things causal. He liked being unattached.

Carrying on through the suite, Gavin searched the faces in the room. Even if everyone wore masks, he didn't doubt he'd spot Abby. Her body had been burned into his memory. Though the more he searched, the more his muscles tensed. Perhaps she wasn't as daring as he thought. He wondered if she'd read the invitation and was disgusted, instead of turned on, which was his initial reaction when he received his first invitation to the masquerade.

Passing by an antique chaise, he spotted the only recognizable face in the suite beneath a yellow and black mask. Jett smiled at him, while he chatted up a stunning redhead in crimson-colored lingerie. Gavin inclined his head, not surprised Jett gravitated toward the pretty redhead. His best friend preferred them.

Gavin continued to scan the crowd, and as a waiter passed by, he grabbed a glass of beer off the tray. Taking a long sip of the ice-cold brew, he strode by more couples who looked comfortable with each other.

Heading past the patio, he glanced out into the warm Boston night. The moment he caught sight of *who* stood in the patio garden, his heart dropped into his stomach. He swallowed the crisp liquid.

The garden had a rustic nature setting with a small pond and waterfall. Along the cobblestone pathway weaving its way through the garden were small gas-lit lamps, giving off a warm glow.

There, out in the garden, was a sight so beautiful it stole his breath. He gripped his beer glass tight, leaned against the French doors, and stared out into the dark starry night.

Even with Abby's back to him, he knew he found her.

Perhaps it was her long, honey-colored hair trailing down her back that he remembered so vividly. Or his mind had imagined her close to what the real thing looked like in the lingerie he'd bought for her. The reasons didn't matter, all that mattered was he knew with total certainty that standing right in front of him was the one and the only Abby Hill.

As he scanned her from head to toe, his cock twitched. The lingerie fit her to a perfection he couldn't have dreamed up. His mouth went dry at how the garter belt, held tight around her hips and clipped to the stockings, fitted her so well.

While the sight of her pleased him, what elated him was that she'd showed up. He had no idea if she'd agree to attend a sex party, which he'd learned had been a two-step process. The first step: He sent an e-mail out requesting she be invited. The second step: A courier had picked up Abby's package from him for delivery.

"Well, now, who is that new treat?"

Gavin turned to the tall, slender brunette, who sidled up with him. Wealth reeked off the gorgeous woman, from her fancy fingernails and toes, to her shiny, long dark hair. "My treat," he replied.

Dressed in lingerie that he suspected cost his month's salary, her pink painted lips curved. "Is she, now?" Her brown eyes sparkled behind her gold mask. "You've never been one to be selfish."

True enough. He had a few ménage encounters at the masquerade. One of them with the woman standing next to him, whom he had named Lady. She'd always seemed like that to him, royalty almost. He also had suspected this woman was the one behind the masquerade.

Lady appeared to be the wealthiest person who attended the parties, always so fancy and done up. Plus, she'd seemed the most comfortable, too. But as always, everything at the masquerade was discreet. He didn't know a single person's name, except for Jett, nor had he ever seen a full face.

Lady took a sip of wine, staring at Abby. "She's lovely. Did you invite her?"

Gavin folded his arms. "Now, now, you wouldn't be asking anything too personal, would you?"

She laughed softly. "Curiosity is all. You've never taken such an interest in anyone in the year you've attended the masquerade. Normally, women are approaching you—not the other way around."

That was true. He never needed to seek out a partner for the night.

Part of him wondered if whoever organized the party had been part of Boston's fire department because of the name of the event, *The Five-Alarm Masquerade*. Or if the person had a thing for firefighters—or if it was all a coincidence that he and Jett were part of the fire department.

Even after a year, they still hadn't pieced together who had invited them. But they suspected whoever it was had met them at a scene of a fire, considering they were invited at the same time.

Lady's gaze swept over Abby again in a slow, appreciative sweep before she turned to him with dark eyes. "I suppose, however, I don't need to ask why there's interest there. I only need to look at her and I've found the answer."

Didn't that say it all? There was something special about Abby—she was so damn sexy. Her appearance portrayed innocence, but she looked comfortable being naughty, too. Not every woman could pull off sexy lingerie.

Abby could.

He'd met her with her clothes on, and it was like a dirty little secret of hers had been exposed, and she liked it. Her chin was high, her shoulders lifted. She obviously loved lingerie, and she clearly loved herself in it.

He agreed, and his raging hard-on proved it.

Lady smirked at whatever crossed his expression, and she tipped her wineglass at him. "Best you go and grab her up. I've already seen her refuse two offers, and it looks like a third is making his move."

Gavin jerked his head to Abby, noticing a distinguished, muscular man, maybe in his late thirties, talking to her. His chest tightened and a hot wave of jealously stormed into him, so intense it clenched his fist.

"She'll refuse him, too. She came to be with me tonight." He grinned tightly at Lady, experiencing that rich hunger to claim and conquer. "She just doesn't know it yet."

Only ten minutes had passed since Abby had taken a glass of wine from the waiter's tray and entered the patio, and she'd already been propositioned twice. The men at this masquerade weren't kidding around—they came tonight to have sex. There was no mistaking it, and they weren't shy about it either.

While it did make her feel good, things weren't going as planned. Where was the hunk she'd always fantasized over? The one she'd feel that instant sexual chemistry with, and the man she'd want to jump his bones in a second flat. Apparently, she'd been revving herself up while getting ready tonight, thinking something *big* was going happen.

So far, she'd rather be eating popcorn and watching a cheesy romantic movie.

Onto the third proposition of the night, the man currently chatting her up wasn't doing it for her either. His body of muscles was nice to look at, but she wasn't finding herself drawn to him in any way that would scream, *Get into bed with him.*

Right down to it, she was bored, and that was damn pathetic. How could she possibly be bored in this situation? Hadn't she come here to spice her life? Do something so daring, her shyness would be forever vanished? Didn't she arrive here to be more like Sierra, and less like Abby?

"I'd make the night worth your while," the brown-eyed man said, wearing a dark blue mask.

Surprised she didn't feel more uncomfortable standing in front of others in her underwear, Abby shifted on her heels. "Why would it be worth my while?" Not that she intended to go with him, but playing along at least provided some entertainment. Besides, she had to show some interest not to be ousted as an imposter. No one had yet to mention that she wasn't Sierra, and she preferred to keep it that way.

The man flashed her perfect white teeth. "I know a woman's body, and what to do with it."

Great! Now she wasn't only getting bad pickup lines, she was receiving bad sexual pickup lines. "Why? Have you had lots of women to study from?"

His smile slowly faded. "I'm not a man-whore, if that's what you're suggesting." He shrugged halfheartedly. "I've read many books about the female orgasm, and had an old partner who let me practice new techniques."

If that didn't take the *P* out of passion, she didn't know what did. "I'm not suggesting you're anything." She sipped her wine, eying the pretty pink flowered tree next to her. "Merely curious, is all." Sure-as-shit disappointed, too.

She decided she had to have a talk with Sierra. If her best friend was sleeping with these men, maybe they needed to get out more. Heck, possibly it was time for that anyway. The fire not only brought memories of the past with it, but it reminded Abby about life, too.

She hadn't been living, not really.

She'd coasted through what she had worked toward and goals she'd set, but that's all she'd done—worked hard to make her business successful. It had succeeded. Abby figured the time had arrived to turn things from business mode, back into personal life mode, which included a healthy sex life . . . maybe even a new boyfriend.

Mr. Muscles in front of her wouldn't be part of either. He closed the distance between them, glancing down to her with warm eyes. "So, what do you say? Are you in for a fun night with me?"

Abby pondered, just to be sure she wouldn't change her mind. She'd already rejected two men, could she really reject another?

She'd shown up tonight, daring herself to do something bold and crazy, like Sierra. She had a *hot reaction* yesterday when she opened the box. It'd been thrilling and exciting, making her feel alive.

Those thoughts had gotten her dressed in the lingerie and brought her to the hotel, wearing a long coat. Sheer stubbornness not to fail on her personal dare had gotten her through the doors and into the Presidential Suite. Now the reality was upon her and she needed to act, and the bodybuilder guy was kind of cute.

A warm breeze at her back caused goose bumps to rush over her skin, bringing forth a surprising shiver, considering the night didn't have a chill. That's when she noticed Mr. Muscles frown at someone over her shoulder.

"Hello," a low, velvety voice murmured.

She turned, and her breath caught in her throat. The man, who stood awfully close to her, wore a silver mask that made his piercing green eyes even more captivating. His face portrayed masculinity with hard edges and sharp lines, and, dear God, he was hot as hell.

The side of the man's mouth curved and he looked to Mr. Muscles. "I'm sorry to say, she's spoken for tonight."

"No problem," the other man replied.

Abby had no clue if bodybuilder guy had left. She found herself glued to *this* man. Tilting her head, she studied him, as something seemed so familiar. Though perhaps the muscles layering muscles making up his impressive physique was something she wanted to familiarize herself with. Yes, so far she'd seen all types of masculine bodies, but his . . .

Good glorious Jesus.

Licking her lips, she scanned him, and he was the entire package—defined eight-pack, squared chest, strong shoulders, and he even had those sexy indents at his hips. Yet, he wasn't overdone like the bodybuilder. *This* man was worthy of a second, third, and as many looks as she could possibly give to him.

When she lifted her gaze to his eyes, a slow grin spread across his face. He stepped in close, circling her and giving her a full once-over. She'd never felt so examined in her life, and she liked it. This man didn't only look at her, he admired her.

He finally stopped, settling in behind her, and the heat emanating off his body was palpable. She couldn't breathe, couldn't move, all she could do was drown in the sheer powerful presence he oozed.

"The lingerie looks beautiful on you." He skimmed her shoulder with a light touch, a hint of pride in his voice.

She shivered, as that touch seemed directly linked to her throbbing clit. Squeezing her thighs to ease the ache, she rasped, "Thank you." If she didn't know better, it seemed like he had picked the lingerie out. Though how could he? She came to the party in Sierra's place.

"Your body tempts me," he whispered in her ear before placing a light kiss on her neck.

Abby swallowed deep, staring out at the other attendees walking by her and watching the exchange. Somehow that increased the flames roaring through her. With everyone watching him touch her with such blatant sexuality, her sex moistened.

"Seeing you like this tempts me to want to keep you here all night," he murmured against her flesh, trailing his nose along her skin and inhaling deeply. "To do incredibly naughty things to this sexy body, for as long as I want."

Her throat dried under the assault of his incredibly talented mouth sliding over the sweet spot on her neck. He brushed her hair over to the other shoulder, placing a kiss on her shoulder blade. She knew she should say something, but the arousal pulsating in her body wouldn't allow a single word to pass through her lips.

She'd never been touched like this—simply, yet with a conviction she couldn't ignore. Though the man didn't care that he invaded her space, he didn't make her uncomfortable. As if he merely showed her what he could give her tonight, offering her a little taste of how he planned to set her on fire.

"You're a striking woman." Pressing himself tighter against her back, his erection rested along her bottom. "Your curves"—he brushed his hand down her side and she squirmed beneath his touch—"they make me so hard."

Feeling his thick cock, she didn't doubt him. The air seemed heavy around her and his finger swiping up her pulse point made her shiver. Her breath rushed from her lungs and she struggled to suck in.

With a low chuckle, he stepped away, and a chill swept through her at his departure. He came to stand in front of her, gazing intently. "Those eyes . . ." Placing a finger under her chin, he tilted her head up. "Eyes that expressive could haunt a man."

Her lips parted, and the side of his mouth arched. "Ah, yes, and those lips . . ." He ran his finger along the plumpest part of her bottom lip. "Luv, that pouty mouth could make a man demand pleasure."

Leaning down, he sealed his mouth across hers, and she couldn't run from his kiss. The power of it took her breath away. For all the compliments he'd given her—more than any man ever had with such blatant intent—his kiss told her he'd meant every word.

His lips were the softest she'd ever kissed, yet determined, too. His tongue licked out in a clear request and she opened wide, welcoming him deep inside. It didn't matter that he was a stranger; she'd kiss him until he stopped.

When he tangled a finger within her hair and tugged, she moaned, wanting him to deepen the kiss. She moved closer, wiggling against his erection, desperate for him to demand more. He didn't—he backed away, giving a final tug on her hair before releasing her.

Brushing his thumb over her lip, he grinned, so dark and delicious. "You kiss like a woman craving to let go."

Abby held his gaze; her electrified body hummed and throbbed for his touch. The warm air brushed against her, reminding her they weren't alone, but she couldn't look away. His presence called to her, urging her to close the distance he'd placed between them. She wanted to tell him she desired to be free from all restraints for one night, but her voice was stuck in the mess of her scorching-hot arousal.

At her silence, the side of his mouth arched ever so slightly, and he extended his hand. "Tonight you're mine. Take my hand, sunshine."

Without his full-on assault on her hormones, her mind snapped into place, and she blinked. "Sunshine?"

He never lowered his hand, staring at her with an arrogance she'd never seen in a set of eyes. "You remind me of sunshine, so I've decided that will be the name you'll go by tonight."

"That's a bold statement," she retorted.

He winked. "Yes, it is."

She waited for him to say more, or to say anything at all, but he merely watched her with that sexy smirk. He hadn't lowered his hand and waited for her to take his as if he had no doubt she would, and that confidence made her belly flutter.

He hadn't asked her a single question like the others had, or had given her any small talk. He spoke to her so directly, so confidently, so dead set on having an evening with her. Apparently, by the slivers of heat building between her thighs, she appreciated his boldness.

Now she found what she was searching for tonight—intensity. A raw sexual attraction to someone based on nothing except the desire to be naked and sweaty. The passion oozing off this man, the power in his eyes, the way he focused entirely on her, it all made her burn.

Though when another couple brushed past and the woman giggled, Abby eyed the man's outreached hand. "Why do you want me to take your hand?"

"To accept me for the night, of course."

Chuckling at his arrogance, she liked the twinkle in his eye. The wind rustled the branches of the tree next to her, fluttering a few of the pink petals to the ground. "You don't think we need to talk first?"

He shook his head, slow and serious. "I'd prefer to do other things with your mouth, as I've just shown you."

His deep voice melted across her, and at the liquid fire racing through her veins, her decision was an easy one. Yes, *this* man was exactly who she wanted to meet tonight. Maybe even who she'd fantasized to meet for a long time.

Sliding her hand into his, she noticed the way his gaze flared. "What do I call you?" she asked.

He leaned in, and his woodsy scent was nearly as sexy as his devilish smile. "Tonight, you can call me G."

4

G escorted Abby to a private hotel room on the same floor as the Presidential Suite. The entire floor had been rented out for the masquerade, which she thought made sense, considering the privacy of the function.

The square bedroom was a little bigger than her master bedroom at home. It had a certain charm to it. While the furniture was simple with a king-sized bed overrun with pillows, it looked similar to her house. From the warm beige color on the wall, to the oak furniture, the room radiated comfort.

She heard the door shut, and turned to see G lock the deadbolt. Yet again, the room vanished as she zeroed in on him. She admired how his shoulders flexed as he lowered his hand from the door, the way his faded jeans hugged his thick hips.

Her heart raced for the obvious reasons that she stood half-naked in a room with a complete stranger about to have sex. The other reason came from the fact that she *did* stand half-naked and was about to have sex. Excitement mixed with nervousness stormed into her so fast that warmth slid down her spine, pooling an intense heat into her loins.

As his gaze caught hers, the fire inside burned under the intensity she spotted in his features. It appeared he experienced the same hunger to devour. Perhaps he even loved the naughtiness of what they were about to do, too.

Two strangers who were feeding off nothing but lust.

Abby could no longer make out the noise from the party only a few doors down, and all that remained was the hammering of her heart. The marble lamps on the nightstand cast the room in a warm, sensual glow, causing shadows to form along G's muscular chest.

When he approached, her breath caught, as that same rush of familiarity sped through her. She tilted her head, watching him, but she couldn't place what looked familiar—it was how he moved . . . or . . . *something*.

One thing was certain: She decided nothing was better in the world than this man walking toward her. She liked—with a total body buzz—being his entire focus, and flames flicked throughout her body.

He closed in on her and she stared up at him, his jaw clenching. As he cupped her cheeks, her breath hitched. The world stopped for a second when he dropped his head and pressed his lips against hers.

Lord have mercy, she'd never had a stranger walk up and steal a kiss right out of her mouth, but that's exactly what he did. Abby didn't know if it was his confidence or lack of hesitation to act that turned her on, or if it was simply *this* stranger, but her temperature rose.

His kiss took her to a place she'd never gone. A high she never wanted to come down from. He wasn't cautious in how he kissed her. His lips were forceful and demanding—commanding her to follow each move he made. And passion poured off every swipe of his tongue.

Unable to stop herself, she inched her way closer. His strong body cradled hers as he held her face in his powerful hands.

The roughness of his jeans against her bare stomach reminded her of the lingerie she wore, sending a wicked burn south.

Heaviness formed between her thighs, her mound clenching and moistening for more. Pressing firmly against his warm, hard body, she wiggled against his erection, craving every inch of him.

He slid his mouth over her cheek and down her neck, where he angled her head. He devoured her as if he'd been starved of her flesh. As if he knew exactly where to kiss her to make her hotter. As if he knew her body better than she did.

"I like how you smell." His tongue slid over her pulse point. "How you taste." Tangling his fingers into her hair, he gave a tug. "How you feel."

The low quality of his voice sent a zing to her clit. Every move he made erased the nerves that had risen and replaced them with a greedy need. Sliding his mouth up her cheek, he discovered her lips again and deepened the kiss.

His fingers tightened in her hair, tugging her close. His body pressing against hers held her still. She wanted to be touched by him, consumed by him. Feeling an equal intensity, she melted into him and kissed him in return with a fevered pitch.

He grunted in obvious approval; then he broke the kiss.

When she opened her eyes, a heat so profound crashed into her. Her body filled with a rich, intoxicating need, and she hummed in rich desire. Some men didn't look any different when aroused. G wasn't among them.

His clear eyes had darkened. The set of his jaw firmed. The power coming off him made her feel feminine, safe, and protected, and the electricity between them almost crackled in the air.

The side of his mouth slowly arched when he took a step back, then folded his arms over his thick, bare chest. "Remove your thong."

She gawked, wondering if she'd heard him right. When his smile became full-blown, she realized she hadn't misunderstood and she hesitated under the demand. Sure, she figured they'd have some raunchy sex, but from his passionate kiss, she expected more *passion*, not a wham-bam-thank-you-ma'am moment.

"Why?" she asked.

He lowered his head, bringing his eyes in direct line with hers. "Because I've told you to."

Abby quivered, not doubting by the hardness in his features that he meant what he said. Part of her was uncertain. The other, stronger part of her wanted to act. She'd come to the masquerade for this reason—for an escape. Maybe a wham-bam-thank-you-ma'am moment was exactly what she needed. Didn't she deserve to do something so crazy?

Damn right I do!

Tucking her fingers into the sides of her thong and keeping her focus on G, she pulled the lacy fabric over her bottom, then removed her panties. As she dropped them to floor next to her, his eyes blazed with heat.

He gave her a once-over, and she noticed he stood a little straighter now. His muscles were stiffer, and the bulge in the front of pants told her something else was rock hard, too. "Turn around," he ordered.

Shivering at the deep command, she turned to face the bed. Images of what he planned next raced through her mind. Would he sheath himself in a condom and take her from behind? All the possibilities made her hot and ready.

When his thick body closed in on her, she didn't need his touch to know he was there, she sensed him all around her. His hand wrapped around her hip, and she gasped at his warm, determined fingers. Her heart hammered, yet a flush so hot slid through her.

He sprawled his fingers over her stomach, his mouth right by her ear. "Are you nervous?"

"Yes," she whispered.

"Beautiful, you have nothing to worry about." He kissed her shoulder, then flicked his tongue up her neck, until he whispered in her ear, "Tonight, you give yourself to me and I'll give you pleasure. That's nothing to worry about, is it?"

"No."

He brushed his lips down her neck and over her shoulder. "Besides, it makes you feel naughty to do something that scares you with a stranger and to give me control, doesn't it?"

She hesitated.

Sliding his lips again over her neck, he brought forth goose bumps across her flesh, and he murmured, "Answer me, sunshine."

"Yes."

He flicked his tongue against her earlobe. "Yes, it makes you feel naughty?"

"Yes."

Inhaling deeply and slowly, he nibbled the base of her neck. "Tell me."

"It makes me feel naughty." She moaned. "I like it."

Her lower half was so heavy that she could only clench her thighs to ease what he was building inside her. Having him do what he wanted, in the way he wanted—this made her so aroused she couldn't stay still. She squirmed and moved her hips with every kiss—with every touch.

Abby had always wanted a man to control her. She craved for so long to be with a man who didn't shy away from the naughtiness, but indulged in wicked fantasies. To know a man who wasn't hesitant with his touches, but arrogant in how he handled her body.

G was that man.

He trailed his finger along the path his lips had taken on her neck, and she experienced the weight of his touch as if he commanded her body to awaken. He was right *there,* so close to her she could feel the heat emanating off him.

There was no noise in the room, it was only his breathing and low voice in her ear. "Your skin feels good, sunshine." He moaned, low and deep, trailing his finger over her shoulder and down her spine. "I like how you move with my touch."

She wanted to say something in return to compliment him, but her voice was stuck as sensation overloaded her. No man had every taken such time to touch her, slow and patient with every single caress of his lips or his fingertip.

His hand slid over her bottom, where he gave her cheek a firm squeeze, and a wicked sliver stormed into her. When G touched her, he meant it. When he spoke, the intent to arouse worked.

G made her burn.

He squeezed the other butt cheek and rubbed his erection against her thigh, making her curious over that bulge. The moisture between her thighs was now a desperate plea. Her clit throbbed for his finger or his mouth. Unable to stand in one spot, she swirled her hips in a cry for more.

"Luv," he practically purred. "If you're going to squirm like that, you'll do it against my cock." Moving in behind her, he pressed himself tight against her bottom, and her mound ached at the feel of his hefty erection. He ran his hands down her arms and kissed her shoulder. "I don't believe I told you to stop squirming."

She rolled her hips, rubbing her bottom against him.

"That's it." He groaned, his breath caressing the sweet spot on her neck. "Yeah, just like that."

G gripped her hips and she moved faster. He didn't assist her movements, but he merely allowed her to rub herself all over him. But when his breath deepened by her ear, he slid his hand over her hip, and she gasped with a start when he caressed her engorged clit. He swirled the bundle of nerves, causing her to freeze, overwhelmed with the tickling sensations.

He pressed hard against her clit in a slight bite of pain. "You don't get pleasure if you stop moving."

Her eyes fluttered closed as the deep press of his fingers was almost as good as the swirls he offered, but she needed more, her body desperate now, and she rolled her hips again. His erection pressed against his bottom, and his fingers moved faster, bringing her higher into ecstasy.

She swirled her hips in the same speed he used with his fingers, mirroring every single move he made. Feeling his cock, hearing his low moans in her ears, was all fuel to her pleasure, making her shift her hips faster, and faster, and faster . . .

G rubbed her clit in quick circles. As he slid her hair over her shoulder, giving him full access to her neck, her breath caught on a moan. His lips were sliding over her neck and he was kissing her, not with sweet kisses, but dominant, devouring kisses.

Each nibble, flick of his tongue, hot press of his lips, and his low, masculine sounds increased her hunger. She lost herself in how he touched her. No, how he commanded her.

Every one of his moves set her aflame. The swirls on her clit left her panting, and the pleasure was coiling tight within. He slid one finger inside her depths and she froze, right on the edge of her climax—almost on the verge of exploding.

Then his finger was gone.

She cried out, half in frustration, half in the highest form of erotic fulfillment.

He said nothing, and she didn't need another order from him. Again, she swirled her hips, not realizing she had stopped. When his finger returned to giving her clit a swirl, she gasped in relief, and his low chuckle followed. "There you go," he murmured.

Continuing to rub herself against his erection, she moved not smooth and fluid, but intense and jerky. He pressed harder against her bundles of nerves, and she screamed, shocked by the sensitivity. When his finger again slid through her wet folds and dipped inside, her entire body trembled.

"I—" She moaned.

"Are going to come for me," he finished for her.

Though he stepped slightly to the side, she continued to roll her hips as he pressed his hardened length against her right buttock. He inserted two fingers and with no gentleness, he pumped his fingers. Thrusting hard and fast within her channel, wet sucking sounds filled the air.

G didn't ease her into climax. When he wanted it, he demanded it, and she had no chance or desire to refuse his order. All the tension inside exploded as she burst into mind-blowing and soul-fulfilling sensations.

She stopped squirming against him.

This time, he let her.

The scent of satisfied, hot, and wet woman filled Gavin's nostrils as he withdrew his fingers from Abby. Her hair was mussed and she looked a mess, and that delighted the primal man inside. He liked knowing he made her that way.

Her head was bowed, and she couldn't catch her breath, making him roar up in pride that he turned her into a boneless woman. He had wrapped his arm around her while she climaxed, and he didn't doubt if he released her, she would've dropped to the ground.

Only when she seemed to gain more control of her legs, standing a little more firmly, did he loosen his hold. Her flesh was damp when he trailed his hand over her flat abdomen, and she quivered under his touch.

Breaking the silence, she gave a laugh soft. "Does 'G' stand for 'God of orgasms,' 'cause, holy crap, you are great at them."

Turning in his arms, she looked up at him with wide, glossy eyes, beneath her mask. He'd never seen anything more beautiful. He smiled, brushing her hair off her damp forehead. "I'll take the compliment, thank you."

Abby leaned into his touch, and he couldn't take his eyes off her. Christ, she was lovely. Her cheeks were a pinkish color. The soft glow of the overhead lighting cast a warm light over the side of her face, illuminating her flawless skin. He ran his fingers over her cheek, then slid his touch all the way down her body until he reached her hip.

She glanced at the bed before she turned to him with a smirk. "Now, it's your turn. Get on the bed."

His cock twitched. "Is that what you'd like?"

She wiggled that sexy-as-hell body against him, only hardening him further. "You're not the only one good at giving orgasms."

Gavin gave her credit for answering, when deep down, he suspected that was difficult for her. Though she owned her sexuality, her blush told him that she wasn't nearly as bold as him when it came to voicing what she wanted. Too bad for her, just because she wanted something, didn't mean she'd get it.

He reached for his belt. "Get down."

Her pause lasted only a second before she did as told, lowering to her knees. Widening his stance, he undid his belt. "I like you there, not on the bed." She might want to control tonight, but she'd never win this game.

Not with him.

Not now.

Once he had his belt open, he reached for the button on his jeans, gazing down at her. The mask, still fitted tight around her face, only accentuated her beauty. Christ, she could be his undoing.

With his free hand, he brushed his fingers over cheek, and he loved when she, once again, leaned into his touch. Her eyes fluttered closed, and he exhaled through his nose, experiencing the same draw to her he had that day at her house fire.

She looked so pure, waiting for him. Quiet and peaceful, offering herself. Her eyes finally opened and a rush of emotion struck him hard in the chest. His fingers froze mid-swipe on her cheek.

I can't take you this way.

He shook his head and told his hesitations, *Yes, you can!*

Determined to do exactly that, he brushed his thumbs over her soft skin and sealed his mouth over hers. Testing, he pushed against the odd hesitation. He moved his lips and tangled his tongue with hers, his cock throbbing to turn off his mind. Yet, the voice in his head kept screaming, *Stop!*

Frustrated, he broke the kiss and regarded her.

Abby, on her knees, wasn't helping either. Seeing her waiting there, offering to suck him off, only increased the battle inside. With his head still screaming at him to stop, he offered his hand. "Come on up."

Once on her feet, she played with a strand of her hair. "What's wrong?"

Turning away, he looked to the bed, which was a place that if his head wasn't being so stupid, he'd be naked and deep inside her hot body. So, why wasn't he?

"Are you okay?" she asked in an uncertain voice.

He thrust his fingers into his hair. Hadn't he wanted this night? Hadn't he planned it? Didn't he want to screw Abby so hard to rid himself of the thoughts of her? Damn straight, he wanted that.

Intent to get his mind back in the game, he took her in his arms. He dropped his mouth to hers, sweeping her away in a kiss that made him forget his hesitation. She was perfection. Her lips tasted so damn good. Her smell tightened his groin.

He wanted her.

Not only for one night.

Breaking the kiss, he grunted, shaking the thoughts from his head. Fuck, what was wrong with him?

"Okay, seriously, what's up?" she asked, breathless. Her cheeks were rosy, her parted lips puffy from his kiss. "Do you not want to do this?"

Gavin rubbed the back of his neck. Here he had the woman he couldn't stop thinking about for two weeks. He remembered that day at her house fire. Her pain had branded itself onto his soul. And he couldn't deny it any longer—this was wrong.

Blowing out a deep breath, he dropped down onto the bed and bowed his head to his clenched hands. "I can't do this as strangers. You need to know me."

She hesitated. "Know you?"

He looked to her, noticing her gaze clouding, going distant. Of course, she would be shocked. She'd clearly not recognized him. Why would she? Who was he to her, a firefighter who had embraced her after the fire? "You've gotten inside my head."

She blinked. "Pardon me?"

Dammit!

He'd arranged tonight to get Abby out of his head, and somehow she only weaved her hold into him further. "I wanted to get my fix of you, and I hoped that would stop my craving you." He paused, choosing his words with care. "It seems, Abby, my being with you can't be as meaningless as I had planned."

She took a step back, the color draining from her face. "H-h-how d-d-do you know my name?"

"We've met before." He reached for his mask, watched her hand fly to her chest; then he yanked the ribbon loose and his mask fluttered to the floor.

She gave him an incredulous stare. "Oh, God."

"Not God." He exhaled a heavy sigh, considering she looked ready to make a run for it. "Gavin Morgan."

"Wait." She finally took a breath, shaking her head slowly. "You were the firefighter at my house."

He nodded.

She gave him a fixed stare and he wished he could read her thoughts. Never, in his entire life had he ever seen a woman look so confused. Even after fires when people were in stunned shock, they didn't look like she did now.

"Is this a coincidence?" she asked with a slow hesitation to her voice. "Like, us meeting here tonight?"

He rested his elbows on his knees, pausing to examine her. "No."

Glancing to the chair in the corner of the room, she noticed that he'd had her long black coat waiting for her. Presumptuous of him, maybe, but hadn't this been his grand ole plan? He hadn't doubted tonight would happen.

She grabbed her coat and dressed quickly, wrapping the tie around her waist. "So, that means you sent me the invitation?"

Gazing with focus at her, he stood and approached her, not liking the cold distance between them. "I did." Christ, he told her this to bring them closer together, not push them farther apart. The second his foot planted on the floor, she took another step back.

"I thought the package was for Sierra." She absently rubbed her arms. "She's the bold one who does crazy things, not me!" Blinking rapidly, she added, "I wasn't supposed to know you."

He crossed his arms in front of his chest. This wasn't what he wanted. "Listen—"

"This doesn't make sense," she continued, as if he hadn't spoken. "How would you know I would pick you tonight? Three other men had asked me to be with them before you." Her hands curled around her middle. "How would you know that I'd turn them down?"

He averted his gaze, realizing the huge misunderstanding facing him. She thought the invitation was for her friend. Lifting his head, he softened his voice. "I knew you would only be with me, because it's the same reason I had to invite you—there's something going on between us."

She pursed her lips in thought. "But how did you know I'd even show up in the first place?"

"I didn't." He hoped what he said next would help, not hurt, his current situation. "After the fire, I was in your bedroom and I saw your books. I assumed you'd be open to the idea of the masquerade."

Her eyes narrowed. "You what!"

Fuck, not help! His hands fell to his sides. "Okay, you're angry about this."

"Of course, I'm angry!" She planted her legs wide, her nostrils flaring. "You went into my private closet and looked at my private things."

"No, I was in your bedroom, making sure there weren't any hot spots where another fire could spark."

She pointed her index finger, glaring. "Which means you shouldn't have looked at my stuff. You should've been doing your job."

"Yeah, I know," he bit off. "That's been the problem. I couldn't stop myself." His voice lost its power. "Listen, I understand why that makes you mad—"

"Good, I'm glad you understand." She sneered. "*Your* feelings are exactly what I'm worried about right now."

He ignored that, and continued. "I sensed something that day between us. Something you clearly sensed, too, since tonight you picked me, when you had refused three others already. Doesn't that tell you something?"

"What? And you think that makes this better?" Her skin became mottled. "Let me break it to you, that *doesn't* make it better."

Christ, he didn't know how to backpedal. Though he suspected he might face an annoyed woman when he revealed he'd seen her private stuff, he hoped she'd see past it. He wanted her to understand the compulsion driving him crazy.

"This was supposed to be for Sierra." She stared at him dead in the eye, with that same icy cold distance. "I wasn't supposed to know you. This was all supposed to be a secret fantasy, nothing more."

"I had meant for our night to be simply that, but I can't do it." He moved into her space, regardless that she clearly didn't want him there. "I won't do it that way." She looked so distant, he clenched his fists. He had no clue how to fix this. "I didn't mean to upset you." He reached out to her. "I want this to be real—"

She flinched, recoiling from him. "I have to get out of here." Brushing past, she headed for the door.

"Abby?" he called.

She didn't look back.

She didn't walk.

She ran.

5

The bookstore, Book Addict, located in downtown Boston, was Abby's piece of paradise. She'd gone to business school with the money from her parents' estate, and after she'd graduated from college, she'd used the remainder of the money to buy her house and her bookshop.

Though *things* were never a replacement for her family, this was how she remembered them. They were woven into the threads of her day-to-day life. They still gave to her, brought her happiness, even from the grave.

She placed a fantasy novel on the bookshelf that had been returned earlier this morning and she turned to Sierra, who sat on the stool near the register. For ten minutes—only interrupted by a couple customers entering the store—Abby told her best friend about her recent *activities*.

By the end, she finished up with the horrifying details of her running out of the room, which she decided hadn't been her finest of moments. "So, that's everything that happened."

"Okay, let me get this straight—" Sierra's mouth twitched before she burst out laughing, gasping for air. "You thought *I* would go to a sex party?"

"Quiet!" Abby snapped, glancing around, glad to see that no customers were within hearing distance.

"I'm sorry, but . . ." Tears filled Sierra's eyes, her face turning a bright shade of red. "Abby, that's so damn funny."

"What was I supposed to think?" Abby folded her arms. "The package came to *your* house. I definitely didn't think it was for me. Remember, I'm the boring one who doesn't do things like answer the front door half naked—which, by the way, was a good thing, since the package was delivered by a woman."

Sierra exhaled, and her laughter blessedly ceased. "Well, that's disappointing, but it sounds like you've got me beat in the naughty department." She plucked at her cotton T-shirt. " 'Cause I sure-as-shit wouldn't do something like that." Her expression became pinched. "Crap, I'm sorry." She looked down, bursting out in laughter.

Abby wished she could crawl into a hole and die. As if the night with Gavin hadn't been embarrassing enough, she had to relive the whole event with her best friend.

Could this get any worse?

She doubted it.

"When you left me a note telling me to meet you here," Sierra said in a high voice, "I had no idea you'd drop *this* bombshell on me." She bit her lip, holding on to her sides, until she erupted into a full belly laugh.

Abby frowned. "You can stop laughing now."

Sierra wiped away the tears of laughter. "I'm sorry, but seriously, Abby?"

Leaning against the bookshelf, Abby threw up her hands. "I realize now how crazy it all is. How was I supposed to know that firefighter would do something like that?"

The bell chimed and Abby glanced toward the front glass door, spotting an elderly couple enter the store. She gave the regular customers a wave as they journeyed to the back of the square store where the nonfiction books were located. Then she turned to Sierra. "I can't believe he invited me. I thought I was going to that party as you."

Sierra's wide grin shifted into her classic sassy smirk, and she wiggled her eyebrows. "Well, Ms. Sexy, you clearly made an impression."

"No, I don't think so . . ." Abby dropped her face into her hands and couldn't even look at Sierra as she muttered, "He saw all my lingerie and my books in my closet. He thought I was into that stuff."

"Um, hello, you *are* into that stuff."

"Not really." Lifting her head, she found Sierra giving her a *duh* expression. "I like to read naughty books and wear naughty things, but it's all in secret. I don't really do those things."

Sierra's eyebrows lifted. "*Didn't do,* you mean? You've already went to the party, so it's past tense."

That was almost worse. "Yes, but I didn't do anything to him. He did . . . *you know* . . . with me; then I ran away like a coward." She probably left the poor guy with a bad case of blue balls. "Which only adds to my embarrassment, since now I'm a total cock tease."

Heaving a sigh, she paced along the front side of the counter, past the empty couch with the wooden coffee tables. Her bookstore resembled a comfy living room with a lot of shelves, exactly as she had designed it. She loved cozy spaces. "What should've been a total fantasy has turned into a freaking nightmare."

Sierra hesitated, giving her a long look. "Maybe it's a good thing."

Abby stopped dead in her tracks and narrowed her eyes. "How is my being humiliated and a tease a good thing?"

Sierra jumped off the counter. "From what you said, he didn't humiliate you. He got you off, so at least you got something out of the fantasy night." She placed her hands in the pockets of her jeans. "And you told me yourself you've been nonstop thinking about him."

Abby regretted she told Sierra that, too. That night after the party, her dream didn't have her running from the room, but instead, had them finishing what they started, until they were both sweaty and satisfied.

Only problem?

The dream version of Gavin wasn't wearing a mask, and all of Sunday, she couldn't stop thinking about him. Before the masquerade, he lingered in her mind. Now, he was permanently fixed there.

Even this morning, his touches seemed imprinted on her body, along with the sound of his voice whispering in her ear. She shivered, then checked herself, and shook the thoughts from her mind. "Yeah, so?"

"So . . ." Sierra drawled, lowering her voice as the customers headed for the exit. "Clearly, by his actions and what you told me he said, it wasn't like he didn't want to go through with it. It was that he didn't want to do it as strangers. Apparently, you both like hot sex." Sierra shrugged halfheartedly. "I'm not sure I'm seeing the problem."

If it were only that simple. Abby waved to the customers, then turned to Sierra. "Yes, but setting up this whole thing? Don't you think that's creepy? He went through my personal property. Isn't there some sort of firefighter moral code for that?"

Sierra's expression became measured. "Dude, you showed up at the party. He didn't force you to go. I mean, really, what are the chances that you would've picked him?" She leaned against the counter with raised eyebrows. "It's . . . I don't know, fate or something."

"Fate?" Abby snorted. "I don't know about that." She sighed, and admitted, "But you're right—it was crazy that out of all the men there, I picked him. I still can't wrap my head around that."

Sierra gave a sharp nod. "Which means . . . ?"

You want him, too . . . and you know it.

Abby ignored the annoying voice in her head. It got her into this crazy position in the first place. "I have no idea," she told Sierra and the stupid voice in her head.

Sierra gave a booming laugh. "Liar."

Abby rolled her eyes. Her best friend didn't miss much, and Abby was curious about it all, now that she wasn't so angry. She wondered why Gavin had asked her and about all the little details to his plan she didn't know.

She heaved a sigh. "Okay, but—"

"But nothing, girl," Sierra interjected. "As far as I see it, he was being sweet—in a weird, horny type of way. He wanted you to know it was him, so that you wouldn't get down and dirty with a stranger. If he was the asshole you're pegging him for, I doubt he would've stopped."

Abby pondered. "Sort of sweet, I guess." Was it really so awful that Gavin actually wanted her to know it was him? She remained undecided. "It doesn't change the fact that he humiliated me."

"*Pfft . . .*" Sierra flicked her hand dismissively. "I wish some smokin'-hot firefighter, not only went total hero by putting out my house fire, but planned a sexy night for me, which included buying me lingerie. Then actually went sweet guy on me, instead of just a sleazy one-night stand stud."

Put that way . . .

Abby gritted her teeth, not wanting to admit defeat. Turning to the counter, she picked up another new paperback from the box delivered this morning and put it on the sci-fi shelf.

Perhaps she needed to focus on the amazing orgasm he gave her, keep it at that, and move on. *You'll never forget his voice, his touch, those eyes . . .*

Cursing the voice she wanted to gouge out of her head, she fixed a book that was out of order on the shelf. She heard the front doorbell chime again, and not a second later, Sierra's gasp startled her.

"Mayday! Mayday! Mayday!" Sierra exclaimed, stepping in front of Abby, bouncing from foot to foot. "Call 911."

Abby scrunched her nose. "What's wrong with you?"

Sierra, with an up-to-no-good smile planted on her face, discreetly pointed over her shoulder. "Find a fire extinguisher and quick—you're about to burst into flames." She hesitated, giggling. "Or at least your cheeks are going to burn."

Abby glanced over Sierra's shoulder and her heart skipped a beat. "Oh, hell . . ."

Gavin strode through the store, decked out in his dark blue uniform. She clearly remembered his muscular body, since she pictured it vividly in her mind. Her fingers itched to feel all those defined muscles under smooth, tanned skin.

Dear God, maybe the whole firefighter thing excited her more than she thought. She couldn't move, couldn't do anything but stand there and experience an entire body buzz under the attack on her hormones.

Heat stormed inside of her, touching every part of her soul. He hadn't been wrong and now she couldn't deny it—there was something between them. She experienced the power of it deep in her center. There was something so real and intense when he looked at her. It was also something she couldn't hide from, and something that didn't make her want to run.

Sierra also had it right, too—a blush crept over Abby's face so fast, she wished she had a fire extinguisher to douse the flames ripping through her entire body . . . especially the ones between her thighs.

Perfection stood only a few feet from Gavin. He liked Abby dressed in jeans and a pink blouse. In fact, he thought she even suited the quaint store, and it resembled what he'd seen at her house.

As he drew closer, he chuckled at her wide eyes, understanding her surprise. He'd messed up, but his parents hadn't nicknamed him Gunner for no reason—he wasn't a quitter. Besides, he also wasn't a firefighter for nothing—he didn't run from a problem, he ran into it until he had it beat.

Once he reached Abby and her friend that he'd seen at her house, he offered her the coffee cup in his hand. "Vanilla mochas are your favorite, right?"

She stared at the cup as if he'd brought her poison. "Ah . . ."

A long awkward pause followed; then her friend jabbed her in the side. "Yes, Abby loves her VMs."

Abby grunted, rubbing her ribcage. "I . . ."

Another pause.

"Hi, I'm Sierra." Her friend offered a bemused smile. "And this is, Abby, who apparently has forgotten how to talk."

Gavin grinned, finding their interaction together cute. Abby's pretty eyes were trained on him, and she was as beautiful in clothes as she was out of them.

He leaned in toward Abby, her sweet, sugary scent overwhelming him. "We've been well acquainted, I assure you."

A flush crept across her cheeks as she reached for the cup. "How did you know vanilla mochas were my favorite?"

His abs tightened in preparation for another lashing and he chose his words carefully, avoiding the word *closet*. "I saw your stickers."

She tilted her head, giving him a long look. "Oh, on my 'Me Wall.' "

Before he had a chance to dig into the meaning behind that, she took a sip of her coffee. The pleasure that washed over her face stirred his cock. At least he'd gotten something right. He couldn't take his gaze off her lips leaving the rim of the cup, but he forced his attention to her suspicious eyes. "I was hoping we could talk."

More awkward silence.

Sierra finally cleared her throat, looking between him and Abby. "Oh, look at that, I . . . er . . . crap, I think I left my curling iron on at home."

Gavin folded his arms, chuckling. Her friend was amusing, considering she had the straightest hair he'd ever seen, making her excuse a poor one. Clearly, Abby agreed. She shot her friend an "Are you kidding me?" look.

Sierra gave a nervous chuckle, tangling her fingers through her hair. Then, without another word, she booked it, letting the front door slam shut behind her.

While Abby watched her friend leave, Gavin couldn't take his eyes off her inability to stand still. He hadn't meant to make her uncomfortable; he came to set things right. He waved out to the two oversized chairs by the bay window. "Come sit with me."

She gave a small nod, stepping into stride with him. After she dropped down in the chair on the left, he settled into the other chair. She looked out the window before she gave him a downcast expression. "Should you be here?"

Gavin's gaze swept out to the engine at the curb, where Jett waited for him. "It's fine. We're on a coffee run. I don't have long, but I wanted to see you."

"I'm not sure why." She crossed her legs, then uncrossed them. "I don't think there's much to talk about."

"Really?" Surprise to him, the past day had been utter hell, and he'd decided this morning that he wouldn't go through another day like that. "You don't think we need to get a few things straight?"

She shook her head, looking down at her coffee cup. "What happened . . . happened. Can't we leave it at that?"

"No, Abby, we can't."

At his low, curt voice, she lifted her head. He leaned in toward her, his eyes coming directly in line with hers. "First, I'm sorry for how things went down and if I embarrassed you. That's not what I wanted to happen."

She snorted softly. "You and me both."

Her hand rested on her knee, and he reached for it with hesitation. She didn't flinch away as he trailed his index finger over the back of her hand. "I want you to know that I've never done that before."

"Done what?"

Heady desire rushed into him at her throaty voice. "I've never invited a woman to the masquerade. I've never taken my mask off." He lifted his head, discovering her dark eyes. "I've never chased after a woman. I've never brought a woman a vanilla mocha to her work, unaware if I'd get a slap in the face if I did."

Gazing over her, he took notice of her other hand trembling around her coffee cup. "Your point is?"

He removed his touch and regarded her. "You make me do things I never would otherwise." He caged his legs around hers and loved the hitch in her breath. "I still want our night—that hasn't changed for me."

She licked her lips. "Why are you so sure about all this?"

He cocked his head, arching an eyebrow. "Because of the reasons I told you." Staring at her mouth, he craved to brand her with his kiss, until she moaned softly. "I *did* invite you to the party. I *did* take off my mask. I *did* chase after you. I *did* bring you a vanilla mocha to your work."

"Oh," was her response.

He sat back in his seat, resting his arms on the back of the chair. His cock pressed painfully against his zipper at the view. Even without the lingerie, she looked ravishing. "So, Abby," he said slow and steady. "Can you forgive me?"

She examined him and he wondered if she planned to refuse him. She finally said with a furrowed brow, "I'm not sure there's anything to forgive. You haven't done anything wrong; it just took me by surprise."

He smiled, as that answer told him one thing. "You liked that it was me?"

She looked to her hands in her lap. "I didn't mind it."

He suddenly felt ultra-awake, rejuvenated by adrenaline. The way she'd left him, he wondered if she'd been horrified that he'd sent her the invitation. He'd never been so happy to be wrong. Tucking a finger under her jaw, he commanded her gaze. "Did you think about me since we met that day at the fire?"

Her chin dipped downward. "Maybe."

"That's a good thing, don't you think?"

She laughed softly. "Possibly, since it appears I wasn't the only one."

God, she was so beautiful. The way she moved, the way the sun from the window beamed across her face. She transfixed him. Making him feel even more like shit for what he'd done. His stomach knotted. "Listen, Abby, I'm sorry about how everything went down. I honestly didn't think you'd react the way you did. I never meant for that to happen."

Her eyes searched his before she asked, "What did you think would happen?"

He lowered his finger from her jaw, wondering how honest to be. Considering she had clearly shown a huge dislike to secrets, he wasn't about to muck things up again. "I thought I'd invite you, we'd fuck, and I'd get my fix of you."

She sipped her coffee, looking at him over the rim of her cup. "Then why didn't you go through with it?"

"I couldn't." He looked out at the engine, seeing Jett tapping his fingers on the steering wheel. Turning to her, he added, "I didn't want it to be just sex. I needed you to know that *I* was with you."

She shook her head slowly, laughing. "But you don't even

know me. I could be a total crazy person, so why was that so important to you?"

"You're right, I don't know you." He held her stare. "But I know myself, and what I want."

She hesitated. "Which is what exactly?"

"Another night with you."

Taking a sip of her coffee, she licked the foam off her lips, which he decided was his punishment for upsetting her. Leaning in toward him, she asked, "Answer me this, then. I thought you said this wasn't about sex?"

He brushed his fingers over her jawline, watching her gaze glossing over. "Oh, it's about sex, Abby, don't think it's not. But I want you to know it's *me* touching you."

Her eyes were soft, filled with an inner glow. "You do realize that's backward if you want to get to know me. Usually people date first, then comes the touching bit?"

"I prefer to get to know you in the most personal manner I can." He slid his thumb along her bottom lip, craving to claim that mouth. "I'd say fucking you is pretty damn personal." At the flare in her gaze, he got right to the heart of his appearance in her store. "Those books you read, those fantasies you have . . ." His fingers ached with the need to keep touching her. "I can give you that."

Her breath hitched. "So, you want another night?"

He grinned. "I'll start with one."

The spark of his radio coming to life caused Abby to start and kicked his heart rate up. He stood, taking the note out of his pocket he'd written up on the drive to her store. "It's up to you now, sunshine."

He placed the paper with his home address into her hand and, without another look to her, he jogged out of her shop. Once he made it outside, the warm sun beamed down on him. He reached the engine, and Jett had already started the truck.

Gavin opened the door, then pulled himself up and dropped down into the seat. "What do we have?"

"Five-alarm fire in Southie." Jett turned on the sirens. "Buckle up."

Grabbing his seatbelt, Gavin cleared his mind of Abby and of the possibility of being with her tonight. Rapid thoughts took over, as they always did on the way to a fire: Was anyone hurt? What was on fire? Did a life needing saving?

Adrenaline tightened his muscles.

This, he lived for.

6

At eight o'clock, Abby exited the taxi and stepped into the warm evening in the Back Bay neighborhood. She stood on the curb beneath the streetlight, and pedestrians passed by in a blur. In front of her, the Victorian brownstone reminded her of her home, but seeing that Back Bay neighbored Beacon Hill, she wasn't surprised. Boston was full of historic row houses, and she loved that about the city.

Boston had charm.

So did someone else.

"Those books you read, Abby. Those fantasies you have—I can give you that."

At her shop and after Gavin had left her, she'd read his note giving his address and what time to meet him tonight. After Abby told Sierra of his plan, she'd received a few smacks in the head from her best friend until she saw sense to give him another chance.

She wanted those fantasies he could deliver.

Hell, she deserved them.

Across the street, music from the Irish pub drifted out into the street. Abby inhaled deeply through her nose and she swore she caught the scent of beer. Making her way up the front steps, she noticed a note tucked into the side of the dark gray door. She grabbed the note and opened the paper.

Don't knock. Come inside.

A shiver slid through her at the promise of what awaited her. Gavin hadn't been wrong—passion so rich and real existed between them. She felt it that day they met, and now she knew he did, too. Only a fool would walk away from something that electric. She was a bookworm and a homebody, but she was no fool.

She tucked the piece of paper into the pocket of her jeans as images of Gavin that night she'd known him as G rushed through her mind. Heat pooled low in her belly, and she turned the door handle.

The door swiftly opened to a foyer, with a dark living room on the right. Though the house was masculine with dark taupe walls, it reminded her of her home. Gavin seemed to appreciate comfortable spaces, too. From the soft mocha-colored couches and an oak coffee table, to the dozens of lit candles lighting up the space in a warm romantic glow.

Kicking off her shoes at the doorway, she shut the door behind her. Behind the foyer appeared to be the entrance to the kitchen, and she glanced at the staircase at the end of the hallway, yet didn't hear any noise. She followed the glow from the candles into the living room.

The moment she entered, she froze.

In the far corner chair on the right side of the square room, surrounded by candles, was a sight so handsome her body awakened. Though she experienced that same buzz in her body in Gavin's presence, it wasn't his gorgeous face bringing forth heat. She leaned against the doorway, smiling. "I see you didn't get changed from work."

"I saw your reaction to my uniform today." Gavin's mouth

twitched, a strand of his hair falling over his brow. "Figured it was in my best interests to keep it on."

She gave him a once-over, dampness spreading between her thighs. She still didn't think of herself as a woman who had a thing for firefighters. Apparently, she had a thing for *this* firefighter. "It definitely was."

Sierra asked her today what it was about Gavin that made Abby so hot, and even then she couldn't think up a solid answer. All she knew was, being in this man's presence did wicked things to her, including making her hormones skip and jump.

Gavin's gaze darkened, apparently noticing something in her expression. "Do I need to remind you of the rules?"

Knowing more of the man behind the mask, she also knew the game they played. Tonight he wanted control and she shivered in anticipation. "No." Perhaps she even liked that he wasn't playing around.

He wanted to control her. She wanted him to take over.

"Good." Approval glowed within the depths of his eyes. "Now, take off your clothes."

His confidence in demands was attractive. She didn't hold the same levels of boldness in her soul. She glanced around his home—noting the silence—before she looked to him. Though his statement caused trepidation, it also sent hot excitement straight through her.

There, before her, sat a man she couldn't stop thinking about—almost as if she were addicted to him. Refusing him, or being shy, wasn't an option. Shutting off her mind, she did as he asked and followed his commands.

Reaching for her blouse, she unbuttoned it. She removed her jeans, leaving her in her black lace bra and panties. At her hesitation, he raised a deliberate eyebrow. "What did I ask you, Abby?"

Her fingers tingled. "To take off my clothes."

His eyebrow arched higher.

Not needing a further command, she removed her bra and lost her panties, all the while taking a calming breath. Arousal so hot stormed into her. Everything low in her body felt swollen and ready for him. Standing there naked, she wasn't embarrassed; she burned with a desire so raw and real, her body buzzed with need.

He scanned her from head to toe, his eyes gleaming. He studied every part of her in a slow sweep of his gaze—from her shoulder, down to her breasts, over her stomach, then to the junction between her thighs. Nothing about how he watched her felt rushed; it seemed as if he had all the time in the world.

She felt admired.

When he lifted his gaze to her face and smoldering eyes held hers, she changed her mind—she felt beautiful.

"Come closer," he murmured.

The candle next to him created an orange hue that highlighted his cheekbone and detailed the curve of those lips she knew kissed her with no regret. She only got a few feet away from him before he said, "Stop right there."

Standing with her arms at her sides, the warmth in the room brushed over her, but her nipples puckered under the weight of his stare. Though he hadn't touched her to create dampness between her thighs, he didn't need to, his presence commanded it.

"Kneel," he stated. "Spread your legs."

She did as told.

He gave a crisp nod of approval. "Before tonight, when you'd think of a man commanding you like I am now, how would you touch yourself?"

Heat flushed right through her, but not in her face, her sex yearned for his touch. "I would—"

"Stop."

She shut her mouth.

He squinted, giving a hard smile. "Show me."

Desperate and aching, she followed his order as simply as if she were alone. Somehow that made it easier, she wasn't thinking about what she'd do or not do. She listened to him, and that shed her nervous edge.

Besides, what did she have to lose?

Nothing.

What did she have to gain?

The best sexual experience of her life.

With that thought on her mind, she grasped her breasts, squeezing them, and working her way toward her nipples. She swirled and rubbed the taut peaks, moving her hips as everything low in her body flamed with fire.

His posture straightened, his fingers forming a steeple under his chin. "I love how you squirm."

The smooth tone he used, matched with his dark eyes, made her run one of her hands down her abdomen, until she reached her swollen clit. She swept along the side of her folds, enjoying her wetness.

Taking the silky-smooth arousal, she rubbed along her entrance, continuing to roll her hips with each touch. She continued to tweak her nipple, giving pinches of sharp sensation that flooded her with desire.

Gavin stayed silent, and somehow having him so attentive made her greedier. Her clit throbbed, and she had enough of teasing. Something he clearly recognized, since he smirked. As she drew her fingers up through her folds to her clit, a soft moan escaped.

The swollen bud was sensitive, and an immediate tremble rocked her. Though she wanted to shut her eyes and lose herself in the sensations, she'd never look away from him. Not when he stared at her as if he was a predator prepping to pounce on his prey.

Swirling her hips in the same rhythm she set on her fingers, she found a pace bringing hot pleasure. She pressed harder against her clit, moaning with each zing ripping through her.

Gavin never took his eyes off her, and she read his thoughts through his distant, unfocused smile.

This wasn't about learning her on-spots; he already had her mapped out. This was about getting her into his control, and she happily tumbled into it. He examined her as if he was reading right through her, and such a study unleashed something deep inside of her—an unknown spark of lust that wanted to come out and play.

She rubbed her clit harder, moved her hips faster, and pinched her nipple tighter, as pleasure coiled tight inside. Her breathing became rapid, her moans harsher, and her inner walls clenched. Her head fell back on its own accord, and she had no power to stop her body from reacting—just as Gavin had controlled her actions, her orgasm stole her thoughts.

The loss of eye contact didn't hinder her rising pleasure; she sensed his intent stare on her every move. His presence was strong and added fuel to her fire, tipping her over the edge and into climax.

With a hard push against her clit, she wiggled her hips as an explosion burst into her, igniting uncontrollable moans from her throat. Riding out each beautiful wave of euphoric satisfaction, she gave little shakes of her hips and quick rubs on her mound.

By the time she stopped trembling, she realized her head was bowed and she was breathless. A finger tucked under her chin, and she discovered intense eyes. "That orgasm, Abby, was how you do it." Gavin's rich voice sent a new round of heat racing through her veins. "Next time, your orgasm will belong to me."

Standing next to the coffee table, Abby peered up at Gavin with a ravishing beauty, making his cock throb to take her. Her show had been the sexiest thing he'd ever witnessed. Little did she know he'd tested her willingness by putting her up against the one thing most women would be nervous to do.

Clearly, Abby came here tonight to play.

Gavin intended to make it memorable.

Keeping his attention on that pretty, pouty mouth, he flicked the buttons open on his uniform shirt, loving how she licked her lips as he exposed his flesh. He dropped the shirt to the floor and hurried to rid himself of his belt. Then he opened his pants, and slid those, as well as his boxer-briefs, over his hips. As his erection sprung free, he took notice of her slight smile as she eyed his raging hard-on.

Tonight, he had a plan, which had already gone to shit. He wanted to draw this night out, tease them both until they could barely stand it. After watching her pleasure herself, he needed to take her. He had waited two weeks to experience the real thing. He wouldn't wait any longer.

Grasping the base of his cock, he closed the distance between them and then angled his cock out. She reached for him, and he brushed his hand over her silky hair as she took him deep into her mouth. The moment her lips closed around him, he threw his head back on a deep groan.

No fantasizing came close to the real thing.

Abby sucked him off as if she'd hungered over him, as he did her. As if she had imagined this exact moment, too, over and over again. Looking down, he grunted and his muscles tightened. Her head bobbed on his dick and her hand followed behind, all pulling him deeper into pleasure. He moaned with each suck she made, and he groaned with each stroke of her hand.

When she swirled her head, matching it with tight jerks on his shaft, his legs quivered. He tangled his fingers within her silky hair, giving a tug of encouragement. Her response was immediate. She moved faster, until he was shifting his hips.

Thrusting both hands into her hair, he gripped her tight as she moved rapidly. He widened his stance, watching her mouth stretch wide to accept him. Those lips were wet, warm, and perfect.

Eyeing her going wild on his cock brought intensity he hadn't anticipated. All the passion he had experienced rose to levels he didn't dare comprehend. The only thing that mattered now, her mouth wasn't giving him enough. He wanted to be buried deep inside her slick heat.

Once she worked her way to the tip of his cock, licking around the head, he forced himself to step back. He pulled his hardened length from between those luscious lips and offered his hand. She stood, and he cupped her face. "When I come, I want to feel you shuddering. I want to hear your screams." He didn't give her a chance to respond, he sealed his mouth over hers, taking the kiss his body demanded.

She smelled of woman.

She tasted like heaven.

His cock throbbed against her stomach as his tongue tangled with hers. Her feminine body against his brought forth urgency. He craved to trap her in his hold, with nowhere to run, but to accept his claim on her.

He kissed her jawline, her neck, and he consumed any bare flesh available to him. He slid his tongue along her collarbone, her raspy breath urging him on. He grasped her breast, taking a taut nipple and sucking it onto the roof of his mouth. Then he moved to other breast, giving it a slight bite, earning him a lovely quiver.

His cock ached as she squirmed against him, pressing her breasts flush against his bare chest. He chuckled, understanding her impatience. Releasing the tight bud, he turned her to face the coffee table. "Put your hands on the table. Do not move."

She flashed him a grin before she turned. The front of Abby knocked the wind out him; the view of her bent over his coffee table, and her gorgeous heart-shaped ass awaiting him, sent a raw, primal need into his soul.

Without pause, he reached for the condom in his pants pocket. He ripped the foil open and groaned as Abby spread her legs, showing off the moisture along her pink folds. More urgent now, he sheathed his hardened length and stepped in behind her.

Running a hand over her soft back, he relished in the feel of her curves. He leaned down, pressed his weight against her, and whispered in her ear, "Has anyone ever taken you hard, Abby?"

"Yes."

A territorially heat flushed through him. He knew the smile on his face was pure predator. "That I don't believe. If they had, you wouldn't have had to read about it." Before she could comment, he pressed his rock-hard cock against her lower lips and entered her.

He moaned, as did she.

Widening his legs, he gazed over the lines of her beautiful form, which were illuminated from the candles glowing in the room. He moved in slowly, warming her up. Her tight heat squeezed him, and watching himself disappear inside her, he knew this ride would be quick and powerful.

Her soft noises sounded in the same rhythm as her inner muscles convulsed around his shaft, all encouraging him to speed up. He gripped her round bottom, spread her cheeks, and moved faster.

"Oh, God . . ." she gasped.

He slapped her ass.

She arched her back. "Yes!"

Another slap.

The sound of flesh meeting flesh, mixed with his slap on her bottom, made him increase his thrusts, until there were only his deep grunts and her loud moans. Beneath him, her bottom was bright red and he gripped her waist, pummeling into her with no worries that she'd break. Abby could take it.

Pressing his chest against her slick back, he reached for her breasts. Every thrust forward, his sac slapped against her clit, and he ground himself into her, feeling shudders run through her. Her screams deepened, morphing together.

He tweaked her nipples, pinching them to a bite of pain, and loving the hitch in her screams. Her hot cunt clamped against his cock with each pinch he offered and became a vise so intense his balls tightened.

Gritting his teeth, he dropped her breasts, running his hands along her gorgeous curves, until he reached her clit. He swirled the bud and her screams now became rougher, louder, and she quivered under him.

The feel of her, the sounds she offered, every move she made, all consumed him. Though this first taste was meant to take the edge off his craving, it failed miserably. She had turned him into a full-blown addict.

Once would never be enough.

Pressing hard against the bud, he pummeled her from behind and she pushed back against him, matching his every thrust. Her fingers gripped the edge of the table, turning her knuckles white.

He wrapped an arm around her waist, pulling her back up against him and sliding his arm across her chest. Trapped in his fierce hold, he pumped into her. He swirled her clit, fast and hard, and he dropped his head into her neck. Her sweet, soft scent of sugar and cinnamon overwhelmed him.

Consumed with passion, more strength carried into his muscles, and he rocked into her hard, ruthless. He released her, and she once again rested her hands on the table. Then he took her like he had wanted to, savagely. He gripped her hips and thrust with all the strength he had in him.

"Yesssss . . ." she screamed.

He tangled his fingers in her hair, angled her head back, and pressed the weight of his sweaty body against her. Her inner walls convulsed around him and he pinned her with the other hand on her hip.

Abby clearly liked it rough.

So did he.

Shifting his hips, he drove in deeper, and she arched into his thrusts. The wet, sucking sounds of their sex hardened his cock further. Her answering moans that had no beginning and no end urged him to move faster.

With his mouth right by her ear, that possessive edge filled him. "Answer again, has anyone ever taken you hard?"

"No," she gasped.

He stopped dead, even if it nearly killed him to do so.

Her shout of frustration blasted against the walls in his living room. He didn't release his hold on her hair, and in fact, he tightened his fingers. Her slick heat was massaging him, pulling at him to keep going.

One second . . .

Two seconds . . .

Three seconds . . .

"Only you," she rasped.

Rubbing his face into her neck, he inhaled her sugary scent that tempted him. "That's right, sunshine." He thrust forward with a punishing strength, and her erotic scream drifted over him with raw power to fuel his muscles. "Only me."

7

As the sleep cleared from Abby's vision, she discovered soft eyes staring at her. The small lamp on the nightstand cast a warm glow in the modest-sized bedroom. Though the room was exactly Abby's style, with the dark oak furniture and gray cotton linens on the bed, the tenderness in Gavin's expression captured her interest.

His gentle look was the direct opposite of the intense and smokin'-hot expression she'd seen last night. Lying on his side, with the sheets at his waist, he brushed her hair off her face. "Hi."

She squirmed closer, running the tops of her feet against the course hair on his leg. "Did I fall asleep?"

He nodded. "For a little while."

"Sorry." She tucked her hands under her pillow, bunching it beneath her head. "I didn't mean to do that. It's been—" She instantly shut her mouth, realizing she hadn't slept as well as she had in Gavin's bed since the fire. "I guess you wore me out last night."

His eyebrows furrowed. "It's all right. You've been through a lot."

That seemed not only directed about the fire, but at an even greater weight of pain. A slight heaviness formed in her stomach, making her aware that last night that tightness in her body had vanished.

Gavin made her forget her pain. His presence eased the ache in her chest; the one that had settled in deep after the car accident. There was something so safe and familiar with him, and she realized, considering she hardly knew him, she'd never been so comfortable in her life. A sense of peace she hadn't felt since being in her family's house overtook her.

Here, felt like home.

She wanted to laugh at herself for thinking such foolish things. She didn't even know Gavin, except that he was hot, kinky, brave, and as far as she could tell, kindhearted. The craziest thing of all, she hadn't planned for a new relationship or sought it out, though as she stared into his warm eyes, it's all she could see.

She wanted to stay with him.

Something her mother once told her whispered in her ear, *"When you meet the love of your life, my darling, you'll just know."*

It all seemed to fall into place and she couldn't refuse the thought. Gavin had pursued her with intent, and that reminded her of something her father had told her during that same conversation, *"And when a man knows he's found his wife, nothing will stop him from making sure that woman remains at his side."*

Abby remembered the sweet look her parents exchanged after her father had said that, and the love they shared. She'd always wanted a loving marriage like they had, and she thought that was the one thing they'd left with her—the memory of what it looked like to be loved, respected, and cherished.

Gavin's eyes glowed, and he brushed a finger over her bottom lip. "Whatcha smiling about?"

"Oh, just thinking." Warmth spread through her and she wondered how he felt, if he had similar feelings, but she wouldn't dare voice her thoughts. She didn't want to be the first one to say, *Is this a friends with benefits thing, or are we dating?* Instead, she went with the safer route. "Did I thank you for the invite to the masquerade?"

He smirked. "By my count, you've already thanked me three times."

It had been a long night, but she welcomed the soreness of her intimate spots. The clock on the nightstand showed four o'-clock in the morning, which was two hours later than when she last looked.

Trailing his fingers down her arm, he took the blanket off her with his touch, and she shivered. His lips slightly parted before he said, "Though I'll happily accept any gratitude you have to offer."

Leaning in toward her, he stole a kiss, quickening her heart rate.

Of all the kisses he'd given her so far, this was the most tender. There was nothing bruising, nothing demanding about the kiss. He simply brushed his lips across hers in a whisper of touch. She relished in the simplicity of such a sweet embrace.

After many more of those kisses, her temperature rose, and he moved away. She smiled, her nerve endings tingling. "So, you are capable of soft touching?" Something she hadn't been sure of until now.

He grinned—one of those *you are my prey and now I shall eat you* smiles. "There's something beautiful in taking you rough." He pressed heated kisses along her neck, while murmuring, "But there's something undeniably sexy about waking up in the morning, rolling over, and landing myself inside a warm woman."

Pulling the blanket away from her naked form, he climbed on top of her, sliding that hard, muscular body against her. She shuddered beneath him, angling her head for his assault on her neck. His cock nudged her entrance and she sensed the latex. She might've had a thought about when exactly he'd put on the condom, but he shifted his hips, dipping inside, and erased all thoughts from her mind.

His breath brushed against her pulse point before he placed a kiss right there. "You, Abby, are a warm, wet woman."

Dragging her leg up over his hip, he moved in deeper, rocking against her. She explored the thick biceps under fingers, relishing in the valleys of his muscles. She inhaled his scent of musky spice, inflaming her desire of him, yet he slid in slowly, as if time didn't matter.

Right now, it didn't.

Every move he made was more addictive than the one before it. Each brush of his lips and slow caress of his body made her simmer in a hot desire. And every inch of his hardened length pushing inside brought her into a higher form of bliss.

Lifting his hips, his cock slid out and he moved down her body, placing kisses along the way. He sucked and teased her nipples. He swirled his tongue over her abdomen. He paid tribute to every inch of her skin. Then he kissed her where she ached.

She had a second to feel his warm breath against her fiery flesh before his tongue slid over her folds. A low, intoxicating sound hummed from his chest, and she arched up into him, embracing each light lick.

Pressing more weight against her thighs, he angled her bottom, and then his licks intensified—intent to unravel her. And she unraveled into nothing less than a woman begging with her moans for him to never stop.

Teasing her, he tickled her cleft with his tongue, then his kisses traveled up to her clit. When she quivered beneath his mouth, he sucked on the nub. Her fingers tangled into the bedsheets and she hung on tight. He drove her higher, circling the bundle of nerves with his tongue and making her go wild.

Glancing down between her thighs, her throat became thick. Gavin kissed her so intimately, bringing forth a surge of passion so hot that moisture flooded her lower lips. Not only in how he kissed her, but the look of him doing it. He personified sensuality, and each touch wasn't without purpose, or without enjoyment.

He loved kissing her *there*.

She didn't want him to stop.

Sliding her hand through his hair, she held him close.

He moaned.

She gasped.

Beneath his mouth, his finger slipped inside her, pumping into her in the same rhythm he set with his tongue. She arched off the bed as he moved faster, determined to send her over the edge, and she became a shuddering mess of sensation.

He inserted another finger, drawing her nub in between his teeth, and flames flicked within. She gripped his hair tight as he moved quicker and swirled the bud, his fingers pumping into her.

Her lower body clenched. "I'm going to . . ."

His mouth vanished.

He slid his hands under her head, cupping her neck, his cock pressing against her slit. Feeling the hard body against her, and pinned beneath his fierce hold, she moaned deeply.

Smiling, a playful grin, he murmured, "Sunshine, when you come, I want to feel it."

He hooked her leg over his thigh, running his hand down to her bottom, where he angled her. As he thrust forward, his eyes were lit with an inner glow. Trapped beneath him, a rise of pleasure she hadn't anticipated consumed her.

Staring into his gorgeous face, spotting the strength mixed with an exhilarating arrogance, no fantasy could top this. With each insertion of his thick cock, she squeezed at him and her body went into convulsions. His smile faded and intensity crossed his features, making her arousal spread out between them.

Beneath her bottom, his hand gripped her cheek, tilting her even farther into him. He moved faster now, but oh-so-sensual.

Every rub of his body against hers was more than just two bodies meeting; it was passion in every sense of the word.

He marked her with his body.

She burned from his touch.

With slow and seductive kisses on her neck, his hardened length filled her, and his pelvis caressed her clit on each thrust forward. He quickened his pace, raising her pleasure and building her moans.

The mattress bounced beneath her as she wrapped her legs around his thighs, and the muscles on his arms flexed beneath her fingertips. She slid his hands down over his shoulders, trailing her fingernails along his back.

He lifted his head from her neck, and dark, primal eyes regarded her.

With her hands urging him on, the side of his mouth arched ever-so-slowly. She knew the danger of that smile; it had snagged her the very first time she saw it. Her body responded to the heat between them, clenching and moistening. Then he was pumping into her, until sweat coated his skin and her pulse hammered.

Meeting him thrust for thrust, she arched up into him. Each hard thrust forward caressed her clit, and her breath froze. Then with a final slam forward of his hips, all the tension inside exploded into wild sensations, leaving her screaming in unadulterated bliss. Gavin's eyes widened and his lips parted before he bucked and jerked, riding her hard during the final moments of his climax.

Many minutes passed before she chuckled softly. "You know, if I'm to prove my gratefulness to you, you have to stop pleasuring *me* and let me pleasure you."

He rested his forehead against hers, his chest heaving. "Sunshine, you have this all wrong." He finally lifted up, looking down at her with positively glowing eyes. "You, in my bed, is all I need."

* * *

Some relationships started out with a slow burn, while others happened as fierce as a backdraft, or so Gavin believed. The fire between him and Abby wasn't one he intended to put out. In fact, he was determined to watch her burn, and for as many nights as she'd allow.

There, lying in his bed and on her side facing him, she looked disheveled. He discovered the more he saw of her, the more he liked each of her looks. Whether she was pretty in lingerie, dressed casually in her bookstore, or now naked and tangled in his bedsheets, he enjoyed the view. More so, he appreciated her company.

He liked Abby.

Though he'd pay for tonight with exhaustion at work in the morning, he'd do it again. The heat between them hadn't been sated, but now burned hotter as he realized this wasn't over for him. He hadn't set out to find a new relationship, yet he also wasn't an idiot when it came to something glaringly obvious right in front of him—Abby and him were meant to be together, of that he was sure.

Knowing what he wanted, and knowing he wouldn't take no for an answer, he set out to prove himself a man she could see herself with—more than what lay between them sexually. He brushed his knuckles across her cheek. "I got something for you."

She sat up, tucking the blankets under her arms. "You did?"

He turned onto his other side and opened the drawer to his nightstand; then he pulled out the picture. With lightness in his chest, he offered it to her. "Here, for you."

Her eyes sparkled as she took the picture. "What is it?" She flipped the photo over and she gasped.

Gavin lay down, resting his head against the pillow and folding his arms behind his head. Though initially, Abby's pain drew him to her, now he'd make sure she didn't suffer another day of tragedy.

When she jerked her head up, tears rimmed her eyes. He understood her lack of words and her emotion, but he didn't have such hesitations. "I fight fires for a living, but I never fix lives." Yanking his hands away from his head, he brushed her tear away. "I know you thought you lost all of your pictures of your family, but this picture had fallen off your desk in the blaze. It did have some damage, so I had it restored."

Looking down to the photo resting against the blanket, she studied the picture that looked to be of her and her family at a fancy affair. She ran her finger over the photo, and her voice thickened. "Did you plan on giving it to me, even if I didn't come to masquerade?"

"I planned to put it in your mailbox."

Her head lifted, more tears rushing over her pink cheeks. "Why?"

He shrugged. "I still don't know." All his behavior since meeting Abby he couldn't explain. He hadn't wanted a girlfriend, let alone would've gone out of his way to do something like this for a stranger.

Watching her touching the photo and seeing her tears clenched his chest in the same way it had the day at her house fire. He reached out to her, moving his fingers over her arm, offering her comfort.

She looked to him, her head tilting to the side. "Was it because you felt bad for me?"

"At first it was. You were so sad that day. It just"—he shrugged again—"affected me, I guess." He glanced up at the ceiling, trying to put into words what he'd been sorting out in his own head since meeting her. "But there was more to it . . ."

"More?"

He turned his head against the pillow. "I wanted to take away your pain."

Her eyes searched his, her slow smile building. "Why would you do that? You barely know me."

"That is the exact question I've been asking myself, and what I keep asking every day since we've met. Why did I have to meet you? Why did I have the picture restored? Why couldn't I have sex with you at the masquerade?" He paused as she leaned in toward him. "The only answer I found was: I just had to, so I did."

She parted her lips, then shut them.

Maybe she understood the crazy impulse that had been driving him, since by all appearances, she had experienced the same intensity, too. The night of the masquerade, she had picked him without a single hesitation, and apparently, she'd been thinking about him, as he had her.

Bowing her head, she smiled down at the photo. "This picture was taken a month before the accident. It might actually be the last picture we had taken together as a family." Her voice broke. "I don't think you could ever know—"

Leaning up on his elbow, he pressed his finger against her lip. "I do know. Not because I've experienced it myself." No, he had all his family—and a huge family at that. In fact, he couldn't wait for his mother to meet Abby—she'd love her. "I know because I can see how happy it makes you."

Her smile was sad, as she lay down beside him and pressed the picture against her heart. "Thank you, Gavin."

He stayed silent.

Gavin hadn't done this to receive a thank you; he did this to ease that despair he'd seen in her at her house. No amount of fires he'd put out, or lives he saved, had ever given him such fulfillment as seeing the contentment on her face.

Many minutes passed and he allowed the quiet, letting her appreciate the moment when she realized not all had been lost. She finally placed the picture on the nightstand table, then turned to him. Her tears were dry, and her smile was sweet.

What he hoped for had happened; she looked to him as more than a lover, she looked to him as a friend. That was a start and something they could build upon. He tucked her hair behind her ear. "Tell me something—what's the meaning behind that wall of stickers in your closet?"

She tucked her hands under her face and the sheet slid from her arm, exposing her silky skin. "After the accident, I put myself into therapy." A flush spread across her face. "In those first couple years, I struggled a bit."

"Understandable," he murmured. "Anyone would struggle."

The fire department provided therapy for any firefighter who needed to talk after a traumatic event, and that wasn't even for people as close as family. He couldn't imagine the pain Abby had suffered, yet he'd seen hints of that misery in her eyes the day of her fire.

Her toes caressed his shin in slow swirls. "As part of my therapy, I was told to make a 'Me Wall' and decorate it all with the things that I loved. It's meant as tool so that every day when I got ready in the morning, I'd see the good things in life that made me happy. It kept me in the present, instead of focusing on the past and on things I couldn't change."

He pressed his lips together. "You felt guilty over the accident?"

She sighed dejectedly. "I should've been in the car with them that night." She hesitated, her expression thoughtful. "It took me a long time to stop thinking about the what-ifs."

He wished this was one thing they didn't have in common. "In my line of work, sometimes I live in the what-ifs, too. What if I got to the fire sooner, maybe I could've saved that life. What if I put the fire out faster, the house wouldn't have been destroyed."

She gave a small nod against her pillow. "Just like my therapist told me, *What-ifs will get you nowhere but not appreciating what you have in the now.*"

He grinned. "Sounds like some good advice."

She paused again, regarding him; then her smile became

ever-so-gentle. "You know, I can't ever say that I'm glad my house caught fire, but . . ."

"It's not bad that it did," he offered.

Laying a hand over his heart, she gave an appreciative sigh. "Yeah, it's not bad that it did."

He placed his hand over hers, gazing over such perfection. Fate worked in crazy ways. Gavin knew that. He had always held on to his belief that things happened for a reason. If he didn't, he couldn't fight fires. He accepted long ago he had no control on the job or over the fact that lives were sometimes lost and homes destroyed, but that's why he liked control in the bedroom.

It kept his head straight.

Staring into her beautiful face, not seeing a single trace of that pain that had consumed his thoughts, he realized that fate had worked its wondrous ways. He wouldn't shy away from what fate had led him to. He intended to wrap Abby in his arms and keep her protected. Pushing off the sheet, he jumped out of the bed.

She sat up, laughing. "What are you doing now?"

"One sec." He went into his closet, got what he needed, then joined her on the bed. "Here, it's a picture of me."

She accepted the photo, then raised her eyebrows. "Which is for . . . ?"

"Once you get your bedroom rebuilt, you can add it to your 'Me Wall.' " He pulled the sheet away from her naked body and slid between her warm thighs. "I'm in your present, so I need to be on that wall." He slid his nose against her neck. "Abby, I plan to be in your future, too."

"Don't I get a say in that?"

He lifted his head. "Nope."

She gave him a silly grin. "Oh, really, why is that?"

"Because we both know the truth." He dropped his weight

against her, pressing his cock against her warm, slick heat. "You need me right here, as much as I need to stay."

With half-closed eyes, giving him a lidded look of satisfaction, she asked, "It's that simple, huh?"

He brushed his lips across hers. "With you, Abby, it'll always be that simple."

If you enjoyed *Hot Shots,* be sure not to miss Lynn LaFleur's

SMOKIN' HOT

An Aphrodisia trade paperback on sale April 2014.

Read on for a special sneak peek!

Voices outside her window slowly dragged Julia from dreams to reality. Through one eye, she peered toward the sliver of light shining through the curtains. It hit the hardwood floor, highlighting dust motes dancing in the air.

She couldn't believe any dust motes existed in Dolly's house, not the way it sparkled. Julia had always considered herself to be neat and organized. The house she'd rented in California resembled a sty compared to Dolly's immaculate home.

The voices drew closer to her window. She couldn't quite make out the words, but she recognized Dolly's voice. A masculine tone blended with Dolly's . . . a nice deep, sexy-as-sin masculine tone. For some crazy reason, an image of the guy from Burger King yesterday popped into her head. The guy with Dolly had the same type of voice she imagined her hunky brunette would also possess.

Julia rolled to her side and looked at the digital clock on the nightstand: 9:07. She blinked and looked again. She hadn't slept this late in . . . She didn't think she'd *ever* slept this late. But she hadn't fallen asleep until almost three o'clock. Since Dolly's bar, Boot Scootin', wasn't open on Wednesdays, Julia and Dolly had talked until well after midnight. After that, Julia's mind had been too full for her to fall asleep. She worried about starting over in a new state. She worried about finding a place to live in a small town where rentals were scarce.

She ached to feel Cole's arms around her, hungered for the taste of his kiss.

Leaving him had been the hardest thing for her to do. But she'd had no choice. After what he'd done . . .

Julia threw off the covers and sat on the edge of the bed. Her stomach rumbled. Not surprising, since she hadn't eaten anything since a snack at nine last night. Dolly had told her to make herself at home, that she could cook whatever she wanted, do her laundry, hibernate in the guest room when she desired privacy. Dolly wanted Julia to think of this as her home for as long as she stayed.

She understood why her mother loved Dolly so much. The woman had a caring heart as big as the state where she lived.

Discarding the large T-shirt and panties she'd slept in, Julia donned underwear, jeans, and a loose short-sleeved blouse. After a quick trip to the bathroom to brush her teeth and hair, she followed the scent of coffee to the kitchen. No more than two steps into the room, she stopped in her tracks. The hunky brunette from Burger King sat at the round wooden table.

He looked her way. Surprise flitted across his face before he smiled and stood. "Hello."

Dolly straightened from peering into the refrigerator. "Oh, good, you're awake. How did you sleep?"

"Great," she answered her hostess while still looking at the man she never expected to see in Dolly's kitchen.

"Are you hungry? I promised Stephen an apple crêpe to go with his coffee."

Julia's stomach gurgled loudly. Warmth crept into her face and she covered her tummy with her hands. Dolly laughed.

"I'll take that as a yes. Why don't you get your coffee and sit down?" She motioned to the hunk. "This is Stephen McGettis. He and his cousin are going to repair my roof. I had quite a bit of hail damage last week when a bad thunderstorm blew through Lanville. Stephen, this is Julia Woods. She just moved here from California."

"It's nice to meet you, Julia."

"Nice to meet you, Stephen."

He remained standing while she got her coffee, not sitting again until she sat in the chair across from him. His politeness impressed her. After working mainly with men who treated her like a kid sister, she enjoyed the bit of chivalry.

Julia watched Dolly place the crêpe ingredients on the counter. "Can I help?" she asked.

"No, I'm fine. I already have the apple mixture, and it won't take me a couple of minutes to whip up the batter. I've made these so many times, I can almost do them with my eyes closed." She glanced at Stephen over her shoulder. "Stephen, you and Julia have something in common."

He turned those amazing cognac-colored eyes on Julia. "Oh?"

Her breath hitched and she had to tighten her grip on the coffee mug before her lax fingers dropped it. The sun shone through the window and touched his long dark hair, giving it reddish highlights. She doubted if this man spent very many Saturday nights alone. Or any other night of the week.

"She was a firefighter in California for the U.S. Forest Service."

A crooked smile turned up one corner of his lips. "No shit?" His smile quickly disappeared. "Uh, I mean, really?"

Julia hid a smile behind her mug as she sipped her coffee. She thought it cute that he didn't want to curse in front of her and Dolly. "My main job was in research, but I fought fires when the call went out for extra help."

"Stephen is a firefighter on our volunteer fire department."

Another point for Stephen. Julia had always admired the men and women who worked on volunteer fire departments. They put their lives on the line without any pay or compensation other than the desire to help others. "How many volunteers on your fire department?"

"Twenty-four men and three women. Are you interested in joining? We can always use another pair of hands."

Part of her wanted to say yes, that she would love to help. Another part of her couldn't face anything to do with fighting fires yet. "I'll think about it."

The skin at the outer corners of his eyes tightened a bit, as if he could read her thoughts and knew she had personal reasons for not jumping in to immediately volunteer. "If you change your mind, Dolly knows how to get in touch with me."

Dolly set a small plate holding a large crêpe in front of each of them. The scent of apples and cinnamon wafted from the pastry, making Julia's stomach gurgle again.

"There are two more crêpes on the stove," Dolly said. "I have a couple of things to do; then I have to head to the bar in time for my delivery." She touched Julia's shoulder. "Come by later. I'll fix you one of my famous cheeseburgers."

"Apple crêpes now and cheeseburgers later? I don't need to gain any weight, Dolly."

"*Pffft.* You're perfect. A man doesn't want to hold a pile of bones. Isn't that right, Stephen?"

A look of apprehension flashed through his eyes. He obviously didn't want to comment on what Dolly said. "I, uh, think I'll refill my mug. You want more coffee, Julia?"

She struggled not to laugh at how quickly he changed the subject. "Please."

Julia and Dolly exchanged grins while Stephen carried the two mugs to the coffeemaker. Then Dolly pushed Julia's hair behind her ear, the way Julia's mother did so often. "I meant what I said. This is your home for as long as you need to stay here."

Hugs last night and touches this morning meant Dolly had to be a physical person. Julia didn't mind that at all. The affection made her miss her mother a bit less. Smiling, she squeezed Dolly's hand. "Thank you."

Dolly left the room as Stephen returned with the full coffee mugs. Not sure what to say to him since she'd met him only twenty minutes ago, she dug into her crêpe instead. One bite and she couldn't stop the moan deep in her throat. Realizing it seemed similar to a sound made while making love, she lifted her gaze to Stephen. She caught him staring at her, his eyes narrowed, his nostrils flared. He quickly looked down at his plate and cut into his crêpe.

She took advantage of his lowered head to study him. He had gorgeous hair. She'd dated guys with short hair, long hair, and various lengths in between. It had never mattered to her as long as the guy kept his hair clean and neat. Stephen's hair fell to his shoulders in gentle waves. She remembered noticing it when she first saw him in Burger King yesterday and thinking how the waves would wrap around a woman's fingers.

Her gaze continued over his face. Oval in shape. A straight nose. Mouth a little wide, with full, well-shaped lips that made her think of kissing for hours.

She could see his mouth better if not for the stubble. He obviously hadn't shaved in at least three days, perhaps longer. Julia had never been a fan of stubble, but she had to admit it gave him a dangerous, bad-boy appearance.

Cole had been a bad boy. Julia never wanted to get involved with one of them again.

Stephen scooped up the last bite of his crêpe. "I'm ready for seconds. How about you?"

Julia looked down at the remaining piece on her plate. "I don't think I can eat a whole one."

Rising from his chair, Stephen walked over to the stove and returned with the plate holding two crêpes. He set it on the table between them. "Take what you want and I'll eat the rest."

She divided a crêpe into two halves and placed one on her plate. Stephen pulled the plate in front of him. She watched his hand as he cut into the half she'd left. Long, thick fingers, bare of any hair. Short, clean fingernails surrounded by cuticles a little ragged . . . probably from the physical work he did as a roofer. She couldn't see his palm, but she wouldn't be surprised if calluses existed there.

She wondered how those calluses would feel scraping over her nipples.

Warmth swept through her body at the forbidden thought. Just because Stephen looked hot didn't mean she would get involved with him. Her messed-up life had to be straightened out before she could have any kind of physical relationship with a man again. Besides, just because she found Stephen attractive didn't mean he felt the same way about her.

"Why Lanville?" he asked.

The image of Stephen's calloused fingers touching her vanished at his question. "What?"

"Why did you move to Lanville? Do you have relatives here?"

"No, I only know Dolly. Well, actually, I didn't know Dolly until I met her yesterday, but I've talked to her many times on the phone. She and my mom went to college together and have been friends for years."

"Dolly's the best. There isn't a woman more caring in this whole town." He laid his fork on his empty plate. "Where did you live in California?"

"East of Sacramento, in the Sierra Nevadas."

"No mountains around here, just hills. Lanville is probably a lot different from what you're used to."

Julia shrugged one shoulder. "I needed a change. Dolly offered me a place to stay and a job."

"You'll be working at Boot Scootin'?"

"No, I turned down her job offer. I'm starting work as a housekeeper at The Inn on Crystal Creek Monday."

His eyebrows shot up, as if what she said surprised him. "You'd rather clean rooms than make great tips?"

"I like to clean."

Pushing his plate aside, he leaned forward and rested his folded arms on the table. "Are you looking for outside work? I lost my cleaning lady a month ago when she cut back her hours. I'd rather eat raw frog's liver than clean a bathtub or oven."

Julia wrinkled her nose at the mental picture his statement created. "Ew."

"Exactly."

She laughed when he grinned. The charm oozed off this man. "I don't know what my hours will be yet. I wouldn't feel right taking other jobs if they'll interfere with my main job."

"Well, if you decide you want to pick up some extra money . . ." He reached into the breast pocket of his T-shirt and withdrew a white card. After flipping it over, he took the pen from on top of his clipboard that lay on the table and wrote something on the back. "Here's my cell number. That's the best way to reach me."

He held out the business card to her. Their fingers brushed when she took it, sending a pleasant tingle up her arm and straight to her nipples. They tightened inside her bra.

Ignoring her body's response, she looked at the front of the card. A cute cartoon man hammering a shingle onto a roof drew her attention before she read, *McGettis Roofing, Dusty and Stephen McGettis, Owners.*

"Is Dusty your brother?"

"My cousin, but we're as close as brothers. He's three years older and we grew up together."

"Do you have any brothers or sisters?"

"Two brothers, both older. One is a lawyer, one is a college professor." He shrugged and flashed her a grin. "They got the brains, I got the brawn."

A single glance at Stephen's broad shoulders, muscular arms, and wide chest proved he definitely got the brawn. However, she had no doubt he had as much intelligence as his brothers. She could tell that from the way he spoke and carried himself.

"How about you?" Stephen asked.

Julia shook her head. "Only child. That was cool while I was growing up since I had all of my mom's attention. Now, I wish I had a brother or sister. That's a bond that can never be broken."

"No father?"

She'd known Stephen for less than an hour. Personal stuff shouldn't even enter into their conversation, yet for a reason she didn't understand, she wanted to be honest with him. "I'm the result of my mother's one-night stand with—according to her—the most handsome man she'd ever seen. He didn't bother to give her anything but his first name. He snuck out of her apartment before she woke up the next morning."

A little uncomfortable at what she'd revealed to Stephen, she decided to change the subject the way he had earlier. "Would you like more coffee?"

"No, thanks. I need to go. I have another appointment in"— he checked the thick watch on his wrist—"fifteen minutes."

Julia rose as he did. He headed toward the back door, so she assumed that's the way he had come into the house. She followed him, holding the door open after he crossed the threshold. Two steps onto the porch, he stopped and faced her.

"Dolly is right."

Confused, she tilted her head and asked, "About what?"

"Your body is perfect."

His gaze dipped to her breasts for a second before he turned and walked down the porch steps, leaving her a little breathless and a lot scared of such a strong reaction to Stephen McGettis.